Rescue R

Book 3 in the Rescue Series

By
Award-winning Author
Heidi M. Thomas

Heidi M. Thomas

SunCatcher Publications

i

Praise for Rescue Ranch Rising

"Sam Moser rescues horses, vets and rebellious teens. But who will rescue Sam from herself? Heidi Thomas does it again as her Rescue Series continues to entertain and educate. Well-paced and satisfying, a wholesome, feel-good contemporary series that deals with real issues. Suited to horse-loving teens as well as adults." ~ Anne Schroeder, award-winning author of *Walk the Promise Road*

"Another extraordinary story by Heidi M. Thomas. She keeps readers spellbound from the beginning to the end of her third book in the Rescue series. Samantha continues to struggle to keep her great-grandparent's ranch prosperous, while using horses to rehabilitate troubled teens and veterans recovering from PTSD." ~ Jane Laurie Hirsch, author of *Murder is Brewing* and *Silent Shots in the Dark*.

"If you like the show, Heartland, you'll love this series!" ~ Laura Drake, award-winning women's fiction author

Other books by Heidi M. Thomas

Cowgirl Dreams series
Cowgirl Dreams
Follow the Dream
Dare to Dream

American Dream series
Seeking the American Dream
Finding True Home

Rescue series
Rescuing Samantha
Rescuing Hope
Rescue Ranch Rising

Nonfiction
Cowgirl Up! A History of Rodeo Women

Children's
The Secret of the Ice Castle & Other Inspirational Tales

Praise for Heidi M. Thomas Books

Cowgirl Dreams (EPIC Award and USA Best Book Awards): "...Brings heart, verve and knowledge to her depiction of the intrepid Nettie. A lively look at the ranch women of an almost forgotten West." —Deirdre McNamer, MFA English Professor, University of Montana, *Red Rover, My Russian,* and *One Sweet Quarrel*

Follow the Dream (WILLA Literary Award): "I enjoyed this bittersweet novel with its accurate depiction of the lives of cowgirls in 1930s Montana and its tender portrait of a marriage." Mary Clearman Blew, award-winning author of *All but the Waltz: A Memoir of Five Generations in the Life of a Montana Family*

Dare to Dream (Book Excellence Award Finalist): "Finding our place and following our hearts is the moving theme of *Dare to Dream,* a finely-tuned finish to Heidi Thomas's trilogy inspired by the life of her grandmother, an early rodeo-rider. With crisp dialogue and singular scenes, we're not only invited into the middle of a western experience of rough stock, riders and generations of ranch tradition, but we're deftly taken into a family drama. This family story takes place beginning in 1941 but it could be happening to families anywhere—and is. Nettie, Jake, and Neil struggle to find their place and discover what we all must: life is filled with sorrow and joy; faith, family and friends see us through and give meaning to it all. Nettie, or as Jake calls her, 'Little Gal' will stay in your heart and make you want to re-read the first books just to keep her close. A very satisfying read."—Jane Kirkpatrick, an award-winning, *New York Times* Bestselling author

Cowgirl Up: A History of Rodeo Women **(Global e-book Winner):** "The best kind of history lesson; Informative and entertaining. Thomas does a great job of showing the lifestyles of these women in a very male dominated world, and how through hard work and determination they gained the respect of many people not only in the U.S., but throughout the world. You can't help but be impressed with the toughness of these women, who competed even with broken bones and other injuries. An eye-opening look at the world of rodeo, and the accomplishments of these women. –John J. Rust, author of *Arizona's All-Time Baseball Team* and the "Fallen Eagle" series

Seeking the American Dream **(Author's Show, Historical Fiction Winner):** "Heidi Thomas's novel grips the reader from the first opening sentence, as her nurse-protagonist struggles to face the wretched suffering in war-torn Hamburg during the final days of WWII. From there, her sweeping saga takes her away from Europe's lurching efforts to rebuild, and into building her own new life in America. From the perspective of a hard-working, and still bright-eyed young woman, we participate in America's own next chapter." –Mara Purl, best-selling author of the Milford-Haven Novels

Finding True Home (Will Rogers Medallion, Book Excellence Awards) "This sequel to *Seeking the American Dream* continues Heidi Thomas' heart-tugging saga of the life of a World War II war bride as she struggles to adjust to life on a Montana ranch, where family is everything and neighbor helps neighbor through the toughest situations. Struggling through isolation, prejudice, and self-doubt, Anna Moser finally finds peace, acceptance, and her true home through a lifetime of love and sacrifice." – Donis Casey, author of the Alafair Tucker series

Rescuing Samantha (**Independent Press Finalist, Book Excellence Award**): "Heidi Thomas brings us a story about a young woman facing life's trials in rugged Montana. But Sam has the gumption of her grandmother and great-grandmother, to persevere and overcome. She is also compelled to rescue horses and young people.

There is drama and true-to-life dialogue in Thomas' smooth writing and the reader will become immersed. It is a joy to watch along with the characters how God brings "mysterious" blessings to their predicaments.

This is also a story of rural America that many of us long for—neighborhood rodeo, BBQ, homemade ice cream, reverence for the Star-Spangled Banner, fiddles and dancing, and (mostly) friendly neighbors. Readers will love this story." ~ Denise F. McAllister, MAPW, Atlanta, GA. Freelance editor, Member of Western Writers of America and Women Writing the West.

Rescuing Hope (**WILLA Literary Award Finalist, Will Rogers Medallion, Book Excellence Finalist**): "If you like the show, Heartland, you'll love this book! Good characters in real-life situations." —Laura Drake, award-winning women's fiction author

~~~

"Samantha Moser has a heart as big as Montana and it seems everyone knows it. Injured dogs, spooked horses, damaged veterans, troubled teens—they all find their way to Sam for nurturing and healing by her compassion and generosity. She sometimes wonders in the quiet of the midnight darkness if there will ever be anyone to love and nurture her and help her achieve her dream of buying her grandparents ranch."—Leta McCurry, author of *Dancing to the Silence*

Rescue Ranch Rising

Copyright © 2022 by Heidi M. Thomas

A SunCatcher Publications book

Cover Design by Jason McIntyre
www.TheFarthestReaches.com

Library of Congress Cataloguing-in-Publication data is available on file.

ISBN: 978-0-9990663-5-5
Printed in the United States of America

10 9 8 7 6 5 4 3 2 1

"For every house is built by someone, but God is the builder of everything." Hebrews 3:4 (NIV)

"In order to rise from its own ashes, a phoenix first must burn." – Octavia
Butler

CHAPTER ONE

Hideous cherry-red flames soared into the night sky like fireworks. Timbers creaked and groaned. Heat radiated. Terrified whinnies shrieked over the crackling roar.

Samantha Moser's body shivered and trembled as the fiery memories raged through her mind. She leaned against a corral fence rail and stared at the blackened expanse where her barn stood only a few weeks before. A dust devil swirled, lifting soot into the air and sending an acrid stench into her nostrils.

She pressed her lips into a hard grimace. The barn her great-grandparents had built in the 1940s—part of her heritage—gone, her dreams up in smoke. In a matter of minutes, before her very eyes.

"Wishing isn't going to get it rebuilt." Brad Ashton's cheerful voice came from behind, startling her back to the present.

She smiled at the man who made her pulse speed up and gave her hope for a future.

"That's true." She brushed the wayward lock of dark brown hair from his forehead, admiring his boyish good looks and winning, confident grin. "I guess what I need to do now is sit down and draw up a plan for a new barn and then find a contractor."

He put an arm around her shoulder and squeezed, giving her a pleasant warmth her jean jacket couldn't provide. "Good idea.

What all do you want to include this time around— a bigger floor plan, more stalls, additional hay storage?"

She leaned into the strength of his six-foot frame. "All of that, and a bunkhouse or cabins too. This is my chance to build my outreach program to work with kids and veterans. And if there are more opportunities to rescue horses, I'll definitely need more room."

"Build it, and they will come," Brad quipped.

"I hope so." This ranch was so far from "civilization"— forty miles to Forsyth, ninety to Miles City, and a little more than a hundred to Billings. Would the children in the group home from Billings and the veterans' PTSD riding program from Miles City want to make the trip? And if they did, how often?

She peered into Brad's dark chocolate eyes. "Am I making a mistake with these plans? Maybe I should simply go into partnership with Clyde—he's already got the facilities."

He shook his head. "I don't think so. It would be hard to combine your dude ranch activities and your healing-with-horses work. You'd have to commute every day, hauling your horses back and forth—or boarding them there—whereas you'd have it all right here."

"But the summer dude program is where it all started. That's where I found Electra." Her gaze shifted to the young teen in the corral who was working with Apache, the horse the two of them had rescued from starvation. With that experience, the troubled Goth persona had changed miraculously. The girl had been hooked on horses ever since, even training Apache to kneel for inexperienced riders to mount, a tremendous asset in working with disabled vets.

"Well," Brad shrugged, "I can't make the decision for you, but I believe this has always been in your heart. Rescuing horses and helping people heal on your own ranch *is* your dream."

Sam's mind flashed back to the beginning, when she'd first leased this ranch—the place her great-grandparents had once owned—and her initial dream of raising Thoroughbreds because of her broken-down racehorse rescue, Sugar.

But her then-fiancé Kenny had turned tail after the first hard blizzard and returned to Phoenix. The harsh climate, finances, and being miles from anywhere put the kibosh on that dream. She chewed on the inside of her cheek. *Maybe that turned out for the best.*

Dreams were fluid. They could be changed. As long as she didn't give up. No way. That wasn't in her blood. Her great-grandma Nettie was a roughstock-riding rodeo cowgirl who defied society's norms. Her grandmother Anna had followed love from Germany, overcoming the cultural barriers of a rural, western life… and then beat cancer. Even her mother Lisa had moved with her dad Kevin to live off the grid in Alaska. These women were her ancestors, her inspiration. She would never give up.

She took in the now-green rolling hills silhouetted against the clear blue sky and breathed in the fresh, clean spring air. Yes, this is where she belonged, and building this ranch and a rescue program was her dream. And now that Jack Murdock, the owner, had finally consented to let her buy the place, what was stopping her?

"Yes, it is. This is my dream, and I'm going to try like heck to follow it through." She squared her shoulders. "Let's go up to the house, and you can help me make some drawings."

Sam set cups of steaming coffee and home-made sweet rolls in the center of the table. April sunlight streamed into the yellow kitchen through sunflower-patterned curtains. Leaning against Brad's shoulder, she tousled his hair. With a lighter-than-air feeling of expectation, she set out paper tablets and pencils. She sketched a rough idea and then took out her ruler to make a scale drawing. "Since I have four horses now, I'll need at least that many stalls, but I'd like to double that…just in case."

Brad listed all her wants, the pros and cons, and researched prices online, "to give you a ballpark figure of what you might expect for materials and building costs these days."

Sam winced. The cost. She still had a pretty good chunk of the money people had donated after Brad's documentary had aired on her rescue operation for Trixi and Apache. But… would that be enough to build what she needed? And, she still needed income to live on. She whooshed out a breath. One need always led to another. She couldn't ask Brad for help. Still recovering from a bad vehicle accident and months in a coma, he was on temporary disability until he could go back to work. His career as a photojournalist, though rewarding on a personal level, wasn't as lucrative as people might think.

When the phone rang, she stood to answer the corded wall unit she'd installed as a nostalgic memento to the past. With no cell service on the ranch, she needed a landline, although Electra had been after her to get a wireless unit.

Murdock's voice boomed through the receiver.

Her chest seized in a habitual reaction to the landlord who had for so long thwarted her attempts to buy this ranch. *No, Sam. He's selling it to you now. You don't need to worry about him evicting you anymore.*

She let her shoulders relax. "Morning, Jack. How are things?"

"Good, good. I thought I should let you know, I've been in contact with my insurance company, and they'll be sending someone out to assess the situation. I'm sure there will be some compensation to rebuild the barn."

A small gasp escaped her lips. "Oh. Wow. That's great. Thanks."

She hung up and stood staring at Brad for a long moment.

He raised his eyebrows. "What? What did he say?"

Trying not to allow a bubble of giddiness grow too much, she strode back to the table and relayed the new information.

"Fantastic! That is awesome." His face lit with a luminous smile.

The kitchen door flew open and in breezed Electra. "What's fantastic-awesome?"

Sam beamed at the clean-scrubbed, boots-and jeans-clad young teen. Moving back to the table, she showed her the plans.

"Yay! That is awesome-fantastic-wonderful news. Ohmygosh, Sam, ohmygosh! Your dream is coming true." The girl bent her head over the drawings. "A big tack room and eight stalls, wow, and you need a bigger floor so we can have barn dances, and cabins, ohmygosh yes, cabins for the kids to stay, and…" She finally paused for breath.

Sam and Brad chuckled over the teen's enthusiastic response.

"Yes, well, it's going to take a lot of money and a lot of work, and then there's still the question, will people come hundreds of miles to participate in my programs?" The old specter of doubt and fear loomed behind her shoulder, casting a shadow over the joyful mania of the moment before.

Brad rose, clutched her shoulders, and peered into her face with widened eyes. "Hey. You've shown me your perseverance in the past. You can do this. Let's not give up before we get started." He grinned. "We'll find out what the insurance will cover, and in the meantime, let's call a couple of contractors to get some bids."

Her heart quivered at his encouragement. "You're right. I'll try not to create failure before I begin. Thanks." She shook her head ruefully. "Kinda too bad Kenny is out of the picture. I could probably hire him for cheap."

"Ah…no. Your ex-fiancé is not setting foot on this place again." Brad snorted and shook his head vehemently.

She heard a hard note of—anger, or fear?—in his voice. "Just kidding. No way I'd invite him back." *Wow. I didn't expect that reaction. But then, why not? Kenny was a lying coward, and Brad is an honorable man.*

A soft tenderness washed through her. She put a gentle hand on his arm.

***

The insurance adjustor came and went, non-committal and non-communicative. Over the next couple of days, she called several contractors, drove to Forsyth and Miles City to meet with them over plans, and waited for bids. The numbers came in, from jaw-dropping heights to too-good-to-be-true lows.

"What do I do, Brad?" She poured over her sketches once again. "I can barely afford the lowball offer."

He gathered up the papers and put them in a cupboard drawer out of her sight. "Well, let's wait till we get the insurance company's information and then decide." He nudged her arm. "In the meantime, let's go for a ride."

Her shoulders relaxed, and she turned her face up to him. "All right. That sounds like the best idea yet. I'll get my boots on." She gave him a quick squeeze and bounded up the stairs.

Electra was already in the corral, brushing Apache as he and the three other rescues munched hay.

"Want to join us for a ride?" Sam gestured to the rolling prairie.

The teen let out a bright squeal. "Yes! Yes, of course. Let's go!" She sprinted to the barn for tack and had Apache saddled almost before Sam could put the bridle on Sugar.

She and Brad exchanged bemused glances, mounted, and headed out to the pasture. Trixi, the blonde trick horse she'd saved from auction, whinnied as she was left behind. "It's okay, girl, you'll get to go next time."

The spring sun warmed her back, a meadowlark trilled, and her spirits lifted. She reached forward and patted Sugar's neck. "This is what we love to do, isn't it?"

Brad rode up beside her on Toby, the horse he had been transporting when caught in a bad blizzard. The accident had left the horse relatively unhurt, although skittish for months afterward. But endless weeks had passed while she hadn't been sure if Brad was going to make it. A pang of the old fear shot through her, remembering his complications of brain swelling, pneumonia, and an induced coma.

She shook the memory from her mind and smiled at him. "You're riding so much easier."

"Yeah, the old, gimpy leg is getting stronger. The riding does help."

Up ahead, Electra twisted in her saddle. "Hey, you slowpokes, c'mon. I'll race ya to the butte!"

"Sure, now that you have a quarter mile head start," Sam called back.

The girl reined in her horse, circled around, and waited for them to catch up. As they came alongside her, she dug her heels into Apache's sides, yelling, "Go!"

Sugar and Toby responded to their riders and the race was on. Whooping and laughing, they arrived almost at a dead heat at the foot of the flat-topped hill and slowed to climb to the top.

Sam slid off her horse and stood, surveying the ranch below and the miles upon miles of nothing but soft green prairie. Deep coulees cut through the landscape, and sandstone hills dotted the distance. Red Hereford cows loafed around the reservoir while their white-faced calves frolicked through the handful of cottonwood trees nearby. She inhaled the fresh, clean air.

"I don't think I'll ever get tired of this view." Brad came up beside her, limping only slightly now.

"Me, either." She leaned into him as he put an arm around her shoulder.

An uncharacteristically quiet Electra stared into the distance. "How are you doing, girl?"

The teen brought her dreamy gaze back to the pair. "Oh, Sam, I just love this place. I can't wait till Mom gets here. Then everything will be perfect."

"Only a couple more weeks." Sam looked forward to her arrival too. They'd become good friends since their meeting a year before where she worked at Clyde's dude ranch. She and her mom were on a vacation from New York to get away from memories of a vehicle accident that killed her brother and caused her dad to leave them. Alberta had seen her troubled daughter transformed by the love of a horse, and had, in a huge leap of faith, entrusted her care to Sam for the summer.

She hadn't known what she was in for, with this headstrong, energetic, mood-swinging young teen. But somehow, they'd made it through the summer without killing each other, and after the girl had gone home for the school year, she ended up running away, back to Montana. Because of Electra's depression, Alberta had relented and allowed her daughter to stay with Sam, as long as she kept up with her schoolwork online.

She walked to Electra's side and gave her a hug. "I'm so glad you came to live here with me." Such a colossal change, from the sullen, white-makeup, black-clad girl who cut herself, to this fresh-faced cowgirl.

If I've ever done something right, this might be it. Sam lifted her eyes to the clear blue sky. *Thank you, Lord. I couldn't have done it without you.*

The trio trotted into the home pasture, where Trixi whinnied, greeting her friends. Sam floated on a bubble of euphoria from the ride. She grinned at Brad and Electra as they unsaddled. Life couldn't get any better than this.

When she entered the kitchen, the answering machine light blinked with a message from Murdock. "Well, good news and bad news. The insurance will cover the barn…but only the original footprint. I'm sorry, I know you want to expand. If I can do anything, give me a call."

With his not-so-great-news message, the respite of their morning ride vanished like a meteor flash. Her chin sank to her chest. Of course. Nothing could be easy, could it?

"Ohmygosh, what does that mean?" Electra was at her side in a flash. "Can we rebuild the barn?"

She raised her gaze to the girl's pale, stunned face. "Yeah. But only a small one. I'll have to use the money I've set aside if I want a bigger facility." She hitched her shoulders. "And I do. I really do."

Brad strode to where she slumped against the wall. "Then you will." He put his hands on her shoulders and stared into her eyes. "You *will*. No need to stress out about it. We'll figure it out together, okay?"

She crossed her arms and clutched her elbows. "But I probably won't be able to build the arena or a bunkhouse."

"Maybe not right away, but you can plan it in phases." He steered her to a chair at the kitchen table. "Let's go over your plans again and see where we can cut costs, and then maybe meet with your low-bid contractor; see what he suggests."

She pressed her hands to her temples. "Yeah. You're probably right. And I'll definitely need to continue working at Clyde's."

No rest for the wicked. Her peaceful mood from the morning ride had been erased by a single swipe of worry.

CHAPTER TWO

Sam and Electra loaded Trixi and Apache into the trailer, and the trio wended their way to Miles City Community College Ag Center. Nick Seward, the ag instructor and veterans' program coordinator, met them at the arena entrance.

"Welcome back. We were all so shocked to hear about the fire. What happened?"

"A freak accident. Newborn calf knocked over a heat lamp." She grimaced.

"But you're okay," the bearded, dark-haired man glanced at the horses, "and all your livestock safe?"

"Yes, thank God. They all got out, even the calf." She forced a cheerful smile. "And we're glad to be back."

Brad headed off for his session with the vet's PTSD counselor. As he strode off with confidence, a weight lifted from her shoulders.

When she and Electra led the horses inside the arena from the loading area, she saw that the group of six had grown by one. "This is Elliot." Nick introduced the newcomer who ducked his head in response.

The regulars greeted Sam and Electra with hugs and handshakes and a chorus of "Welcome back. Glad you're okay."

Sondra, the lone woman in the group, raised wide eyes to Sam. "Are you...really? Okay, I mean?"

"Yes, I'm fine. I'm a little overwhelmed with the idea of rebuilding right now, but other than that, life goes on, right?" She touched the woman's arm. *Sweet of her to be concerned. Maybe she thinks I have PTSD now too.* "Well, everybody, are you ready to go to work?"

The group replied with enthusiastic whoops and "Yeah, let's roll." She got the men started with Electra and Apache, and she took Sondra and Elliot to work with Trixi. Sondra had been gradually working her way toward becoming more comfortable with the big horse. But after almost slipping off at her first attempt to ride, the petite soldier had not yet tried again.

Elliot didn't have any prosthetics, but he did have a red, mottled burn scar on his neck. Sam assumed, like the rest, he also suffered from PTSD—the deep injury that couldn't be seen. She kept a cheerful face and talked about the horse, what to expect from her and the program, and asked Sondra to demonstrate brushing.

"You move at your own pace. You don't need to do anything until you're ready."

The muscled veteran watched with an intense gaze as Sondra rubbed Trixi's face, ears, and neck and spoke to her softly. She offered the mare a cake pellet on the flat of her hand. The tense lines in her face faded, and her shoulders relaxed. Then she picked up a brush and stroked the horse's coat, seemingly lost to the world around her. Trixi bent her neck around to encircle the woman.

Sam explained everything Sondra did, how she gained the mare's trust by petting her and talking to her, how she brushed in the direction the hair grew, gradually working from front to back. "Horses are very intuitive. They pick up on your mood, and I believe they want to comfort you when you need that."

Elliot snorted. "And kick you when you least expect it."

She jerked her head in surprise. "Sounds like you've had a bad experience."

11

"Yeah."

"So, what brought you here?"

He shrugged. "Nick thought it'd be a good idea. Confront my demons and all that, ya know. Wrong place at the wrong time's all."

She nodded. Probably referring to both his horse and war experiences. "Yes, you have to be careful not to startle the horse by coming up behind them. But most are really quite forgiving if they've been treated right. And Trixi is a champion at that."

"Okay. If you say so." He made no move toward the horse.

"Do you want to try feeding her a treat?"

He stood, silent for a moment, rubbing the scar on his neck. He finally nodded. "Sure."

Sam gave him a pellet and showed him how to hold it out on a flat palm.

He strode forward, shoving his hand in Trixi's face. The mare snorted and threw her head back. The vet jerked, dropping his arm and the pellet. He swore, barely under his breath.

"Easy now." She spoke as much to Elliot as to the horse. "Approach slowly. Let her smell you and trust you."

"Nah. Ain't gonna work." He turned his back, his shoulders rigid.

"It's okay. When you're ready." Although she wanted to grab those tight shoulders and shake him, she forced herself to relax. "All right, Sondra, what would you like to do today? Are you ready to ride yet or just watch?"

The woman's wide eyes stood out in dark contrast to her pale face. She swallowed. "I… uh… I think I'll watch."

"All right." Sam nodded. "Hey, Electra, one of your students want to come over here and ride?"

One-armed Linc broke away from his group and sprinted toward her. "I would!" His face beamed. "It's hard to get a turn, with all those guys wanting to ride now."

"Great. Let's demonstrate to Elliot how this works for riders who have trouble mounting." *Boy, I sure hope this goes better with him than the other two.*

Elliot barely moved his head to watch.

She gave Trixi the signal—tapping her own leg—the horse kneeled, and Linc slid into the saddle. He gave the next signal—tapping at the point of her shoulder—the mare rose, and with Sam close beside, walked around the arena.

As they came around to where the two watchers stood, Elliot, with his back to them again, swiveled his head to look.

"It's great fun," Linc called out as they circled once more.

After he'd ridden several laps, he dismounted, gave Trixie a pellet, and stood rubbing her face. "You're such a good girl, yes, you are."

Well, at least one showed some progress today. Her heart ached for the trouble that had caused the new guy to react so aggressively and negatively and for Sondra's continued fear. "Okay, that's enough for today. Good job, everybody." She tried to inject an upbeat note into her voice. Too bad their session was up for the day. *Maybe if I had more time, more experience, more insight to their issues… Maybe I could make more of a difference.*

While Electra and her students unsaddled and brushed Apache, Sam did the same, with Sondra's and Linc's help. Elliot stood back by the bleachers, one side turned toward them, observing out the corner of his eye.

Her first two veteran charges—Del in his wheelchair and Garrett with a prosthetic foot—approached, along with Nick. The two vets were effusive in their praise for Electra and Apache.

"Good session today." The ag instructor nodded his approval. "How'd it go, Elliot?"

The veteran ducked his head and grunted.

"That's okay. Small steps, remember?" Nick turned back to Sam. "Is there anything we can do to help you, um, with cleanup or rebuilding your barn, or anything?"

Warmth rushed through her. "Oh, thank you. I appreciate your offer. The cleanup is pretty much done, and now I need to find a 'cheap' contractor." She explained the insurance situation.

"Well, that sucks." He huffed a breath. "You let me know, okay?"

She smiled. "I will. Thanks."

Brad returned from his counseling session and helped load the horses. "Why don't we have some lunch at the 600 Café and then stop by that contractor's office with the lower bid?"

"Yeah! I'm starving." Electra bounded into the pickup and slid to the middle of the cracked vinyl seat.

"You're always hungry." Brad poked her with his elbow as he fastened his seatbelt. "Sam?"

She nodded. "Yeah, I could use some sustenance."

"You look a little downtrodden. Something happen?" He leaned forward to peer around the teen.

"It was a little rough with the new student. He's got major issues, very negative, very aggressive." She sighed. "I don't know about this one."

"He'll come around. They all do eventually. Just look at Garrett and how reluctant he was at first. It took a lot of patience on your part, but now he's almost as enthusiastic as Linc and Del."

She shifted gears and steered toward downtown. "Yeah, I suppose. I hope so."

After Sam found a large parking lot space for the truck and trailer, the trio headed for the landmark restaurant, where Brad ordered steak and eggs and Electra a hamburger and fries. Sam dipped her spoon into a hearty chicken noodle soup, and then tipped it, letting the broth slowly cascade back into the bowl.

Although she felt a bit shaky and knew she needed food, her stomach churned.

Would this new man be her downfall, her failure in the program?

Elliot's demeanor plagued Sam as she drove. *You've got to be patient with him,* she reminded herself. After all, Garrett had been extremely reluctant to get close to the horses at the beginning, although he had contacted her to work with him. But she'd given him slack, the time to warm up to Sugar and Trixi, and along with his friend Del, he finally came around to the idea of riding.

Even though he'd fallen off and injured his knee because she hadn't been vigilant enough, Garrett had, by that time become hooked on horses. *Elliot will come around too. He's got even deeper problems.* Maybe she should call Nick and talk to him about how to deal with it all. And with Sondra too. Sam had hoped for more, but the woman's progress seemed stymied.

As she drove the lane toward home, She caught a glimpse of a beat-up green pickup with a faded silver trailer backed up to her chute. "What the…?"

Electra and Brad leaned forward to peer through the windshield.

"Ohmygosh, they're unloading a horse." Electra's voice rose.

Parking beside the visitor's vehicle, Sam got out. "Hello. Can I help you?"

The person at the chute turned a leathery face toward the trio. Wispy strands of gray hair escaped from under a greasy, crumpled hat. "Oh, hullo there." A woman's voice, raspy and as weathered as her face. "I heared you rescue horses. An' I got one for ya." She gestured a tobacco-stained hand toward the small, black pony that peeked out from the back of the trailer.

"Well, yeah, I have several, but—"

15

"Um… This here's Money. He's a Welch-Shetlan' cross, an' I got 'im fer my granddaughter, but he ain't workin' out. She's only eight, an' he won't go. Poor lil thang, she jis sits on 'm and cries." She shook her head, more stringy wisps flapping. "An' then when I got on 'm, he perceeded t' buckin' like an ol' rodeo bronc. Ain't no horse fer a lil gal."

Sam didn't know much about the Welsh pony breed, but Shetlands could be quite stubborn. "Yes, but…I'm not set up for more horses." Sam pointed toward the blackened spot in the corral. "My barn burned down recently, and I don't have—"

"Wull, I cain't keep'm. I'd jis have t' shoot 'im."

Electra gasped. Sam's abdominal muscles tensed.

The woman reached through the trailer window, slapped the pony on the rump, and he ran kicking and whinnying into the corral. Then she climbed inside and unloaded two bags of oats and four bales of hay. "This here oughta help feed 'im… Fer a few days anyhow."

Sam's mouth dropped open. No words would come as the woman jumped into her truck and ground it into gear. "Oh, ya might wanna keep 'im separate from yer other horses," she called out the window as she drove away.

"No!" Sam yelled after the retreating trailer. "I can't…"

Too late. The woman was gone.

She faced Brad and Electra and threw her arms out wide. "*What* the heck just happened?"

"I think you got yourself another rescue." Brad's mouth turned up slightly at one corner.

"Ohmygosh, he's just the cutest little thing." Electra was over the fence and in the corral, approaching the pony before Sam could say anything. He stopped mid-lap, his front feet planted forward, his ears back, blowing and snorting. "Hey, little fella, c'mere. I have a treat for you." She offered a pellet on her palm as she slowly approached him.

16

Money snorted again, whirled, and kicked. His hind legs barely missed Electra's outstretched arm. She shrieked and jumped back.

Sam clambered over the rails and ran to the girl, wrenching her out of the way as the pony kicked again. They hustled over the fence while the little horse galloped 'round and 'round the corral, kicking and blowing.

"Ohmygosh! He's an ornery one." Electra's eyes were moon-sized in her pale face. Her thin shoulders trembled as Sam squeezed an arm around her.

"Are you all right?" Brad peered into her face. "Did he get you?"

"No. I'm fine." She shook her head. "I just… wanted to… give him a treat… make friends…" Her voice hitched.

Sam rubbed the girl's arm. "I know. It's okay, honey. He's a different sort." This was the first time Electra had come up against a horse that wasn't friendly or a sucker for a pellet. "He might have been abused." The little black's mane and tail were extraordinarily long and matted and his hooves overgrown and cracked.

The teen sniffed and swiped at her nose with the back of her hand. "Yeah. Poor little guy."

"At the very least, not well taken care of." Sam scrunched her face. "It's probably going to take some time to win his trust. And…we have to be prepared that maybe he won't come around."

Her shoulders tightened. *Just what I need, a problem horse.*

17

CHAPTER THREE

After watching Money nip and kick at the other horses across the pasture fence, Sam set up a small pen with panels at one end of the big corral to keep him separate. Electra helped her drag in a tub for water and threw in a flake of hay. The pony snorted and sniffed, approaching the feed with caution, as if it contained a rattlesnake. Then he grabbed a bite and stepped back, chewing as his eyes rolled from Sam to Electra. They stood quietly, simply watching.

When Money didn't sense any movement or danger from them, he stretched his neck out and grabbed another bite. Soon he ignored them, greedily snuffling and chewing the hay.

"He acts like he's starving," Electra whispered.

Sam nodded. "He does look a little skinny." *I think he has been neglected as well as abused.*

After the pony had eaten and drunk his fill, he retreated to the far end of the pen, again eyeing them suspiciously.

"I think we'll leave him be for now." Sam headed toward the other horses. "Let's take care of these guys and maybe take a short ride." She threw a glance toward Brad at the corral fence. "You up for that?"

"Definitely." He walked, limping slightly, to the gate and joined them.

The late afternoon sun slanted, stretching their horseback shadows into long, comic caricatures as they rode toward the reservoir where the cows were undoubtedly gathered. A hawk

18

gave a piercing cry above and glided across the pure blue sky toward the horizon.

Thoughts of the day buzzed through her mind like a bee looking for a flower. First, Elliot's angry pain and Sondra's lingering fear of riding. *Is this program worth the time and travel? Is it really going to help them?* She gazed at Brad and Electra ahead. Her little "family." She had helped them, so maybe there was hope for the veterans' program as well.

Second, meeting with the contractor hadn't panned out. A note on the door of his small, beat-up trailer office stated he was "out on a job." She'd left him a note to call her, but doubts and frustration to get the barn rebuilt were winning over patience and planning. She huffed a snort. Now her plan to build a larger barn and an indoor arena had turned into a mountain-sized obstacle.

And then, coming home to this unhappy, unruly pony. The nerve of that woman, simply dropping him off. *What does she think I am?* The blood in her neck and face heated and pulsed. She'd been so shocked, she hadn't even gotten the old biddy's name. Or thought to ask about papers or bill of sale. *That was stupid.* She ground her teeth. Now she had another horse to feed and to—maybe—gentle and train. An audible groan escaped.

Brad turned his head toward her and rode back. "I heard that. What's up? Are you chewing your cud over what happened today?"

She bridled at his joke; however, couldn't help but allow one corner of her mouth to curve slightly. "Are you calling me an old heifer?"

He grinned. "Naw. But I know you by now. I see your shoulders up around your ears, and almost see steam coming out."

"I can almost feel it." She allowed herself a small chuckle. "Oh, Brad. This day has just overwhelmed me. All these events—the barn, the vets, this new horse—seem like too much to deal with."

"Yeah. Taken all at once, it is. But you know what 'they' say in self-help circles, one step at a time."

She wrinkled her nose. "Now you're turning my own advice back on me."

"If the shoe fits…" He repeated the need for patience and listed the success she'd already had with several of the veterans, with Electra and him, and with her other rescue horses. "Especially Toby."

"I know, I know." She rolled her eyes. "Yeah, as soon as we—you, really—got him over his fear of going into the barn, it had to burn down."

"A freak accident. You know that."

"Yeah, I do. But now getting the barn rebuilt, along with the expansion I'd hoped for… It's all a bunch of pipe smoke. The insurance money will barely cover the original barn, much less anything else."

Brad shrugged and reached across to give her arm a quick squeeze. "Your dream going to happen, one way or the other. Maybe not all at once, but it will. You have your ranch now, and that was the first step. Next step, the contractor will call you, and you'll go from there."

Her shoulders released with his encouraging words and affectionate touch. She let herself sink into the rhythm of Trixi's gait, the softening spring air, sounds of awakening insects, and the watercolor wash flowing across the horizon. *A little more time and patience, Samantha Moser. There's always hope.*

***

As the days passed, the little black pony continued his tirade against the pen, other horses, and any attempt to gain his trust. Sam stood at the panel fence, watching him pace and buck and snort. This had to be more than just stubbornness. How did that woman even get an eight-year-old girl on his back if he was this bad? She ground her teeth. *Because the old so-and-so probably beat him, that's why.*

Money would only come to eat and drink after any human had backed far enough away, so there was no holding out a tantalizing pellet to get close enough even to pet him. She couldn't win his trust this way. She let out an exasperated sigh. *I don't have the time for this.* On her long list, after her own chores: the weekly class with the veterans, Clyde was gearing up for dude season, and the group home kids were clamoring to come out and ride. And, of course, the barn needed to be rebuilt.

She stomped to the house and punched in the contractor's number once again, listening to the endless ring on the other end. As she took the receiver from her ear to hang up, a voice came over the line. "…lo?"

"Oh! You're there. I was about to give up on you." Sam repeated her name and the information about the barn.

"Yeah." Papers rustled in the background. "Okay. Yeah. This is Bob. Joe's out on a job, but yeah, he told me to give you a call. Sorry. Things have been a little crazy."

"So, Joe gave me an estimate, and if that's still good, with the insurance settlement, I'm wondering about a slightly bigger structure. Could somebody come out and take a look?"

"Sure." Rustling papers again. "How about tomorrow? We can both be there."

She gave him directions and hung up. Maybe she should get someone else to come out as well. But the next lowest bid she'd received was still way too high.

Slamming her fist against the wall, she recoiled from the pain. She stomped out to her pickup, bootheels grinding in the dirt. "Electra! Brad! I'm going over to Clyde's."

The girl's voice came from the pasture where she'd ridden up on Apache. "Okay. I'll stay here and finish chores with Brad."

"All right. See you guys later." She started the truck, put it in gear, and spun a cloud of dust behind as she drove away.

The fifteen miles to the dude ranch gave her time enough to alternately pound the steering wheel, take deep breaths, yell out loud, and take more breaths. She opened the window and let the wind blow her hair, the smell of new grass and sage filling her nostrils. The low hillsides were now dotted with fragile pink and white bitterroot flowers, and occasionally a meadowlark song drifted through the window. Gradually, her foot eased off the gas, her shoulders lowered, and the peace of the spring countryside overcame her anxious thoughts.

Clyde wielded a hammer, repairing a corral gate, as Sam drove in. He pushed his hat back and gave a nod. "Mornin'."

"Hi." She got out and surveyed his handiwork. "Thought maybe you'd need a hand getting ready for the season."

"Yup. Sure could." The middle-aged rancher shifted his attention back to the gate. "Hand me that short board from the back of the pickup, would ya?"

She grabbed the wood and handed it to him, wincing as a splinter slid into her palm. "When is your first bunch coming in, and what would you like me to do?" She pulled the splinter out with a fingernail.

"Next week." He spat tobacco to the side. "Maybe organize the tack and see if anything needs repair."

"Okay." She turned toward the barn.

"How's the barn plans comin'?"

She shook her head and huffed. "Don't ask." Then she chuckled. "I do have a contractor coming out tomorrow. But now, guess what I found when I got home from Miles City last week?" Before she realized she needed to, she had spilled the story and the frustrations over the poor, stubborn, little pony.

"Good gawsh-amighty." Clyde spat again, hitting a dirt clod. "The nerve of that ol'... uh...woman. And you have no idea who she is?"

22

"No. None."

He snorted a laugh. "Well, I guess your reputation as horse-rescuer has spread. I'd let Sheriff O'Connor know, just in case she'd decide later to come back and accuse you of stealin' her horse."

Sam grimaced, remembering when she and Electra had rescued Apache. She'd written a check and a bill of sale and given it to the owner's nephew, but the owner then had reported his horse stolen and took it back. The anger, disappointment, and anxiety over appearing in civil court rose up from her insides like bile. Fortunately, the judge had sided with her, and she got Apache back.

"Yeah, that's a good idea. I'll do that. In the meantime, I guess we just need time to win this pony over." She strolled back to the barn.

When Sam drove into the home yard, she saw Brad standing at the makeshift pen. She frowned. *What is he doing?* She got out of the pickup and strode to the corral gate. Then she saw what he was watching. Inside the pen, Electra sat about six feet away from the pony's feed bucket, her back to the horse.

Panic ratcheted up from Sam's belly. Oh man, what do they think they're doing? What if Money turns and kicks at her again? *Oh no, no, no!* She forced herself to walk with calm and quiet steps, all the while tamping down the urge to yell, "Get out of there!"

Brad faced her with a grin. "Hey," he whispered. "Glad you're home."

She locked her hands around the panel rail, knuckles white. "What do you think you're doing?" Her words hissed through clenched teeth.

Electra looked up from a book. Her face beamed.

The pony stared at the bucket and the human beyond. Sam's breath caught. They were trying the approach Brad had used to

23

lure Toby into the barn after the gelding had been traumatized by the accident and was afraid to enter enclosed spaces.

Money took a step forward, snuffling at the tantalizing pellets just outside his reach. Then he swung his head around toward Sam and Brad, whirled, and ran back to the far side of the pen.

"How long has she been at this?"

"A couple hours, I think."

Sam raised her voice a notch. "Electra, I think it's time to give him a rest."

"Aww." The girl's mouth turned down.

"Yeah. Probably a good idea. You can try again tomorrow." Brad opened the gate for her to come out.

Sam put her hands on her hips. "I don't know if that *is* such a good idea. This pony is so unpredictable. We don't know what he might do. I can't let you put yourself in danger. I don't want you to continue with this."

"Sa-am!" Electra's forehead knotted. "I wasn't in danger. He isn't going to hurt me. Brad was right here all along. I *want* to work with him." Her voice rose to a high pitch and her wide eyes glistened. "Pleeease?"

"No. No way can I allow you to put yourself in harm's way. Your mom would absolutely *kill* me if you got hurt." She narrowed her eyes at Brad. "I'm surprised at you, letting her in there. You saw what happened before."

His eyes registered shock. "It was okay, honest, it was. He never showed any signs of aggression today."

"Yeah, we made a lot of progress. He was getting closer and closer." The teen delivered her words with a marked tone of sincerity. "He just needs time and patience. You're always saying that."

"I know. But this is quite a different situation." Sam faced her squarely. "I don't want you doing this again. You understand?"

Electra's shoulders slumped. "Yeah."

Sam stalked to the house.

In the kitchen the phone light blinked, with a message from Alberta. She would be arriving in a week, and she left her flight number and arrival time. A blanket of relief wrapped around her. Soon, she could let Electra's mom take over. She took hamburger out of the refrigerator and began preparing supper.

The teen slinked in, toward the stairs with head down.

"Your mom called." Sam caught her in mid-step.

"Okay," a small voice answered.

"You can call her back, if you want." She gave her a sympathetic look as the girl plodded into the kitchen. "But don't tell her anything about this pony, all right?"

Electra nodded, her face like a storm cloud about to release rain.

"Hey." She put an arm around the teen's shoulders. "I'm sorry if I've upset you, but I hope you understand why. I care about you, and I don't want you to get hurt."

A sniffle and a nod.

"Okay. Call your mom."

That brought a smile, and Electra punched in the number. Soon she was squealing with happiness at the news that her mother would be there in a few days.

When Brad came in, he headed for the bathroom to wash up, also avoiding her gaze. She rolled her eyes. It was like dealing with a couple of little kids caught red-handed. "Supper's ready," she called. "It's spaghetti, your favorite."

He came out, chuckling. "Yeah, except it isn't leftover spaghetti."

She gave him a playful cuff on the shoulder, remembering the first time he'd shared a meal with her and how he'd joked about the dish being better the second day. That was when she'd begun to warm up to him and his quirky sense of humor. It had been a long time since she'd seen glimpses of that side.

"Well, it will be tomorrow." She gestured to the table with her head. "C'mon, dish up before it gets cold."

***

Pleasantly surprised, Sam did a double-take when Bob and Joe from JB Construction arrived the next morning in a beat-up, mud-splattered work truck. She'd almost expected a no-show. *Maybe this is a good sign.*

She grabbed her papers and bounced down the porch steps to meet the men with a handshake. "Good morning."

"Mornin', ma'am." Joe nodded, his sun-browned face half-hidden by a battered, dark-stained Stetson. "Sorry I didn't get back to you sooner. It's been a busy month."

"That's a good thing…for you, I guess." She gestured toward the corral where the barn once stood. "Come, take a look at the area, and I'll show you what I have in mind." Mentally crossing her fingers, she led the way. *I sure hope they can do it.*

Brad and Electra, who had been with the horses gathered at the pasture fence, joined the group. "Are you going to build our new barn and arena and bunkhouse?" The teen inserted herself between Sam and the men.

Joe chuckled. "Well, missy, we're goin' to take a look and see what we can do for ya." He held out a hand to Sam. "Let me take a look at your plans."

She gave him the sheaf of papers. He and Bob studied the blueprints she'd downloaded from the internet, with added sketches and figures, propping them against the rail.

The morning sun shone toasty on her back, but the prickly sweat in her armpits was not from the heat. She shifted her glance between the men hunched over the papers and Brad and Electra standing close by. Brad raised his eyebrows and gave her a nod, as if to say *Calm down. It'll work out.* Electra fidgeted and chewed on a hangnail on her thumb. Sam bit at the inside

26

of her cheek, trying to send telepathic thoughts to the teen. *Stay back. Don't go giving them suggestions now!*

"Okay, so you want to increase the size of your original barn by half and attach an indoor arena?"

Sam nodded. "Yes, that's what I'd like to do if I can afford to. But I'd like separate bids for the two. I'd like a bunkhouse too, but that will probably have to wait."

"Sure." Joe strode toward the corral gate, addressing Bob over his shoulder. "Get me that big tape measure from the truck, wouldya?"

"Yup." The other man soon rejoined him, and they walked the still-blackened spot and beyond, measuring and jotting notes.

The trio stood back, watching with an air of anticipation. Excitement and dread dueled inside. Brad took her hand and gave it a squeeze. Electra's big, dark eyes sparkled with eagerness.

Finally, the two men returned to the group. Joe folded the papers and tucked them in his shirt pocket. "All right. We've done the walk-around and measurements. Bob here will study your blueprints to get an idea of how much material is needed, and I'll call you with the new bids."

"Okay." Sam had hoped he could at least give her a ballpark figure right away. "Do you know how long that'll take?"

"Not long. Prob'ly two-three days."

She nodded. "All right. I look forward to hearing from you...soon."

The old truck bounced away down the road, raising a plume of dust. "How come they didn't tell us right now?" Electra expressed the disappointment Sam didn't dare say out loud.

"Well, they have to figure it all out, how much lumber they need, and how much time it'll take, and all that." She sighed. "Hurry up and wait."

"Yeah. That's the way it goes, I guess." Brad patted her shoulder. "Let's go for a ride before you have to head off for Clyde's."

"Sounds good."

They saddled up and rode out through the gullies, the sunshine and breeze easing her impatience. "Whatever happens, at least I'll get the barn rebuilt, maybe a little larger."

"Yeah, you will, and that'll be great."

"Even if I have to wait to do the other projects, I guess I can do one at a time." She allowed a thrill to lift her thoughts.

"Absolutely. I'm excited for you." Brad peered at her from under the brim of his hat. "Hey, are we okay?"

She tossed a frown his way.

"I mean, because I let Electra work with Money without checking with you first. I'm sorry about that."

"Oh that. Yeah, we're okay. I may have been a bit snappish, but gosh, it scared the bejiminies out of me."

"I didn't realize it would upset you, but I do understand why. You've had a big responsibility with this girl. She's come so far, sometimes I forget that she's only fourteen." Brad snickered. "Until she gets excited over something."

"Me too." Sam laughed with him. "I'll be glad when her mom gets here next week. Then *she* will be in charge of her."

CHAPTER FOUR

When Sam arrived for the next veterans' riding class, she quickly scanned the group standing in one corner of the arena. Counting six heads, she looked again more closely. Nope, Elliot wasn't there. While her heart sank with disappointment, relief lifted it again. At least she wouldn't have to deal with his anger issues today.

Del waved from his wheelchair, and Garrett strode to meet her entourage. "Good morning." He gave them a quick nod and a smile.

"Hey there. You look eager to get started." She grinned back. What a big difference from the first few times he'd come for horse therapy at the ranch.

"Yeah. We all are." He took Apache's reins from Electra and led him to the group.

As Sam approached with Trixi, the mare whinnied as if greeting them. "Hi, everybody. Good to see you here." She reviewed techniques for mounting and reining and answered questions. "Okay, if you're ready to start, Sondra, Garrett, and Jimmy, come with me. The rest of you are with Electra."

Her group followed to the other side of the arena, Garrett limping slightly with his prosthetic foot, and Jimmy dragging a bit with his artificial leg. She took Trixi's halter off and held out a bridle. "Who would like to try putting this on?"

Garrett looked from Sondra to Jimmy. "I've done this before. You guys take a turn."

The young woman vet hung back, her eyes cast down. Jimmy stepped forward. "I'll try." He took the gear, put it behind his back, and approached the horse slowly, his hand outstretched until he was able to stroke her neck. Then he pulled out the bridle, put the reins over her neck, and as Sam had previously demonstrated, inched the headgear over her nose, and placed the bit at her lips. Well-trained as she was, Trixi stood quietly while the veteran fumbled and nearly dropped the gear. His face flushed bright red, and he cast an apprehensive glance toward her.

"It's all right." She reassured him with a soft tone and a nod. "Try again. You don't need to be nervous. Talk to her, use your right hand to pull the bridle up and your left to encourage her to take the bit."

He took a breath and murmured to the mare, rubbing her nose and face before he attempted again. This time he was able to get everything aligned exactly right, and Trixi opened her mouth to accept the bit.

"Oorah," Garrett said softly.

"Good job, Jimmy." Sam encouraged him through fastening the chin strap. "Now, who wants to saddle her?"

With a glance at Sondra who shook her head, Garrett stepped to Sam's side. "I'll give 'er a try."

He spoke to Trixi, caressed her face and neck. Holding the reins in his left hand, he smoothed the hair on her back and then reached down to pick up the saddle blanket. That in place, he patted and talked to her some more. Then he studied the heavy saddle sitting nearby. "So, how do I hang onto her and put the saddle on at the same time?"

Sam chuckled. "That can be a trick, but we'll tackle that at a later date. Trixi is so well-trained that you can go ahead and drop the reins to 'ground-tie' her. Other horses you might want to tie to a corral fence. But she's the perfect horse to practice on."

"Okay, glad for that." Garrett picked up the saddle and with a grunt, heaved it onto her back. It slipped back a little, and he pushed it upright.

"All right. Now make sure it's not too far back or too high on the withers." She eased the saddle into place, showing her group where it should sit. "Now, reach under her belly and grab the cinch."

He gave her a look of disbelief. "O-kay..." With an eye on the mare's hind legs, he reached to the other side, grabbed the strap, and brought it toward him. "Huh. Glad she's not a kicker." He gave a nervous laugh.

"Most horses you'll encounter have been saddled so often they won't object—unless you're doing something that hurts them." She instructed him how to tighten the cinch and check the saddle to make sure it didn't roll off to the side when he was ready to get on. "I learned the hard way about getting the cinch tight enough—got out to the pasture, leaned to one side while chasing a cow, and it rolled under the horse's belly. I landed butt-first in a big cactus patch."

"Ow!" Her three students spoke as one.

"Yeah. Not fun." She grimaced.

"You can stick your foot in the stirrup and put your weight into it to see if the saddle does give any." She demonstrated, the saddle shifted slightly, so she tightened the strap once again. "Some horses are tricky and will take in a big belly full of air when you tighten the cinch, so you have to wait a bit and then tighten the strap some more."

"Oh my gosh. That's a lot to remember." Sondra's face scrunched in an I-can't-do-this frown.

"You don't have to remember it all at once," Sam reassured her. "We'll keep practicing. We have all the time in the world."

"Well, okay... I dunno..."

"You can do it. Don't worry about what might happen down the road. Let's just go with what we are doing right now."

She huffed a private snort. *Listen to me. Maybe I ought to practice what I preach.* "So now we're saddled and bridled. Who wants to ride first?"

When no one spoke up, Garrett nodded. "I'll go."

"Do you want to try mounting while she's standing, or do you want her to kneel?"

He chewed on his lower lip a moment. "Well... I'd like to try with her standing, but I don't know about..." He glanced at his left foot, the one he would use to step into the stirrup.

"Let's give it a try from her right side. Most horses have been trained only to be mounted on the left, so they might object. But again, since Trixi is a trick horse, she doesn't mind." Sam led the way to the other side.

Garrett stuck his boot into the stirrup, boosted his body up, left leg over, and landed in the saddle. "Right side up!" He flashed the group a bright look.

"Go ahead." She nodded to the track.

He adjusted himself in his seat. Then he gave the reins some slack, nudged his heels against the mare's sides, and rode forward.

Sam walked alongside, making sure he didn't slip out of the saddle. *Like he did that first time.* She shook her head. *Only I was stupid enough to have him ride bareback then.* She'd learned her lesson, sitting in the waiting room at the ER.

She glanced at Electra's group. Apache had kneeled for Del to transfer from his chair to the saddle. It looked like they were doing well. How would she ever do this without her girl?

After several laps around the arena, Garrett dismounted to applause from the others. A huge smile gleamed on his flushed face. "Awesome!"

"You've come a long way. Good job." Sam turned to the others. "Anybody else?"

Jimmy stepped forward. "Sure. I haven't tried mounting a standing horse yet."

32

She glanced at his legs. "Which one?"

He patted his right.

"Okay, great. You can get on from the usual side then, the left."

The blond-haired vet gave a couple of heave-ho's before he landed in the saddle, clucked his tongue, and rode forward.

"Doin' great!" Garrett called out.

As she walked beside them, the tension she carried in her face and shoulders eased. *They really are doing well today. This is fun.*

The other two veterans applauded when Jimmy finished his laps.

"That was great!" Sam joined in. "You looked like a pro."

He slid out of the saddle, a pleased look on his face. "Huh. When I was layin' in that hospital bed with one leg gone, I never pictured myself as a cowboy."

Garrett clapped him on the back. "Like 'back then I couldn't spell it, but now I are one'?"

"Yeehaw!" Jimmy let out a guffaw.

"Yeah, I can see you with a pair of fancy chaps and alligator boots." Sondra giggled.

The three broke into laughter, joshing, and high-fiving each other.

Sam's chest expanded. *This is more like it!* This program could be a good thing after all. She caught Sondra's glance and raised her eyebrows toward Trixi.

The woman kept her smile but swallowed hard before she nodded. "Okay. My turn."

Yess! Sam did an inner fist-pump. She helped Sondra put her foot in the stirrup and gave her a gentle boost onto the saddle. The young veteran checked her right boot to make sure it was in the stirrup on the other side, squirmed to get a firm seat, and clutched the reins in one hand and the saddle horn in the other.

She took a lungful of air and held it a moment before releasing. Her smile quivered, and her eyes were wide and bright.

"Lookin' good up there," Garrett encouraged.

"Whenever you're ready." She patted the woman's leg. "I'm right here beside you."

Another breath. Another audible exhale. Her face pale, she squared her shoulders and nodded. Then she loosened the reins and pressed her heels into Trixi's sides. The mare moved slowly forward. Sam strode beside them, her hand on the cantle behind Sondra.

At first the young woman held her back and shoulders in rigid tension, but half-way around the track, she visibly sank into the horse's rhythmic motion. They continued around the arena in silence, but when they got back to the guys, Jimmy waved a hand in the air as if he were twirling a rope. "Ride 'em, cowgirl!"

Sondra's optimism returned, and she allowed herself a chuckle.

"You really *are* doing great. I'm proud of you."

Another lap. More banter from the men. The woman vet's face beamed as she indicated she wanted to keep going. Sam stayed calmly beside her, but she wanted to leap high and click her heels and yell and cheer.

When Sondra completed her last circuit, she reined the mare up beside her group, and dismounted in one smooth motion. "Oorah!" "Hoo-Ah!" Garrett and Jimmy whooped. With a grin as big as the moon, Sondra swept her arm out and bowed. "Thank you, thank you very much."

Again, the three veterans came together with hugs, fist-bumps, and laughter. Like a proud mom, she stood back and watched their bonding and spirited camaraderie.

Nick came up beside her, followed by the other group. "Looks like you had a successful session."

34

"Yes, we did. Really good." Her face heated with his compliment. "You guys too?"

She glanced at Electra who also grinned like the Cheshire cat. "Yeah, awesome!"

A door slammed like a shot, Sam jumped, and eight pairs of eyes focused on the entrance. A man staggered toward them, his brown hair sticking up in all directions, shirttail half-untucked.

Sam gasped. Elliot!

He held a bottle high. "Greetingsh! 'm I late?" Taking a swig, he let out a chilling gale of laughter. "Betcha all havin' fun, ridin' the lil horsies." He stumbled, almost fell, but waved the bottle to catch his balance, cursing. "Buncha big, brave veterans, huh? Horsies get yer goat?"

Nick sprinted forward, followed by the other guys.

Elliot swayed. "Who'sh teacher's pet t'day? Huh?"

Beside her, Electra squeaked. Sam grabbed the girl's hand, her heart pounding like a bass drum. *Oh my gosh! She doesn't need to see this!* She wanted to cover Electra's eyes, scoop her up, and get her away. But frozen to the spot, she was unable to take her gaze off the spectacle.

Catching the man's arms as he pitched forward, Nick and Linc eased him down onto the bleachers. The ag instructor took the bottle from the vet's hand and spoke in a low but firm voice. "You're okay, Elliot. It's all right. Had a little slip, huh?" He patted the veteran's back, and the man burst into anguished, angry howls.

She only caught a few words, mostly four-letter jeers and ugly bursts of bile, as the men gathered around him. Elliot flailed against their embrace, screamed, punched, and kicked.

All the while, she held a protective arm around a shaking Electra.

The door banged open again, and Sondra came in with the counselor, Brad close on their heels. They joined the group surrounding Elliot.

Long moments stretched. Electra's body thrummed against Sam's embrace.

The group spoke to the man in calm, soothing tones until he at last fell back, his venom spent.

When Nick and the counselor stood, they held Elliot between them, and escorted him out of the arena. His head hung low, and he stumbled as he hung on to their arms.

"Ohmygosh. Ohmygosh." The teen's breathless comment echoed Sam's own thoughts.

She hugged the girl closer, rubbing her back. "It's okay, honey, it's okay." She spoke in a soft tone, but inside turmoil churned. What if she'd been by herself when this happened? What if Elliot had hurt someone…or himself?

Brad hurried to their side and joined their embrace. "Are you all right?"

Both nodded but squeezed each other harder.

Nick returned to the arena and gathered everyone around.

"Is Elliot going to be okay?" While still scared out of her wits, she had to know.

"Yeah. The counselor's got him. He'll get him some assistance." Nick rubbed the back of his neck. "Good job here, everybody. Thanks for your help in getting him calmed down."

The other vets nodded and exchanged glances. "There, but for the grace of God…" Del spoke into the palpable silence. Again, everyone else nodded, staring at the ground or into the distance.

Sam's heart felt like warm putty. All these veterans had their own story, their own horrible nightmares to deal with. She wanted to reach out to each one with a hug and tell them how important they and their healing were to her. *If my horses and*

Electra and I can be a part of that… Her throat closed and eyes stung.

"Elliot's going to need our support now, more than ever." Nick addressed the vets. "So, if any of you would be able to reach out to him over the next few days, that is going to be so important. Counselor Higgins will be available to you as well, either later today or tomorrow."

He aimed a sympathetic gaze at Electra and her. "I'm sorry you had to witness that. I know it was a scary thing. It's not something that happens often, but it can. And you did the right thing, Sam, keeping Electra safe."

She gulped. "Well, I do know horses, and the unexpected can happen with them as well. I just hope he'll be all right, and that maybe…someday he might be willing to come back and try this again."

A chorus of "yeah" echoed from the group. Del wheeled forward to shake her hand. "Thank you for sticking with us." Garrett followed suit, and everyone lined up to shake hands and offer thanks or a word of encouragement.

Sondra was last. She peered into Sam's face for a moment and then gave her a quick, hard hug. "Thanks for today." She ducked her head and turned away to head for the door.

"You were great!" Sam called after her. The young woman looked back over her shoulder, her face flushed pink, and she gave the slightest smile.

After the vets had gone, Nick and Brad helped load the horses. The wind whipped up a dust devil in the corral. Although the sun shone bright in the blue sky, the breeze sent a chill through her body.

"Again, thank you." Nick stroked his beard. "If you feel like you'd like to talk to Higgins too, you would be most welcome to do that."

"I'm sure we'll be okay, but thanks." She glanced at the silent Electra. *I hope so anyway.*

37

"Or call me if you want to talk." The ag instructor patted the side of the horse trailer.

"Okay." She got into the driver's seat, while Electra and Brad climbed in on the other side. "See you next week."

Several miles of highway hummed beneath the old truck before Brad broke the stillness. "So, you had a little excitement huh?"

Sam snorted a laugh. "Just a little."

"Gosh, my heart about leaped out of my chest when Sondra burst into the office, yelling for help." He shook his head. "Higgins knocked his chair over and hightailed it out of there so fast, I could barely keep up. I was so scared for you two."

Electra sat still, not responding.

"Are you okay, honey?" She put a hand over the girl's.

"Yeah." Her voice squeezed out the word in a squeak.

"I don't know if you'd like to talk about it right now—we're both here with you—or if you want to later." Uncertain how to help, Sam groped for the right words. *Lord, help me. What do I do now?*

"Yeah. I was scared." She rubbed her knuckles into her eyes. "It…it was like my dad… He…" she hiccupped. "After the accident…he would get drunk…and come in…and yell at us…and call us names." A tear rolled down her cheek. "I know that wasn't really him." Another tear followed.

Shock zinged through Sam like an arrow. She pulled the truck to the side of the road, shifted into park, and embraced her. "I know, honey."

"No, that wasn't your real dad." Brad patted her back and rubbed her arm. "And today that wasn't the real Elliot either. Both men have problems they can't face, and they turned to alcohol to numb their pain." His gaze met Sam's over the girl's head.

Electra nodded against Sam's shoulder. She hiccupped a couple more sobs. "I miss my dad."

The three sat in a quiet embrace, simply rocking and absorbing what peace they could from each other.

CHAPTER FIVE

The sight of her white, two-story ranch house brought Sam a pleasant rush of welcome. *My home. And it* is *mine now.* She glanced toward the corrals to see if Sugar and Toby were waiting. "Hmm. We have company."

Horace Jones' truck sat by the corrals, her seventy-something neighbor leaning against the cab. "Hey, Horace," she greeted him as she got out of the truck.

"Howdy." He pushed his hat back and gave her his trademark grin. "Hadn't seen you guys in a while so thought I'd come over and see how you're doin'."

Brad exited the pickup and shook the man's hand. Electra drifted toward Horace and wrapped her arms around him without a word, burying her face in his chest. He raised his bushy gray eyebrows at Sam over the girl's shoulder.

"Later," she mouthed.

Electra let go the hug and still without saying anything, trudged toward the barn.

Sam went around to the back of the trailer to unload the horses. Trixi and Apache trotted out to the pasture, immediately lowering their heads to graze on the greening spring grass.

The men leaned against the corral rails. "The girls had a bit of drama at the veterans' class today." Brad glanced toward the barn where Electra had disappeared.

Horace cocked his head at Sam. "Oh yeah?"

"Yeah." She told him what had happened with Elliot, her stomach knotting.

"A shame." He clicked his tongue. "Lotta them vets have a terrible time readjusting."

She blew at a feather that had landed on a post. "I was kind of in lala land, thinking the horse program was working its magic with everyone, and that he would be caught up in it too."

"But you had a really good day with Sondra." Electra had quietly returned to the group.

"Yeah. That made me feel good, like I was finally making progress." Sam stared off to the rolling horizon. "It does give me hope. And I do think I—you and I—can make a difference." She cupped the teen's chin in her hand. "*You* are a big part of that success."

Horace removed his hat and ran a hand over his iron-gray crewcut. "Oh, heck yeah. You've already made a huge difference for Garrett and Del. I've seen that for myself."

"And for me too. I can't pretend I totally understand what they're going through." Brad picked at a loose sliver of wood on the rail. "But from the issues I've had since my accident and rehab… I do get how some of them might react to 'normal' people and life around them when they come back." He glanced at her. "I sure did have my share of resentment and rebellion. I put my family and this gal through a bit of hell for a while."

He slipped an arm around her, and she leaned into his shoulder, happy those days were in the past. "Well, you're doing lots better now. And you never resorted to drinking or abusive behavior."

"I have you pushing me to thank for that." He gave her a gentle squeeze. "Higgins—that counselor I've been seeing there at the center—" he explained to Horace, "says so many of the vet PTSD clients he sees don't have that kind of support system. Or their families don't know how to relate to them."

The older man nodded. "Yup. And doctors and the VA system don't know nothin' either."

"Or they're just too overwhelmed with cases. Higgins told me there's one and a half times more risk of suicide among veterans than in the general population—comes out to about twenty a day."

Sam's midsection constricted. *Oh my gosh. What if Elliot is suicidal? What if he'd done something in front of all of us?* She knew, of course, some of those statistics from the study she'd done for this equine rehab course, but so far it had only been numbers on sheets of paper.

"Do you think Elliot…?" Electra's small voice expressed her thoughts.

She drew the girl into her and Brad's embrace. "Oh, honey, no. I don't think so. He's in good hands with Nick and Higgins. And he did reach out to the program. So I think he's trying."

"I hope he comes back." The teen sniffled. "I think we could help him."

From your lips to God's ears. "Oh, yes." She rubbed Electra's back. "I think we can too." How was this young girl going to deal with all this? How would *she*, for that matter?

A hunger pang prompted her to glance at her watch: 2:30. "Gosh, we missed our lunch in town. I'll go in and fix some sandwiches. I'm sure you're all hungry."

"Yeah. I am." Brad nodded. "Too late for lunch, too early for supper—is it lupper?"

Electra's face animated. "Or slunch."

"How about slupper?"

Horace guffawed, and the back-and-forth banter continued as Sam moved toward the house. Her shoulders relaxed, and she smiled. Brad's old sense of humor had returned and rescued the tense moment.

Of course, that didn't mean she wouldn't have to address the subject more with Electra, but maybe the girl wouldn't be quite so upset from today's event. Maybe it was time to take her back for a visit with Robin. The counselor at the group home in Billings had helped her before. Electra had been cutting herself and ran away from her home in January, buying a plane ticket to Montana with her mom's credit card. Sam grimaced, remembering the upheaval. Alberta had been none too happy and was ready to scoop her up and take her back home. But seeing how her daughter blossomed at the ranch, she agreed to let her stay.

While they ate, Brad and Horace kept the conversation light, and as the food filled her belly, an emotional wellspring bubbled inside too.

Electra broached the subject of the pony. "He's such a cute little guy. I wish I…we could get him to trust us." She glanced toward Sam.

Horace shrugged his wide shoulders. "Time. Just gonna take time."

"Something I have so much of." Sam made a wry face.

The teen's face brightened. "Well, if you would let me work—"

She shook her head in a hard no. "We've already talked about that, how dangerous it could be."

"But he was starting to…" Electra's voice rose into a whine.

"No! That's my final word." She gave the girl a piercing stare. "I'll work with him a little more this afternoon and whenever I can, and if he shows signs of not wanting to kill anything that comes near him, maybe I'll rethink things."

Electra's mouth turned down, and she huffed.

"It's gonna work out." Horace smirked at them. "Why don't I come out and take a look at 'im too."

Sam left Electra to clean up the lunch dishes, while the rest of them tromped out to the small round corral where Money stood at the far side, his head hung low. "He's been so neglected, but of course, I haven't been able to groom him or even get to the point where I could take him to a vet to get checked out."

Her neighbor clucked his tongue. "Yeah. He's not very pretty right now."

As they approached, the pony snorted, planted his feet, and raised his head in a defiant stance. Sam got a small bucket with cake pellets and rattled it as she entered the corral. When she got closer, Money blew hard and moved away, hugging the fence as he paced around the enclosure. She set the bucket in the center and continued to move him around and around. Then she took out a bandanna and waved it in his face to make him switch directions. After working him this way for about half an hour, she stood quietly by the bucket, and with trepidation, turned her back on him. *Let him not come up and kick me!*

The pony continued to run in his circle, snorting and blowing. When he stopped, it was as far away from the humans as he could manage in a round corral. Sam reached down and rattled the bucket. He snorted, turned, and kicked the corral fence.

She drew a quick breath and sneaked a look behind her. He showed no signs of interest in the cake bucket. The defiant stance remained. They stood in deadlock for what seemed like an hour before she finally gave in with a deflated sigh and trudged back to the fence where Horace, Brad, and Electra stood.

Only then did Money move to the center of the ring to grab a mouthful of pellets. But he immediately retreated to the far side again.

Sam shook her head. "Lunging usually wears them down, but nothing I've tried so far has broken the barrier."

"I see that." Horace shrugged. "Some of the old-school cowboys would just tie him up and buck him out." Apparently seeing her look of horror, he quickly added, "But I know that's not your style."

"No way!" Electra spoke up beside them. "We think that old lady did that kind of thing and maybe even beat him." She sniffled. "We can't hurt him anymore."

The old man's face softened. "I know, little gal, I know. Sorry I mentioned that. You do need to help him trust you, and that will just take time. That's all I have to suggest... Time."

Sam's shoulders slumped. This would be a huge challenge. Maybe she should give him to someone who had more time to work with him. She gave herself a mental shake. *No. You can't give up on him. He needs you!*

The following day, Sam and Electra drove to the Bruckners' to meet the new group of dudes. She thought back to her first season when she'd applied out of desperation for an income after Kenny left her high and dry.

"Remember the first time you and your mom came to the dude ranch?"

The teen snickered. "Yeah, me the sad little Goth girl who hated everybody."

"True, but it didn't take long for you to become a real-life cowgirl after you met Apache." A bubble of happy emotion rose inside. "I'm sure proud of how far you've progressed since those days."

"I guess." She cocked her head. "I sure like living here better. And I really like working with the dudes and the vets and when we can, with the group home kids."

She playfully cuffed the girl's arm. "I like having you here too. You're a big help."

Clyde met them at the corral, where his horses milled, some dozing, some pacing, some with heads hanging over the fence, waiting for a pat or a treat.

"This is a corporate retreat," the rancher explained. "They're doing some 'touchy-feely' meeting right now, but when they're done, they want to come out and meet the horses."

"Okay. You want us to start them out as usual with brushing and then saddling?" Sam hooked her boot on the lower rail.

"Yeah. Some have riding experience, but some don't, so we'll start them all out with the basics."

She and Electra retrieved the grooming aids and brought out saddles and bridles from the barn. Each horse received a scratch and a few words of greeting as they waited. "Hey, Ginger, are you ready?" The teen smoothed the mare's mane and gave her a hug. "You're my favorite, yes, you are." The chestnut bobbed her head and rubbed against the teen's shoulder.

A door slammed and boisterous voices came from the meeting center as a group of five men and one woman headed for the corral. "Yeehaw! We're ready to ride." The apparent leader approached.

"That's great." Clyde touched the brim of his hat and gave them his big "dude rancher" grin. "This is Sam and Electra, and they'll be takin' you through the steps before lunch. After that, we'll go for a ride, if you're ready."

Electra gave them each a handful of cake pellets, and Sam introduced Ginger. "This is how you approach...slowly." She held her hand out flat and let the horse lip the treat from her palm. The other horses gathered around, rumbling whickers, and stretching out their necks. "Okay, each of you pick a horse and go ahead with your treat."

A couple of the men, apparently the ones with experience, stepped right up and fed their chosen animal, caressing its face and down the neck. The woman also approached the mare without fear. "Hi, Ginger. My name is Jill. Don't bite me now." She spoke quietly. "I haven't done this before, but I can tell you're a nice girl." She giggled a little when the soft lips touched her palm and glanced at Sam. "You didn't tell us it tickles."

"Yes, they're very gentle, and they won't bite." Sam chuckled. "You're doing well." She picked up a brush. "All right, folks, Electra will give you each one of these, and you can get to know your horse even better." She demonstrated the proper technique and then gave the brush to Jill who stroked Ginger's neck and withers.

Sam ambled around to each of the men, giving a word of praise or advice, and another encouraging pat to the horse.

"Hey, this is great," one of the men commented. "Beats the heck out of the office."

"That's why I love this lifestyle." She nodded. "This *is* my office." She certainly was blessed to have the opportunity to do what she loved.

As she showed them how to bridle and saddle, Irene rang the dinner bell on the big front porch. "Lunchtime. We'll pick up where we left off after you eat." She unsaddled Ginger as the group trekked to the house, laughing and teasing each other.

"This is a pretty cool bunch." Electra helped set the tack in the shade of the barn.

"Yeah. So far, so good. You hungry?"

"Race ya!" The girl took off at a run, and Sam followed at a more sedate trot.

After a hearty lunch of grilled chicken and salad, with oatmeal raisin cookies for dessert, Clyde led the group back out to the corral. The men who had ridden before bridled and saddled their horses under the rancher's supervision, but she and Electra tacked up the others.

The mid-April sun beamed almost hot, while a cool breeze lifted the horses' manes and tails as they rode through the greening prairie. Here and there a patch of yellow sweet peas or purple violets appeared. Jill pointed at a delicate, pale pink flower. "That's beautiful."

"The bitterroot," Sam told her, "our state flower."

A meadowlark trilled its happy melody amid the horses' clomping accompaniment. She breathed in the fresh spring air, glad she could relax with this group and not be on the constant lookout like she was with the vets.

A gray grouse fluttered out from the sagebrush in front of Ginger. The mare quickly sidestepped the flopping hen who must have had a nest nearby. Jill, who had twisted in the saddle toward Sam, lost her balance. She shrieked, dropped the reins, and slipped. The well-trained Ginger stopped immediately. Before Sam could even think, she caught the woman, who hung stiffly off to the side, panting tiny sobs.

"Jill! You're all right." She leaned over and boosted her back into the saddle center. "You're fine. You're fine."

"Oh-oh-oh." Her eyes were wide, and she continued her panting.

The men turned their mounts around and circled the two women. "Are you okay, Jill?" the corporate leader asked.

"Oh-oh-oh."

"She's fine." Sam spoke in a soothing tone, as much for the men as for the woman. "Take a deep breath, Jill. C'mon now, deep breath, and let it out slowly."

Finally, the woman calmed herself with several inhales and was able to speak. "I'm okay." She swallowed several times. "Thanks. That…scared…me. Sorry."

"You did great. You didn't fall off. You're just fine." She reached into her saddlebag and retrieved a bottle of water. "Here you go. Take a drink."

Jill gulped half the bottle and then managed a weak smile. "Better now."

"Good. Do you feel like continuing?" Sam returned what she hoped was a reassuring smile.

48

"Yeah. Okay. Let's keep going." Jill straightened in the saddle, picked up the reins, and touched her heels to Ginger's sides. "I'm okay. I'm okay…" She continued the mantra as they rode onward.

***

"So much for a no-drama ride." Sam settled herself into the well-worn seat and pointed the pickup toward home.

"No kidding." Electra giggled. "That lady's face was so white… I thought she was going to pass out."

"But she didn't. She really was a trouper; I have to give her that. Kept on going and actually enjoyed the ride."

The teen shook her head. "I guess we always have to watch everybody, all the time."

"Yep. That's for sure." Split-seconds could lead to disaster. One little glance away and Sondra had slipped. Not saddling the horse and Garrett had fallen. One little sage hen and an almost-wreck for Jill. But, things had turned out all right. Sam had to keep believing in that.

Her stomach grumbled. "So, what shall we fix for supper?"

"I dunno." Electra shrugged. "Maybe Brad's cooking something."

"Maybe. He has been known to rustle up some grub on occasion." She grinned.

They settled into silence as the dirt road unwound beneath the truck. The day waned into dusky blue-gray shadows below the rolling hills and along the washes. It *had* been a good day, and Sam looked forward to an evening curled up with a good book and her little "family."

"Whoa!" Electra leaned forward to peer through the windshield. "What's that?"

"What's what?"

"Stop. Something's on the side of the road." The girl twisted in her seat to look back.

She braked to a stop and backed up. A dark form materialized just off the road. A bundle of rags? She leaned toward the passenger side window. "What is that—a coyote?"

The animal lifted its head but didn't move to get up.

"It's hurt." Electra opened the door and slid out before Sam could object.

"Wait!" she yelled as the girl wrenched her door open and hurried around the side of the truck. "Don't go near. If it's hurt, it might attack you."

Electra gasped. "It's not a coyote. It's a dog." She approached cautiously, speaking in a soft tone. "Hey little doggie. Are you hurt? It's okay. We're gonna help you."

The dog growled but still made no move to get away.

"Don't touch him." Sam moved closer, her pulse pounding. "Looks like it's been hit." The black and white dog was covered in blood and its leg bent at an odd angle. *Oh dear, oh dear.* "Poor little guy. C'mon, baby, it's okay." She gestured to the pickup. "Go get that blanket from behind the seat."

The girl dashed to the truck and retrieved the blanket. Sam covered the dog, still speaking in a soft, soothing voice. "Open the tailgate, please, I'm going to have to get him into the back."

Electra hurried to comply. Sam wrapped the cover around the animal and lifted it in her arms. It whimpered as she carried it to the pickup bed. A couple of hay bales were left in the back, so she and Electra arranged them around the animal.

"Can I ride with him?"

"No, he'll be all right. He's not in any shape to try to jump out, and the bales will keep him from sliding as we drive." She jumped into the truck and threw it into gear as Electra balked momentarily and then got in.

"What are we going to do?" The teen's eyes were wide.

"Gotta take him to the vet in Forsyth. Looks like he's injured more than I can take care of." She pushed the gas pedal toward the floor. "Call Brad and let him know."

He had, indeed, cooked a roast and baked potatoes. "I'll keep it warm for you," his promise echoed over the phone speaker. "Are you two okay? Do you want to pick me up on the way? Or I could meet you there."

"No, we'll be fine. Just have that dinner ready when we get back."

Electra disconnected. "Oh, should I call the vet and make sure he's there?"

"Yeah, better do that." Sam grimaced. How could she have forgotten? "Also, call the Jersey Lilly and see if anyone is missing a dog. Let Billy know what we found."

Close to an hour of revving the old truck over the speed limit, and they arrived at the vet's office.

The light was on, and, as promised, Dr. Price waited.

He helped carry the dog inside, examined him carefully, and took X-rays. "The leg's pretty badly broken. I'm going to have to do surgery." He paused. "If I have your go-ahead."

While she hesitated, mentally reviewing the status of her checking account, Electra vibrated beside her. "Oh, yes, we have to, Sam, don't we? Yes, please say yes!" Her face had turned pale, her eyes like full moons, and a tear drifted down her cheek.

"Yes." Sam huffed a sigh. "We can't let the poor thing suffer. Go ahead, Doctor."

The kindly, middle-aged vet dipped his chin. "All right. I'll get him patched up and will call in the morning."

Back in the truck, the teen sniffled. "Will he be all right?"

"I'm sure Dr. Price will get him fixed up, good as new." Sam gulped. *Sure hope we can find his owner. And that he can pay the vet bill.*

CHAPTER SIX

The next morning Sam cleaned up breakfast dishes while Electra did her schoolwork and Brad went out to feed the horses. When the phone rang, she nearly dropped a plate in the sink.

"Mornin', Sam. Dr. Price here."

Her neck muscles knotted. "How is…?"

"Doggie is doing okay, went through surgery fine, but I had to amputate the leg. Too much damage."

"Oh no." An odd sensation of grief ran through her. "Poor thing. But he'll survive…?"

With eyes like dark pools in her ashen face, Electra stared over her textbook.

The vet assured Sam the dog would survive and be able to get around fine on three legs. "I want him to stay here for a few more days though, so I can keep an eye on him. Any idea who his owner might be?"

"No. I need to get a picture to put up in the Jersey Lilly." Dollar signs danced behind her eyes.

"I'll take one and email it to you."

"All right. Thanks, Doctor." She gave him her address, hung up the receiver, and slumped into a chair across from Electra.

"What…? Is he okay?" The teen's voice quavered.

Sam told her what the vet had said.

"Three legs? Ohmygosh! How is he going to run and play and…?" A tear trickled onto her cheek. "Oh, the poor little dog. Are we going to take care of him?"

"I don't know, honey. Dr. Price is going to send a picture, and we need to put it up in town so the owner will know he's been found."

After a few minutes, waiting for dial-up internet, she checked her email and printed out the photo. "Let's go." She headed for the corral to tell Brad the news.

His brow furrowed. "Aw, that's too bad. Okay. You run on to town. I'll finish up here."

Grinding the pickup into gear, she bumped down the dirt road to Ingomar.

Electra sat in silence for a few miles. "What if we don't find his owner? Can we keep him?"

She grimaced. "Well, let's not cross that bridge just yet. I hope we *will* find his family." Otherwise, that vet bill would take a big chunk out of her savings.

At the Jersey Lilly, the owner Billy Cole taped the picture to a prominent place on the wall. "Haven't heard of anyone missing a dog. Course, a lotta times people from Forsyth or Miles come out this way and dump unwanted pets."

Electra gasped, and Sam's hope sank. Like the way she'd ended up with Money, the problem pony. People these days—nobody wanted to take responsibility. "A throw-away society," she muttered.

"Yeah. So true." Billy clicked his tongue in sympathy. "Can I get you a cuppa joe?"

"No thanks, just had some." She turned away. "Guess we'd better get home."

Neither spoke on the way back until her cell rang. Electra answered and put it on speaker.

"It's Joe from JB Construction. Howya doin'?"

Oh gee, she'd nearly forgotten about the bid for the barn, with everything else going on. "Good. You have some numbers for me?"

"Yeah." He quoted her a price that made her mind click into high speed.

If the insurance covered part of it, then she could pay the rest from the money she'd received last year after the documentary on her rescue of Apache and her effort to buy Trixi. The mare's owner Miss Ellie was disabled and moving into an assisted care facility. People who watched it sent in money to help save the trick horse from being auctioned.

She chewed the inside of her cheek. Building the cabins or bunkhouse might not be feasible right now, but a new barn would be a start. "Okay. Let's go ahead."

"Great. I'll get the materials ordered, and if I could stop by and get a check from you to cover that…"

"Sure. I'll be home this afternoon."

"Thanks, Ms. Moser. I'll send Bob out to collect. You have a nice day." He disconnected.

She expelled a lungful of air. "Well… we're going to get the barn started."

"Awesome." Electra grinned for the first time since they'd found the dog. "That's some good news for a change."

"Yeah. Finally." She smiled back. "What d'you say we work with Money a while this afternoon?"

"Really?" The teen bounced on the seat. "Yay!"

Brad met them at the corral fence and pumped his fist when she told him about the contractor's call. "All right!"

Sam opened the gate from the small pasture where the pony was isolated from the other horses and shooed him into the round pen. Standing in the center, she started the free-lunging process—directing him in circles and then changing directions—hoping he would eventually begin to trust and follow her cues. No way she could get a line on him yet. She had her doubts whether this was the right method, but it would have to do until she could think of something else. Around and around, back and forth, she ran the horse through its paces until he stopped, blowing and snorting.

"Are you getting tired?" She took a step toward him with a handful of pellets from her jacket pocket. His dark eyes peered warily through his long, scraggily mane. "C'mere, boy. Are you going to let me get close today?" She took another step and another. He pushed his rear into the fence and blew again, shaking his head. Another step, and he took off running.

Her shoulders slumped. "Not even for a treat?" What was wrong with him that he wouldn't respond to food? Rolling her eyes, she turned her back to him and walked to the fence, where Brad and Electra watched.

"He sure is stubborn." Brad kicked the toe of his boot in the dirt.

"Do you think he has PTSD?" Electra leaned over the top rail, studying the scruffy little pony.

"Could be, especially if that woman mistreated him."

Brad squinted. "Don't look, but he's coming toward us," he whispered.

A prickly sensation rose between her shoulder blades as she sensed him getting closer, blowing and fluttering his nostrils. Had the technique worked this time?

Then she felt his head next to her shoulder. Holding her breath, she pivoted part-way and inched her hand to pat his nose.

He snorted hot, moist air on her neck. His teeth chomped down on her shoulder, and he ran off again.

The shock nearly knocked her over. "Ow! That little bugger!" She spun, raising her hand as if to slap him, but stopped in mid-air. No, that wasn't the way to react. Besides, he was hugging the far side of the fence, head down as if he knew he'd done wrong.

"Ohmygosh, Sam, are you all right?" Electra's face was pale and drawn.

55

"Did he hurt you?" Brad lifted her sleeve to look at the site.

"Yeah, it hurts." She twisted her neck to see the teeth marks on her upper arm. "But it doesn't look like he broke the skin."

"You'll probably have a pretty good bruise." He patted her back. "Put some ice on it. Do you have any Arnica? That should help with the swelling and bruising."

"I think I do. I'll go in and look in a bit. You guys, don't worry. I'm okay. The bite was as much a shock as pain." She shook her head and repeated, "That little bugger."

"Maybe that's why the woman treated him bad." The teen's eyes still stared, big and round.

"Or she mistreated him, and he turned mean." Her initial anger melted into sadness. "Oh my. What are we going to do with him?"

Sam hiked the incline to the house, her entourage following. Finding the cream, she applied a liberal amount, again shaking her head in wonder at the large circle of angry red marks.

She returned to the kitchen, where Brad and Electra sat at the table, discussing the pony. "I think the best medicine right now is some coffee and chocolate chip cookies."

"Yeah!" The girl leaped up and rummaged in the cupboard for the sweets.

Brad gently pushed Sam into a chair. "You sit and rest. I'll make the coffee."

As they ate their snack, her friends threw out ideas about Money. "Maybe he needs a muzzle, like a dog," Brad offered. "Or maybe he should be tied up."

"I still think I could tame him, if you'd let me." This from Electra.

"And risk you getting bitten or kicked? Uh-uh." Sam wagged her head emphatically. "Maybe I'll talk to Dr. Price. He might have some ideas."

An engine revved outside as a truck pulled in front of the house. "Oh yes, that'll be Bob. I almost forgot him again." She stood. "Go let him in, and I'll get my checkbook."

The sunburned construction worker sat at the table, dunking a cookie in his coffee when she came downstairs. He ducked his head in greeting. "Hello, Ms. Moser."

"Call me Sam. So, you need some money down for the materials…"

"Yeah. Joe placed the order, and it should be in next week. We're finishing up a project, so maybe the week after, we can get started here."

Excitement bubbled up inside, and she could barely sit still. "That's great. I'm looking forward to that."

Beside her, Electra beamed and squirmed in her chair. "How long will it take? Are you going to build the barn and the arena and the cabins and…?"

Bob chuckled. "Well, I guess we're going to start out with the barn, right, Sam?"

"Yes, the barn and a roof for the arena. We may have to wait to enclose it." She grinned at her young friend's enthusiasm. "We'll see what happens as we go."

She wrote the check, and Joe gave her an invoice and receipt. "Thanks for the coffee and cookies. See ya in a couple weeks."

After he left, Sam sat in euphoric disbelief, staring at the other two. "We're gonna get a barn!"

Electra whooped and high-fived her, and Brad leaned from his chair to give her a one-armed hug. "You're getting a barn."

CHAPTER SEVEN

Rays of the early rising sun woke Sam the next morning. Her first thought was of the new barn, and she raised her arms in a happy stretch.

"Ow!" Pain in her upper arm reminded her what happened with Money the day before. She sat upright on the side of the bed and looked at the bruise—dark purple with a crescent of dark-red tooth-shaped marks. Groaning, she padded downstairs to the bathroom to retrieve the pain cream and a couple of aspirin.

Coffee on to brew and bacon sizzling in the pan, she lifted the phone to call the veterinarian's office. Although early, the receptionist answered with a cheery voice. "Let me see if Dr. Price can come to the phone," she offered when Sam identified herself.

After a minute or two of listening to bland Muzak, the line clicked, and he came on. "Mornin', Ms. Moser. Doggie's doin' fine. He came out of the anesthesia great and ate and drank last night and this morning. I want to keep him another night, but you can come pick him up tomorrow. Unless you've found his owners."

She gulped. "No, not yet. I'll check with the Jersey Lilly again today, and if I haven't found anyone, I'll come get him."

"He's a nice dog, very friendly and sweet. Somebody's pet, I reckon. Real lucky you found him."

Darn. She bit her lip. Why on earth would anyone simply dump their pet? He had to be lost. Surely the owners were looking for him. "Yeah. Poor little guy. Well, I'll keep hoping…

58

Anyway, the other question I have for you involves an ornery horse." She told him about Money and what she'd done so far.

"Hmm." A moment of silence. "Sounds like you're doin' the right things. I know how stubborn Shetlands are, and if he was abused, it may simply take more time. Guess I'd suggest getting back out there right away and showing him you're not afraid of him."

She huffed a breath. "Right." Normally, she was not afraid of any horse, but this guy...well, he certainly was a challenge.

"Ya know, you might get on the internet and check out Monty Roberts or Pat Parelli. They're supposed to be some kind of big-name horse trainers. Maybe there's a video that'd give you some ideas."

"Thanks, Doctor. I'll do that. See you tomorrow."

As she blotted the bacon on paper towels and cracked eggs into the pan, Electra came yawning down the stairs. "Were you talking to Dr. Price? Is the dog okay?"

"Yeah, he's doing great. We can pick him up tomorrow. But in good conscience, I think I need to put an ad in the Forsyth paper, just in case."

The teen's lower lip jutted forward. "Aww."

"If he was your pet, and you lost him, you'd want to know, wouldn't you?"

"Yeah... I guess." She grabbed a piece of bacon, her face brightening again. "I'm hoping nobody claims him though."

"Of course, you do. Let's just add to our menagerie, right?" She shot her gaze to the ceiling. And at what cost? One step forward and two back in the finance department.

"Who are you adding to the zoo?" Brad shuffled into the kitchen and grabbed a cup.

Electra giggled. "The dog we found. We can go get him tomorrow, and I hope we can keep him."

He sat at the table with his coffee, eyeing Sam. "You ready for this...in addition to Money?"

59

"What choice do I have?" She set the platter of bacon and eggs on the table, grabbed her coffee cup, and sat. "I suppose we could take him to the Humane Society in Miles after he heals."

"No!" The teen choked on a bite of food. "We can't do that! He's only got three legs now. Nobody's going to adopt him, and then they'll have to...have to..." Her voice broke with a sob.

Guilt snaked through her gut. No way she could disappoint Electra, nor could she ever leave the dog to an uncertain fate. "Honey, don't worry about it. We won't let that happen. We'll bring him home and take care of him until we can find his owners." She patted the girl's arm. "Okay?"

"Okay." The girl sniffled and stood to throw her arms around Sam. "Thank you. You're the best."

Exchanging a bemused glance with Brad who whispered, "Rescuer extraordinaire," she returned the hug. Rescuer, indeed. How did that happen?

After breakfast and chores, Sam stood at the pasture fence. The problem pony canted his neck just far enough that he could keep an eye on her. "Money, Money, Money, what are we going to do with you?" She spoke in a soft voice. "Once upon a time you must have been a nice horse. Huh? Were you? Were you a good boy once?"

He cocked an ear back toward her but remained standing, his tail switching.

"I'm not going to hurt you, I promise. I want to be nice to you and pet you and groom you and feed you treats." Picking up a pail of pellets, she took one out and tossed it within a few feet of him. She had deliberately not fed him this morning.

He stretched his head toward the pellet, flared his nostrils, and sniffed. Again, he sniffed and blew. Then, with his left ear and eye still on her, he took two cautious steps, picked up the cake, and crunched.

60

"Good boy. That's a good boy now." She threw out another, again just far enough away to force him to move closer.

He hesitated, head lowered, and stepped forward, snuffling the ground until he found the pellet.

She kept talking to him and praising him with each step. "That's a good pony. There's more of these for you. Come, get your treats." Each time she tossed another pellet closer to where she stood, she held her breath. Would he keep coming?

He kept a wary eye on her, but the lure of the food enticed him. Closer and closer. She crossed her fingers. How close could she get him? And what would he do—bite her again?

"C'mon, Money. Here's another one." She dropped it a scant yard from her.

His breathing became ragged. He snorted and pawed at the ground where the last pellet had been.

"It's okay, boy, c'mon. You can get one more, just one more. C'mon."

He stretched his neck as far as he could without taking a step. But it wasn't close enough.

"C'mon, Money. C'mon. You know you want it."

He glared through his long, stringy forelock, flaring his nostrils and searching for the scent. Then he lunged forward, grabbed the pellet, and galloped away to the far corner of the small pasture. He stood crunching, and she could've sworn he grinned at her.

"All right. That's good for now. You came much closer than you have before, other than biting me." She tittered. "But that wasn't fair. My back was turned. We're gonna get to know each other, and you're gonna find out I'm not a bad mom. And I know you're a good boy. I just *know* it."

She ambled back to the corral where Electra and Brad perched on the top rail. "Hey, that's progress." Brad touched the brim of his hat in a snappy salute.

"That was cool!" The teen's face was all smiles.

"Yeah. A teeny-tiny bit of progress. Maybe." She wasn't about to believe it yet. "Well, I've gotta get going to Clyde's. You guys good here or you want to come along?"

"I'll come." Electra headed toward the pickup.

Brad shook his head. "I have some phone calls I need to make. I'll hold down the fort here."

"Okay. Hey, would you call the Jersey and ask if anyone is missing a dog?" She gave him a peck on the cheek and stepped toward the truck.

"Sure." He pulled her to him in a hug. "Have a good day."

"Thanks." Stunned, she lifted herself into the pickup, shifted into gear and drove away. She glanced in the rearview mirror to the sight of him waving. Where did their relationship stand? She never knew if he was going to be affectionate or back away. She sighed, a yearning expanding in her chest.

After a hard day of repairing fences, readying tack, and helping Irene Bruckner bake and cook for the next group of dudes, Sam and Electra wound their weary way home.

Brad sat on the porch with a pitcher of cold lemonade. "Hi. Toasty day for mid-April. Thought you might need some refreshment."

"Thanks. I am a bit parched." *Wow, what a thoughtful guy. I could get used to this.* She cocked at eyebrow at him. "Any news?"

He shook his head. "Nope. Nobody from around here is missing a dog or recognizes that one. And I called the *Independent* in Forsyth to double-check on your ad and make sure they have the right phone number. They said it's running, but you haven't had a call all day."

She grimaced, while Electra hopped up and down, a big grin on her face.

***

A soft knock at the bedroom door woke Sam the next morning. "Yeah?"

"Are we going to pick up the dog today?"

She chuckle-snorted. "I guess so." Glancing at the clock, which read 6:30, she scooted to the edge of the bed and stretched. The arm wasn't quite as sore this morning. "I'll be down in a minute."

Boots thundered down the stairs. She laughed and put on her robe to follow. In the kitchen, Electra measured out the coffee grounds. After Sam had washed her face and brushed her teeth, she knocked on Brad's door. "Mornin'. Time to rise and shine."

A grunted "okay" came from the other side. She went into the kitchen and stirred up batter for pancakes.

"So, your mom is arriving next Saturday?" Brad slid onto a chair, coffee cup in hand.

The teen gave a little squeal. "Yeah! I can't wait."

"I'll bet. It's been a while since you've seen her." He glanced at Sam. "You glad too?"

"I am." She set a stack of pancakes on the table. "It'll be fun to have Alberta around again."

"Is she going to stay here?" Brad slathered butter over his flapjack. "I s'pose I'd better vacate that room for her."

"Oh." It hit her like a mule kick. She hadn't thought about the logistics of having so many people in her tiny house. "Gosh, I don't know."

Electra took a bite and spoke around it. "She's, um, going to um, work for Clyde, right? So she'll prob'ly live there."

"Ye-ah. That's right. I never thought to talk to him about that yesterday. I'm sure she's been in touch with them." She sat. "I'd better give him a call today, and you should call your mom too."

***

On the drive to town, Electra vacillated between bouncing excitement over the dog and her mom and moments of silence. During those quiet moments, Sam's thoughts jumbled. If Alberta lived and worked at Clyde's, she'd want Electra with her. There had been times when she couldn't wait till the girl was under her mother's care. But now… Her stomach seized up. She simply wasn't prepared. Plain and simple, she'd been in denial.

Was Electra prepared to leave the ranch? Of course she'd want to be with her mom. But it would be so quiet without her. She would miss the squeals, the exuberance, the girl's bouncy personality, her help with the horses and cows.

A breath hitched. She'd be left alone with Brad. That might be awkward. On the other hand, maybe time together would be a good thing. Could they rekindle their budding romance, or was it dead ashes like the barn? His accident, brain injury, and coma had taken his lively, fun-filled persona from him. He'd said he cared for her, but what exactly did that mean? Sorrow washed over her with a cold wave. *I want my old Brad back.*

***

After parking in front of the veterinarian's office, Sam followed Electra inside. The receptionist, with a name badge reading "Shelly," greeted them. "Have a seat. I'll let Dr. Price know you're here."

They moved to a set of plastic chairs in bright, primary colors. She gazed around the waiting room at posters of horses, dogs, and cats. A lop-eared gray and white cat eased from behind the counter and wound itself around their legs with a "meow."

"That's Einstein, our office cat," Shelly explained.

"Oooh, he's so cute." The teen smoothed her hand over his back and was rewarded with a loud purr. "Aww, Einstein. You're so soft." She scratched his head and lifted her wide eyes to Sam. "Can we—"

"Don't *even* think it!" Sam huffed. "We're bringing home a dog already. Besides, this is *their* cat."

Electra stuck out her bottom lip. "I know. But he's so cute and soft and cuddly." She continued to murmur to Einstein, who had curled up in her lap, still vibrating with his purrs.

"He wins everybody's heart." The receptionist exchanged an amused glance with her. Then she placed some papers on the counter. "Here's the instructions for the dog's care and your invoice."

Sam stood and shuffled forward, swallowing past a gigantic boulder in her throat as she took in the bottom line. Oh boy, this was worse than she'd anticipated. Biting the inside of her cheek, she pulled her checkbook from her purse and wrote the check. *Oh Lord, please bring the owners forward!*

Dr. Price stepped from the back, carrying the dog bundled in a blue blanket. "Hi there, ladies. Here's your boy. He's doing great. Shelly give you the care guide?"

She couldn't speak, but simply nodded.

Electra, who had followed her to the counter, was already at the vet's side patting the dog's head and crooning to him.

Dr. Price winked. "I can see he's going to get the best rehab ever." He cocked his head toward the door. "I'll carry him out to the truck for you."

The teen raced to the office door, and she followed to open the pickup. The vet placed him gently in the center of the bench seat and stepped back. "Give me a call if you have any problems. This is one lucky mutt, that you found him. He probably wouldn't have made it otherwise."

Aww. Empathy surged through her. She fought the urge to hug the dog. Instead, she stuck out her hand to the vet. "Thanks, Doc."

Slipping onto the seat beside the black and white dog, Electra put a hand on him and then stared out the window at Sam and the doctor. "Lucky! That's a great name for him."

65

Sam rolled her eyes. *Here we go. Once you name something…*

"I'd say so." Price grinned. "You ladies have a good day now. Drive safe."

Electra turned all her attention to the dog, petting and murmuring to him.

Thoughts somersaulted through Sam's mind as she drove. The dog would require a lot of time and care. Would he actually recover and be able to run around like normal? And the vet's bill. She'd have to transfer more money from her reserve account to cover the check she wrote. Better call the Jersey Lilly. Maybe someone would see the ad in the paper and call. She chewed on her cheek again. Electra would be heartbroken though.

And the barn project. Would this expenditure set back her plans for expansion?

Her thoughts switched gears again to Alberta's imminent arrival and her young friend leaving to live with her mom. Hot, stinging tears rose in her eyes, and she blinked them back, gritting her teeth. *No, not going to think about that right now. I have too many other things to deal with.*

CHAPTER EIGHT

As Sam parked by the house, a pleasant sensation rose inside, seeing Brad ride in from the pasture on Toby. Riding out by himself was several huge steps forward from when he'd first arrived, broken, depressed, and on the verge of giving up.

He dismounted and ground-tied the horse as she and Electra got out of the truck. "How's the dog?"

"His name is Lucky," the teen announced.

Sam gave him a lopsided smile. "I guess he has a name. Doc said he's doing great. We'll have to fix him a bed on the porch, and I have a list of instructions for meds and changing his dressing and—"

"On the porch? No!" The girl put her hands on her hips. "He can't stay outside in the cold. We have to let him be inside."

She glared at the teen, about to broach a counter argument.

"That way, he'll be closer if he needs something. I'll sleep on the couch and take care of him during the night." Electra thrust her earnest face forward. "I will. Please?"

Shaking her head, Sam closed her eyes for a moment. "All right. I see your point." She reached into the truck and slid the dog out. He gave a soft whine but settled in her arms as she carried him up the steps to the house.

Electra had already run ahead and now galloped down the stairs, carrying a large quilt. "This okay for his bed?" She folded it into the corner next to the sofa.

"Yes, that'll be fine for now. Maybe we can get him a horse blanket later. But go to the closet in Brad's room and get a sheet to put down in case he bleeds or pukes or something."

The girl was off like a flash and back with the sheet. Sam lay the dog down. "Okay, now… Lucky. You be a good boy. Stay here and get some rest." She raised her gaze to see Electra's face-splitting grin.

"You called him Lucky," she squeaked, and her upper body squirmed in delight.

Yeah, I did. I'm such a pushover. The dog raised his head and whined softly. Her heart melted like butter in the sunshine. She squatted beside him and stroked his head, murmuring, "You're all right, little guy. You're going to be fine. We'll take good care of you." Scratching his ears with one hand, she pulled the blue blanket up to his neck with the other. "You just rest now. Go to sleep, Lucky."

She stood and gestured with her head toward the sofa. "Sit down a minute, Electra."

The girl sat, wide-eyed and expectant.

"Okay. I admire your love for horses, dogs, cats… I do too. I can't stand to see anything suffer." She eased into the rocking chair. "But we have to be realistic. Rescuing this dog has cost me a *lot* of money. And that may mean giving up some other things I had planned."

Electra's face paled. "Yeah, I know. I saw the check you wrote. That *is* a lot. I'm sorry. It's my fault. I made you stop for Lucky."

"No, it's not your fault." An ache rose in her chest. "We certainly could *not* leave him there, injured, to die. I would never, ever want to do that. And I'm really glad we did save his life. But I want you to be prepared—we might find his owner, and we will have to give him back."

A tear slid down the young cheek.

"And we probably can't rescue every creature we come across."

"I know." She raised her gaze to Sam. "Thank you for saving him...and Apache and Trixie and Toby...and me."

Aww. Her insides turned to putty. She rose to sit on the couch beside the girl and put her arms around her. "You're welcome. I'm glad for all of them and especially for you."

They sat entwined in their embrace when Brad came in the house. He smiled. "My two rescuers."

"Hmph." Sam disengaged and stood. "Well, time for some lunch, and then we need to get to work."

The next several days wove themselves into a pattern. True to her word, Electra slept on the sofa near the dog, gave him his medications, and changed his bandages. Lucky gradually grew stronger, sitting up longer, wagging his tail, and licking the hands that cared for him.

Sam continued working with Money. Some days he would take the pellets and come closer, others he ignored them—and her—altogether. When she free-lunged him, he responded to her directions, but would never come to her. She wracked her brain and studied horse training videos on the computer, trying to think of ways to win his trust. According to them, she was doing the right thing. Only it wasn't working. She fluttered frustrated past her lips. *Time, Sam, give it time.*

She and Electra went to Clyde's in the afternoons, doing whatever chores he needed and working with his current group of clients. That, at least, took her mind off her finances, Money, and Lucky worries—for a few hours.

Saturday morning, she awoke to Electra's voice and knock on her bedroom door. "Time to get up, Sam, we gotta go get Mom!"

"Okay. I'm getting up." She glanced at the clock: 6:00. They didn't need to be at the airport until 10. Well, she couldn't blame the girl for being excited to see her mother. Anticipation winged through her. She was eager to see her friend again, but… She shook off the thought that Electra would be leaving before the consequences of her leaving could fully form.

After breakfast and chores, the two climbed into the truck for the trek to Billings. "Drive safe." Brad gave her a peck on the cheek through the window.

Why can't there be more? Right now, we're not much more than roommates. With a sigh, she drove down the dusty road. Was something wrong that the two of them hadn't jumped into a relationship headfirst? Well, yes of course, there was. The accident. But how much longer would that serve as an excuse? Was it Brad? Or was it her? Did they both have a fear of commitment?

She gradually became aware of Electra's chatter beside her. "…and for her to meet Lucky and Money and see how much Apache has learned and…and what the vets are doing and we can go riding together—all of us—and…"

"Yeah. That'll be great," she murmured vaguely. "It'll be fun."

At Billings Logan Field, they watched through the lobby windows as the plane landed, and then Sam ambled while Electra sprinted to the arrival area. The teen stood on tiptoe, peering over the small group of people deplaning. "There she is!" She gave a squeal and ran forward to meet her mom with arms outstretched.

Affection spread through Sam like a smooth-running stream. A yearning for a family of her own bubbled up inside.

Alberta, an older version of the teen but with long, dark hair, took her daughter's arm in hers and came toward her with a big smile. "Hi! So good to see you."

The two look so much alike and Electra is nearly as tall as her mom now. She pushed aside the yearning. If she was destined to remain single, at least she had a family—her horses, maybe even a dog. That should be all she needed. She stepped forward to embrace her friend. "I'm glad to see you too."

"Whew, am I glad this flight is over. I'm home." Alberta held her at arm's length. "And how are *you* doing? You've had a rough couple of months."

"I'm all right. We're making headway." Sam followed them to baggage claim and retrieved the suitcases.

"Is this all, Mom? I thought you were moving here for good?"

"That's it. I have a moving van coming in a few days. For now, I rented out the house in New York partially furnished, and we'll see what we need in the future if we rent or buy here."

Sam helped load the luggage into the back of the pickup, and they piled in. "Early lunch at Jakers?"

"I'm not really hungry yet. Let's wait and have one of those delicious burgers at the Jersey Lilly when we get to Ingomar."

"Yay! I love their burgers." Electra wiggled closer, keeping a snug hold on her mother's arm. "I just can't wait to show you everything, all the horses, and what Apache has learned…" And she was off on one of her bubbly monologues, keeping them entertained on the trip home.

At the café, they settled at a scarred wooden table, and Billy came from the back of the huge dark cherry back bar to take their orders, his round face beaming. "Great to see you again, Alberta. You back for good?"

"I am. And it feels good."

Sam glanced at the poster of Lucky on the wall. "Nobody's come forward missing their dog, huh?"

71

"Nope, 'fraid not. Sorry." The proprietor stuck his pen behind his ear into the thick mop of reddish-brown hair. "I'll get your food out shortly."

"So, a dog?" Alberta leaned back in her chair.

"Yeah, he's *so* cute, he's black and white, part border-collie we think, and his name is Lucky and I've been taking care of him and giving him medicine and he's getting better every day and…"

Billy brought their burgers, and they tucked into the food like starving ranch hands.

"Um…" Sam cleared her throat. How to approach the subject? "Do I take you directly to Clyde's, or are you coming to my house first?"

"Oh yes, that. I'm sorry I haven't told you my plans." The woman took a sip of her Coke. "If it's okay, I'll come with you and stay the night. We'll have to pack up Electra's things anyway, and then tomorrow we can move into the cabin Clyde has for us."

The teen's eyes opened like a cavern's maw. "Move?"

"Yes, honey, you'll be coming to live with me." Her mother's forehead wrinkled in a puzzled frown. "I assumed you'd want to."

"Well yeah…but…"

Sam sensed the wheels churning in the teen's head, as they were in her own. *Here it comes. Who will win this round?* Pain clutched her mid-section with icy claws. In the past few months, she had grown to love this girl, like a daughter or a younger sister.

"But, Mom…I have to take care of Lucky and there's training Apache and going with Sam to the vets' classes in Miles City and I help her with chores and…" Her voice rose to a higher pitch.

"Sweetie. Think about it a second." Alberta leaned forward and peered into her daughter's face. "I'm your mother. You can't live with Sam forever. She's already gone above and beyond with taking care of you and helping you keep up with your schoolwork and everything."

Electra's face crumpled. "I know, Mom. I want to be with you." She raised her gaze to Sam. "But I want to be with you too."

Her insides liquified, and she fought back tears. *I want her to stay.* But the girl did belong with her mother. She reached down into her strength reserves and grabbed hold with all her might. "It's okay, honey. I'm still working for Clyde, and I need your help with the veterans' classes and with the horses. We'll see each other all the time."

Alberta clasped the girl's hand. "I wanted to move to Montana to give us both a better life. You have already changed and grown so much—thanks to you, Sam—and I hope I can learn to relax here and find balance in *my* life."

"Yeah. You will, Mom." The teen's face brightened. "It's such a great place and the people are all so great and the horses, oh, well, they're all great too." She giggled. "We can ride together as often as we want."

"Okay, then it's settled." The woman dipped a fry into the last of the ketchup and held it aloft. "Here's to a new life in Montana."

"Hear, hear." Sam raised her glass to the toast, forcing a smile. "If it's all right with you, maybe Electra can still come over to my place and help out a day or two a week."

"Sure. I think that would be fine. Once I figure out what my job with Clyde entails, I'll know the schedule, and we'll figure it all out."

"Awesome!" Electra threw both arms in the air.

After lunch, with thoughts and emotions jumbling in her brain, she drove them to the ranch, where Brad waited by the corral. Having him there to welcome her home stirred hope.

Even if Electra was leaving, she still had him, in whatever relationship they could settle into.

As she parked, she jerked her head back in a doubletake. Near him was a barn-sized pile of lumber. She leapt from the truck and ran toward it. "It came! I can't believe it."

His face held a satisfied grin. "The lumber yard delivered it this morning, not long after you left. There's the beginning of your barn."

Electra danced beside her as they all gathered around the stack of wood. "Yay! I can't wait, can you? I just can't wait!"

Sam allowed a surge of giddy anticipation to wash away the earlier murky feelings of loss. "Me too. I can hardly wait either." Grabbing the teen's hands in hers, she joined the dance. Brad and Alberta applauded the spontaneous jig, their laughter providing music for the celebration.

Finally, the dizzying whirl came to a halt, and Sam bent at the waist, panting, and laughing. "Whew! Well, now, let's take your bag up to Electra's room, and then I know she's got a ton to show you."

Quick as a flash, the girl sprinted to the pickup and pulled out her mother's large, floral suitcase. "This one, Mom?"

"The smaller one, honey. Thanks."

"You can sleep in my bed and I'll get the sleeping bag and sleep on the floor and..." Her voice trailed off as she led her mother toward the house.

Sam pivoted once again to gaze at the lumber. Then she entwined her arm with Brad's, and they strolled up the incline. "I'm excited for you," he said. "Maybe the fire was a blessing in disguise. This way, you'll get the barn you really want."

"Hmm. That's one way of looking at it, but yes, you're right. Maybe in stages, but it'll be all new and fresh." With a wave of satisfaction, she envisioned the red and white structure, with a covered arena to the side, filled with horses and kids and veterans, all bonding and riding and being healed. *That's my dream, and maybe it's coming true.*

Inside, no message light blinked, so she called JB Construction. No one answered, and she left a message that the materials had been delivered, asking for a callback to let her know when they would be starting the project.

Electra thundered down the stairs, her mom following in a more sedate fashion. "C'mon, Mom. I'll show you what Apache's doing and maybe we can go for a ride. Is that okay, Sam?" She slammed out the door without waiting for a response.

Alberta rolled her eyes and chuckled. "I've missed that exuberance."

A sharp pang shot through Sam. *I'm going to miss it too.* But she gave her friend what she hoped was a cheery smile. "I'll bet you did. You go ahead and take a ride, do whatever you need to unwind."

"Thanks." The woman enveloped her in a hug. "You've been a lifesaver for us, and I want you to know I appreciate it." She headed out the door.

A sudden weakness caught her off guard, the room tilted like a seesaw without the second rider, and she folded into a kitchen chair. Brad came into the room from the hallway. "Are you okay?"

She forced another smile. *Fake it till you make it.* "Yeah, yeah. I'm fine. It's all a bit overwhelming—Alberta's here, and Electra is leaving. I didn't think it would hit me so hard."

Sitting in a chair next to her, he put an arm around her shoulders. "I was a little afraid it might. We've both gotten used to having her around. She does perk up the spirits, even though sometimes it can be a bit wearing."

She huffed a laugh. "That's true. And how often did I find myself counting the days till her mom got here and could take responsibility for her wild tangents. But now..." Tears burned behind her lids. "Now, I don't want her to go. I wish I had room for Alberta to live here, but that doesn't make sense either, since she'll be working for Clyde."

"It's not like you won't ever see her again." Brad swept a strand of hair from her face.

His tender touch nearly undid her. She blinked back tears. "I know. I'm being stupid and emotional over nothing." She expelled a sharp breath. "Thanks for being understanding."

"Of course. That's what I'm here for." His face leaned closer to hers, and she closed her eyes with a pleasant tingle of expectation.

The phone rang, and they jumped apart like teenagers caught doing something wrong.

Dang! Just when things were showing promise. She rose to her feet, her face heated. When she picked up the receiver, Clyde's voice boomed through the line. "So, is there a certain young CPA in the country?"

"Yes, we got home a while ago, and she's out with Electra and the horses, of course."

"Oh yeah, I'll bet that little gal has so much to tell and show her mom." He gave a deep belly laugh. "Well, have her give me a call when she comes in. I just wanted to check to be sure she made it in all right."

"Okay. I'll give her the message."

"I've got some more dudes coming in next weekend, if you're available to help."

"Yeah. You bet. I'm happy to. Thanks." She hung up and strode to the door, with a sideways glance at Brad. "Well, I guess I'd better check on the ladies and do some chores."

He followed, brushing her arm with a tender caress. "I'll help."

After supper, the group spent the evening catching up on New York life and Sam's work with the veterans, interspersed with Electra's amusing asides. Lucky snored in his blanket bed beside the sofa next to where the teen sat, her hand trailing over his back.

As the wall clock inched toward midnight, Brad yawned and stretched his arms above his head. "Well, ladies, not to be a party-poop, but I'm going to bed. Don't stay up too late, gossiping."

Alberta laughed. "Yeah, I'm pretty beat too. Electra, you go on upstairs. I'll be up shortly."

Finally winding down, the girl stood from the couch, her eyelids drooping. "Okay, Mom. See you in a minute." She stopped to kiss Sam's cheek. "Love you." Then she climbed the stairs.

I love that girl too. "I'm going to miss her being around all the time." Her eyes misted over.

"I know. I realize this has to be difficult for you." Her friend leaned against the back of the sofa. "I mean, after all, I've left her here with you for several months, taking on full responsibility for her well-being and her studies. You've practically been her mother." She lifted her eyes to the ceiling. "Don't think for a moment that I haven't agonized over the burden I put on you."

"Oh. Well, I was glad to do it. I knew how miserable she was in New York, and I sure didn't want her to get back into that self-destructive behavior."

Alberta brought her gaze back to peer at her. "I know you were. I didn't want that either. But I want you to know I realize how attached you've become to her—and her to you—and I want you two to spend as much time together as possible."

Gratitude and relief washed away sadness. *Thank goodness. Alberta could've been jealous of our relationship.* "Thanks. That would be great. She's welcome here anytime, and like I said before, I value her help with the veterans' school and…" she sniffled, "and with everything. She has stepped up and really become my gal Friday."

Her friend gave her a smile. "I know. She's changed so much—winter to summer, night into day. I have my bright, bubbly girl back. And it's all because of you."

They both stood and rocked in an embrace.

"Thank you," Alberta whispered as she turned to go upstairs.

Sam went to the window, where the moonlight played tag with the clouds. Her heartspace ebbed and flowed. Big changes loomed on the horizon.

CHAPTER NINE

The next morning, after the women did chores, Sam suggested a ride to check on the cows.

"That would be great." Alberta brushed straw from her jeans.

"Yippee!" Electra responded in her inimitable style, dashing for the barn to collect bridles.

Transitioning from April, May had donned a bright costume of wildflowers amid a carpet of green grass. Horses' hooves clopped along the path worn by winter feeding, and the warm air smelled of spring freshness. Sam filled her lungs.

"Thanks for being understanding," she said to her friend. "I'm so happy you're here, but I hadn't really thought through what it would mean, that Electra would be moving in with you." She made a wry face. "How silly of me."

"No. Not at all." Alberta clucked to Trixi and reined her around a clump of spicy sage. "I understand. I've missed her terribly the past few months. So glad to be with her again. I feel a huge weight lifted off my shoulders out here, and I'm very much looking forward to starting a new life."

Electra swiveled her head and waved at them from ahead. "C'mon, you slowpokes!" She kicked Apache into a faster pace toward the reservoir where the white-faced cows lolled with new calves by their sides. "Aren't they cute, Mom?"

The livestock all present and accounted for, they headed toward home, riding along in pleasant silence, broken only by an occasional meadowlark trill or an exclamation from the teen. "It's so pretty out here, isn't it, Mom?"

"Yes, honey, it is beautiful and very peaceful."

After a leisurely lunch and dishes washed amidst teasing and laughter, Alberta cleared her throat. "Well, I hate to be the bad guy, but we'd better get our stuff packed up and moved over to the Bruckners'."

Electra's grin faded and her shoulders slumped. "Okay, Mom." Her voice dropped from excited to resigned. "I know we need to go, for your job." She trudged up the stairs, her mother following.

Sam drifted into the living room where Brad nursed a cup of coffee and sat next to him on the couch. He put a comforting hand over hers. They sat in silence, her biting the inside of a cheek to keep the tears at bay, until the two came down with their suitcases.

Electra dropped hers by the door and scurried to the corner where Lucky lay in his bed. He raised his head and licked her cheek as she bent close and murmured.

"Well…" Alberta spoke after a couple of minutes had passed.

The teen shifted her gaze upward. "Oh, Mom…Sam…?"

Her mother shook her head sharply. "No."

"But—"

"Absolutely not. Sam has footed the bill for this dog, and so it rightly belongs to her. Besides, its real owners might show up anytime."

"I know it cost a lot. Sorry." Her lower lip quivered. "Bye, Lucky. I'll be back to visit you…soon. You be a good doggie." She rose and took reluctant steps toward the suitcases. As she did, the dog pushed himself onto his haunches and then took a ginger step on his one front leg, attempting to follow.

A fist squeezed Sam's lungs. She couldn't breathe, couldn't swallow.

"Holy cow, look at that." Brad leaned forward.

Electra looked back to see Lucky walk toward her, one tiny, awkward, hopping step at a time. She mewled and rushed back, squatting beside him. "Oh, Lucky, you're walking! Ohmygosh, Mom. Did you see that? Sam, did you see?"

"Yes, I did." Sam knelt beside them, stroking the dog's back. "Good job, Lucky. Good boy." Her gaze rose to the girl's mom who turned sideways and wiped her eyes.

Alberta squared her shoulders. "That is amazing, honey. You did so well, taking care of him… But we need to leave him here right now. Okay?" She picked up her luggage. "Come along. Let's go."

Brad scooped the dog into his lap and nodded to Sam. She opened the door and led the way to the pickup, Electra, chin on her chest, lagged behind, her suitcase dragging in the dust.

***

With Electra gone, a heavy discontent hovered over her. Even the horses seemed to realize something was missing and displayed less enthusiasm in their greetings in the morning.

Strangely, Brad seemed more distant than ever, and tension thrummed between them. *What is going on with him?* She had thought they would be able to talk more and maybe begin to develop their relationship, with just the two of them at the ranch.

During the next couple of days, she threw her full attention to the livestock and chores. She rode Sugar or Trixi to the pasture, counting the new calves that frolicked in the grass. Checking the fence line, she repaired broken wire and replaced staples. She packed a lunch and stayed away from the house all day, aware she was avoiding Brad.

Thursday morning, Alberta brought Electra over so she could go to Miles City and help Sam with the vets' program. The girl leaped from the vehicle almost before it stopped and galloped to the corral to envelope Apache's neck in a hug. "Oh, I've missed you, boy, I've missed you *so* much!"

With a laugh, Sam greeted Alberta from the porch. "Want a cuppa before you head back?"

81

"Sure." The woman cut a glance toward her daughter. "That's all she could talk about the last three days—Apache, Apache, Apache."

"I'm sure she does miss him. They have that special bond." Sam led the way into the kitchen and poured coffee for her friend, filling a travel cup for herself and one for Brad. "She'll get her 'fix' today."

"I hope so. When she gets her mind on something…" Alberta shook her head. "You know how she is."

"I do." Then she called down the hall. "Brad. Are you ready to go?"

"Yup." He trudged into the kitchen, accepting the cup. "Hi, Alberta. Getting settled in your new place?"

"Sort of. Our cabin is cute and comfortable—if somewhat small. When my load of household items arrives, I may have to store some of it in Clyde's barn. I like it though. I already feel more at peace."

"I'm so glad." Sam squeezed her friend's arm. Alberta did look more rested, the lines around her eyes less pronounced than when she'd first arrived. "Well, we'd better get going. I'll bring Electra back tomorrow when I come over to help get ready for the weekend guests."

Despite a background niggle of worry about whether Elliot would be there, the trip to town buoyed her spirits with the teenager's nonstop barrage of stories about the Bruckner ranch. "…the horses and chickens and goats and I'm going to help with any kids that come and I think Sapphire and the group home kids will be out the next week and Mom's been helping Irene baking tons of goodies and she's started studying their bookkeeping stuff and…"

Catching Brad's quirked mouth from the corner of her eye, Sam exchanged an amused look. She patted Electra's knee. "I've missed this, even though it's only been a couple of days."

"I know, right? I miss you too…" the girl looked back through the rear window at the horse trailer, "and I miss Apache. I miss him *so* much."

At the college, Nick met them and helped unload the horses. Brad silently headed to the counselor's office.

The ag instructor's gaze followed his departure. "Is he doing okay?"

Sam shrugged. "I don't know. He's been withdrawn, very quiet."

"Well, Higgins'll get him squared away, I'm sure." He led them into the arena, where the veterans waited.

A quick perusal of the small group eased the tightness in her chest. Elliot was not there. While a part of her wanted desperately to help the troubled man, another part—her chicken part—reassured her this visit would be much easier without him.

"Hello, Sam." Garrett limped toward her with a hand outstretched, while Del followed, his strong arms maneuvering his wheelchair through the dirt. The rest of the group also welcomed her and Electra with handshakes, and Sondra gave her a light, quick hug.

"Good to see you all. It's been a little while. I hope you're all doing well and are ready to ride." She gestured to the horses. "Grab your brushes and let's get started."

Sondra, Garrett, and Jimmy gravitated to Trixi, and Linc, Al and Del went to Apache. The woman vet paused at the mare's face, stroking her nose and up to her forehead. A tingle ran through Sam as Sondra pressed her cheek against Trixi's and her shoulders visibly relaxed. *Good. She's getting more comfortable,*

After a few minutes of grooming, Garrett volunteered to tack up, with the other two double-checking the cinch and saddle position. Then he stepped back, arm out, with a flourish. "Madame?"

Sondra's eyes widened, and her shoulders rose again. "Um, no thanks, you go first."

Aw, geez. She'd done so well last time. Why was she hesitating now? Sam tamped down an urge to veto the woman's decision and insist she get on. *No, gotta give her time.*

Garrett ran a hand over his sandy crewcut. "Well, I'm game. I managed to get on from the right last time, so is it okay if I try that again?"

"Of course." She stepped to his side as he mounted with only a slight bobble. Patting his knee, she encouraged, "Good job." She walked alongside as he urged the horse forward, at first holding onto the saddle horn with his left hand and then cautiously lifting it away. He flashed her a raised-brow glance, and she gave him a salute, which elicited a grin on his flushed face.

Proud-mama emotions welled till she thought the snaps on her western shirt might pop. Wow, what a huge difference from the first several times he'd come to the ranch. His confidence had grown from hesitant baby steps to cowboy strides. She smiled back.

Jimmy rode next, and even kicked the mare into a short trot. His boyish enthusiasm radiated to the roots of his blond hair. "Hoo-ee! That was fun," he chortled as he lifted his right prosthetic leg over the saddle and kicked his left foot out of the stirrup to slide to the ground.

"You'll be galloping in no time." Sam clapped him on the back and then swung her gaze to Sondra.

The woman nodded. "All right. My turn, I guess." With another face and neck caress for Trixi, she stuck her boot into the stirrup and mounted in one smooth motion.

"Very nice." Sam followed her as she rode around the arena several times. "You're feeling much more relaxed, aren't you?"

"Yeah. It doesn't seem quite so far to the ground this time. But thanks for sticking close by."

84

"You bet."

The two groups finished by unsaddling and brushing the horses again. As Sam and Electra led the mounts toward the exit, the doors from the lobby opened. Brad entered, followed by a stocky, brown-haired man.

Elliot. A lead balloon sank to the bottom of her stomach. *Oh no. Now what? Is he drunk again?*

Nick moved to their side as the two men approached. Apprehension rippled up her spine.

Elliot removed his Navy Veteran ballcap and stood in front of her. "Um…" He cleared his throat. "I want to…apologize to you both…for my actions and um…language…the other day."

Beside her, Electra gasped.

Wow. She swallowed. This was not what she'd expected.

"I'm sorry for causing trouble. I know I was wrong." The man cast his gaze toward his feet. "I've been working with Higgins, and um… I don't know if I'm ready…to come back here, but maybe, sometime… If you'll allow me."

Before she could speak, she inhaled a fortifying breath. "Thank you, Elliot. I accept your apology, and I hope you *will* consider coming back to work with the horses."

"Yeah. You should. They help *so* much." Electra spoke up, an eager lilt in her voice.

Sam extended her hand.

After a moment's hesitation, he took it. "Thanks for being patient." His red face was washed with a sheen of perspiration.

He walked to the exit, his head down.

Nick gave her a thumbs-up and followed.

Slowly, she put a hand over her mouth, swung her gaze from Brad to Electra, and then to the group gathered around.

"Oorah," Del uttered softly.

"How… Where…?" Sam couldn't find the right words.

"He was waiting when I came out of Higgins' office," Brad explained. "He said he wanted to apologize to you but needed a bit of moral support."

And Brad helped him. Her scalp tingled. *A big step for him too.*

"That took guts." Garrett nodded toward the doors.

"Yeah." "Awesome." "About time." The others spoke at the same time and then took their leave, shaking Sam's hand or patting her back.

"Ohmygosh, can you believe that?" Electra's eyes were still saucer-wide as they loaded the horses.

"I honestly didn't think he'd be back." Sam closed the trailer gate. "And I never expected an apology."

Brad opened the pickup door and let the teen slide into the middle.

"Would you like to drive?"

"Um, sure. You trust this gimpy ol' leg?"

"If you do."

He got in the driver's seat but remained quiet as he drove away from the center.

After a few miles, she glanced at him. *What is he thinking, feeling? Is he getting better?* Sometimes she thought so, and then… She broke the silence. "So, how did your session go?"

"Fine." He huffed a laugh. "Nothing quite as profound as with Elliot."

"But…it's helping?"

He shrugged. "Yeah. I think so."

"I still can't believe it." The teen swiveled in the seat. "I'm so glad he's getting help, and I really, really, really hope he'll come back and work with Apache and Trixi."

Sam couldn't help but smile. "Me too." Her insides were still shaky gelatin from the encounter, her body and emotions expecting one thing and then the unexpected happening. *I hope he will too. I would like to be able to help him.*

86

CHAPTER TEN

The next morning, she drove Electra to Clyde's, where the girl gushed to her mom about their experience with Elliot. "That's good. Glad to hear." Alberta grabbed her daughter and pulled her close. "I know that was a scary time for both of you."

"It was."

"Yeah, really scary." Electra scrunched her face. "Kinda like when Dad…" Then she grabbed Sam's arm. "C'mon. You gotta see our cabin. It's so cute."

Alberta hesitated a moment and met Sam's gaze before stepping onto the porch. "It'll be nicer when we get our own things." She opened the door to a cozy log living room with a rock fireplace and a kitchenette to one side. Two bedrooms sported horse-themed quilts and curtains with colorful braided rugs.

Sam wandered through the cabin. "I like it." She took in the small round dining table covered with ledgers and papers. "I see you've already started working on the books."

"Yes. Trying to get a feel for how they've been doing things, and then I need to get it all computerized." The woman sighed. "Irene has started the process, but she doesn't have the time, what with cooking and taking care of guests."

"I hope you'll like it here." She hugged her friend. "Well, I'd better go see what Clyde wants to me do before he comes looking for me."

***

Brad was on the phone when she walked into the house that evening. "Yes, that sounds good. Okay, I'll see you then." He hung up. "Hi. How was your day?"

"Good." She described the Luccis' cabin and what she'd done to help get ready for the weekend dudes. "How about you?" Wrinkling her forehead, she waited. Who had he been talking to? See who when?

"Fine." He took steaks from the fridge. "Rode Toby again."

"That's great. He seems more and more comfortable with us." She gathered salad ingredients to chop and toss.

Without replying, he headed toward the porch and the barbecue.

Lucky skip-hopped from the living room and nuzzled her leg. She bent to scratch his ear. "Good boy. You're getting better every day." She glanced out the window at Brad hunched over the barbecue. *Is he getting better? Why won't he talk to me? It's like pulling hen's teeth, as Grandpa used to say.*

Since the May evening was too chilly to eat outside, Brad brought the steaks in, took potatoes out of the oven, and set the platter on the table. He poured two glasses of red wine.

Sam added the salad, and they sat. "This was so nice of you to cook tonight. What a great meal."

He brushed at his dark hair now growing out from being shaved in the hospital, the familiar lock curling over his forehead. "You work hard. It's the least I can do."

"Well, thank you. I appreciate it." She speared a bite of steak and chewed, waiting. When conversation wasn't forthcoming from his side of the table, she asked, "So, how was the ride? Is your leg bothering you?"

"A little. Not as much, though. It's getting stronger." He poured bleu cheese dressing on his salad.

"And Toby? He seems calmer."

"Yeah." He chewed for a moment. "Yeah, he is. He's a pretty nice saddle horse. I'll bet Electra could teach him to kneel."

Her fork halted half-way to her mouth. "Oh, wow. That's a great idea. Especially since he's younger. The other two horses are getting up in years, and I don't like the wear and tear on their joints, doing that so often."

"She'd love it." He grinned.

"I think she would."

For several long minutes, the only sound was forks clinking on their plates. Sam raised her gaze occasionally to catch Brad sneaking a glance at her, then quickly averting his eyes. She took a sip of wine. "So. What's up with you? You've been giving me the silent treatment. Have I done something? What's going on?"

He cleared his throat, took a drink, and set the glass down with deliberate precision. Then he turned it slowly by the stem, staring into the burgundy contents. "I'm sorry. We do need to talk."

A chill raked over her.

"I think it's time I go back to work." He peered at her from beneath lowered eyelids. "I've been mooching off you long enough, and I'm not contributing anything."

She cocked her head. "No—"

He held a palm up. "Hear me out. I've been here a good two, two and half months. You've been feeding me, supporting me, cheering me on, and helping me beyond what I could ever thank you for. And I'm just a blob. I've been bad-tempered and grumpy, and you're right, I've been giving you the silent treatment. And you don't deserve that."

Needle tears stung behind her eyelids. "But…"

"Talking to Higgins…he thinks I'm depressed, that I do have PTSD, even though I think that's a crock. What I went

89

through with a stupid vehicle crash is nothing compared to what those vets have been through." He raked his hand through his hair.

"But it's *your* issue, *your* recovery, and that makes it just as important as theirs." An ache chiseled a chasm in her chest. She touched his hand lightly. How could she alleviate his pain?

He shrugged. "Yeah, I s'pose. But I can't see it that way. I need to leave. I need to find my own way, not keep dragging you down with me."

The air thinned. Her breath locked in her lungs. She stared at his square-jawed, handsome face. Finally, words choked themselves out. "You're not."

"Oh, but I am." With a low moan, he studied the floor beside him. "I can see how your spirit has dimmed. I know you've been through a lot, with the barn and the horses, with Lucky, and Electra, but I believe the biggest weight on your shoulders is me."

"Brad." Her voice rose in anguish. The chasm widened, the ache deeper, sharper. "That's simply not true."

"I know you care about me, and you want to help me— heck, you're helping everybody and everything that comes into your path. And I care about you too, but right now, I can't give you what you need—a stable relationship. So, I think I need to give you some space, and I need to go."

Her world spun out of tilt. Wind roared through her head, and her heart flapped like a trapped bird. "Brad..." The desperate need for answers propelled her racing thoughts. "I-I don't *want* you to go."

His smile slanted sadly to one side. "It's not forever. I'll be back." He took her hand in his. "I need to find a purpose to my life. I've been talking to the station manager in Billings, and he wants me to come work for him, part-time at least, until I've healed up more."

Tightening her grip on his hand, she struggled to breathe normally. "Yeah." She tried to force her voice into calmness. "I understand." The needles poked her eyes. *No, I don't.* "I thought…you were healing here…with Toby, with Higgins…" she barely choked out the words "…with me."

His chocolate eyes held her gaze. "I am. You *have* helped. Just look at where I was a couple months ago—I was trapped in my own head, didn't want to do the PT, didn't want to rejoin the world." His look seared her soul. "Look at where I am now—riding again."

The ache grew to prairie-sized proportions. She withdrew her hand and wrapped her arms around her middle as if to hold herself together. "What do you want, Brad?"

"I don't know…for sure. I have to go—to find out."

A steel band tightened around her chest. "Well, let me know when you do." She rose from the table and rushed up the stairs, slamming her bedroom door behind her, and threw herself onto her bed.

She should have known this was coming. He couldn't stay here forever. He needed to go back to work, to his world. But where did that leave her? Where was that budding growth of a relationship, that possibility of someone to share her feelings and dreams and life with? She didn't want another "rescue case" or roommate. She needed a soul mate, needed him to tell her he loved her, needed her.

Was that all simply a pipe dream? She wanted more, yearned for more, for intimacy and love. Call her old-fashioned, but she knew what she wanted, and it wasn't a quick thing. She supposed Grandma Anna's influence, as well as Aunt Monica's, set her moral compass. Sure, she and Kenny, and now Brad, had technically "lived together" in the same house, but she simply didn't go along with the current jump-into-bed-live-together mentality of today. She wanted a serious commitment—a till-death-do-you-part covenant. However, his signals were anything but that.

The needles prickled and built and surged until the dam burst, and she buried her face in her pillow and let the sobs erupt.

She awoke in the pale dawn to the sound of a vehicle outside. Brad's voice and someone else's. She curled into a ball. *He's leaving.*

The screen door bumped, and footsteps echoed up the stairs. Her bedroom door creaked open. She squeezed her eyes shut.

Brad's fingers gently caressed the hair from her forehead. She lay rigid, pretending to be asleep. His spicy, clean-soap smell enveloped her as his breath feathered her ear. "I'm going now. But I'll be back. Soon. Don't give up on me." He brushed a kiss on her cheek, and then he was gone.

If he leaves and finds his compass, will it lead back to me? Or would he find happiness out there without her?

Hot tears oozed from her clamped-together lids. *I don't care. I don't care. I don't care.*

But she did. Her whole body shook with the hollow ache of loss. She lay, still curled into a fetal position, until she fell back to sleep on her damp pillow.

The sun's rays streamed through the bedroom window. Opening her eyes in gradual increments, she unwound from her ball and sat on the edge of the bed. Brad's kiss ghosted her cheek. *He's gone.* Her body moved robotically, as if she'd had a giant shot of Novocain.

Coffee made, toast choked down, horses fed, she found herself in the truck driving to Clyde's. After all, she had a job to do. The dudes were arriving today.

The rancher met her at the corral, gave her a sidelong glance, but when she shook her head, he went on as if nothing was wrong. "The group came last night, and after lunch, they want to go for a ride." He peered at her again from beneath the rim of his sweat-stained hat. "You and Electra up to helping out with that?"

"Of course." Sam pasted on her fake-it-for-the-dudes smile. "Bring 'em on."

She wasn't sure how she made it through the afternoon. Everything around her seemed to happen in real time outside her own slowed senses. Somehow, she went through the motions with Electra, visited and bantered with the women in the group, gave them pointers, and took them for a short ride. The ladies hugged her and thanked her for a "fun time" and "we want to do it again tomorrow."

After the horses were untacked, brushed, and put out to pasture, she headed directly to her truck without stopping at the house to say goodbye.

After chores, the autopilot Sam heated leftovers, and she hunched over her plate, not seeing what she ate. Everything was flat, tasteless, as if Brad's absence had removed all the flavor.

Someone washed the dishes—she assumed it was her when, startled, she saw them piled in the drainer—and she drifted to the living room to slouch in her rocker. Her arms like lead, she couldn't even pick up her book. She sat as the dusky shadows grew long, hearing only deafening silence.

The next two days slow-mo'ed their way through a fog. Sam attended to her chores, to the dudes, and her job at Clyde's. His questions, "Are you all right? Anything wrong?" drew only a shake of her head and a curt, "No. Fine." Even Electra's chatter failed to break through the gelatinous layers surrounding her.

Sunday evening, she sat unmoving once again, drowning her thoughts in the dark. She wouldn't think of him. Wouldn't think of the future. Wouldn't think of the what-ifs. Every time one arose, she tamped it down decisively, like tobacco in a pipe bowl.

When the phone rang, she nearly fell out of her chair. She stumbled to the kitchen. "'Lo?"

Teresa Knudson's cheery voice lilted over the waves. "Hi, girlfriend. I haven't seen you in a month of Sundays. Thought I'd better give you a call, see if you're still alive and kicking."

"Hi." Sam's voice rasped like a rusty gate, and she cleared her throat of the hard stone that had taken up residence there. Teresa, her real estate agent when she found this place, was now one of her best friends. "Yeah. It's been a while. How're you?"

"I'm great. Busier than a one-armed paper hanger." Her laughter tinkled. "But you sound…off. Is everything okay?"

"Yes. I'm fine. Everything's fine." Her voice rose to a falsetto.

"I don't believe you." Teresa's voice held a note of concern. "What's happened? Tell me. Please."

No, no, no, I can't talk about it. I'll disintegrate. Her breath came in shaky intervals. She slid down the wall to the floor.

"Sam. It's me here. C'mon. What's wrong?"

Her heart clenched until it felt as small and hard as a shriveled peach pit. But it knocked around until she thought it would poke a hole through her chest, and all her emotions would pour out like entrails of a dead animal on the prairie.

"Sam. Sam? Are you still there?"

She gulped a mouthful of air. "Yeah. I'm here. Um…well… Brad left." Wrapping her arms around her middle, she squeezed to hold it all in.

"Oh." A sharp intake of air. "Oh my. Listen. I'm coming over. Hang on, girl. Be there in forty-five minutes." The phone line went dead.

Sam held the receiver clutched in one hand until the persistent beep brought her back.

CHAPTER ELEVEN

True to her word, Teresa arrived in less than an hour, carrying a small cooler. She opened it, and with a flourish, took out a half-gallon of Rocky Road ice cream.

Sam managed a weak smile.

Her friend grabbed two spoons from the silverware drawer, and they sat at the kitchen table.

Sam scooped a bite of the cold, creamy comfort and let it melt in her mouth.

"So, did something happen between you two? What's going on?"

"Nothing happened." She spoke around a tongue as icy as her heart.

"Well, what then? Something has you in its clutches. You are not your usual self."

"That's just it. Nothing was happening. He froze me out. Then, he said he needed to get back to work, find his purpose, that he was just a burden on me, and couldn't give me what I needed." The words came at last in a rush.

Teresa pushed a strand of long, blonde hair behind her ear as she peered intently into Sam's face. "And…?"

"I don't know. My head says I'm reacting like a stupid teenager, that what he said is true—he can't hang around here forever. He has to make a living, feel like he's doing something worthwhile, continuing his recovery. But in here…" She put a hand over her chest, then spooned another bite and stared at it. "It doesn't understand. I feel…crushed, broken, abandoned."

Teresa covered her hand with a warm palm. "So, you love him."

"I don't know." She squeezed her eyelids shut against a cocklebur of emotion. *No, don't cry. You don't love him. He doesn't love you! It's as simple as that.*

"Oh, honey. Your heart knows."

Despite her resolve, the tears flowed. "This is stupid. I'm being stupid." She hiccupped.

"No, you're not." Teresa came around the table to sit next to her and put a gentle arm around her shoulder. "You're hurting. That feeling of abandonment is real. I know your history with that issue—your family, your friend Jace, Kenny. Now you feel like Brad's left you too."

"It's not logical. I'm blowing this all out of proportion." She sniffled and took a tissue from her pocket.

"Emotion isn't logical." The young woman pulled the ice cream closer. "Here, have some more medication. You know the old saying, 'If you love something, let it go. If it comes back to you, it was meant to be. If it doesn't...'" she paused, "'hunt it down and kill it.' Want me to go hunt him down and beat him senseless?"

Laughter bubbled up around the knot of tears. "Yeah." She took a big bite of Rocky Road. "I'll go with you."

Both women burst into giggles.

"Okay, so let's go through the logic." Teresa took a pad and pen from her purse. "Number One: Brad was in a seriously bad accident and in a coma for more than a month. Number Two: he's been out of the hospital only a couple of months. Number Three: he's been crippled up, unable to work, unable to do much of anything but let you take care of him. That is a huge ego-buster for a guy."

Sam nodded. "And, Number Four: his counselor says he has PTSD, although he pooh-poohs that." And what if, once Brad was fully established in his pre-accident life, he would grow away from her, no longer need her help?

"He would. It's going to take time. You know how that is—you work with problem horses. You have the patience of Job. Practice some of that patience on Brad. Give him space and time. I've seen the way he looks at you—there's no way he's not in love with you."

The lump of ice in her chest melted. She took another bite of ice cream, thinking about her own rocky road.

Teresa spent the night and had coffee brewing when Sam came downstairs. She accepted a cup from her friend and inhaled the earthy, life-stimulating aroma before taking a sip. "Ahh, thank you. You're hired."

With a grin, Teresa joined her at the kitchen table. "So, how're you feeling this morning?"

Sam took a quick inventory of her emotions, surprised to find how calm she felt. "At peace. Thanks for coming to my rescue with the ice cream and for providing your shoulder to cry on."

"Anytime, girlfriend, anytime." Her friend smiled. "Relationships are difficult at best. I know, with my own long-distance one with Alan. But throw in what Brad's gone through and what you've been dealing with, and you've got yourself a real knotty situation."

"You *are* right, though. I have to be as patient with him as I am willing to be with my horses. Trust doesn't happen overnight."

Teresa sipped her coffee. "And, remember, if that doesn't work, I can always hunt him down…"

They both dissolved into laughter.

After breakfast and helping with morning chores, Teresa left to meet a client. Since Sam didn't have to go to work anywhere, she did laundry, washing loads of sheets from all the company she'd had recently. Lucky followed her outside and lay in the warm sun as she hung them out for that fresh-air smell.

"You're getting around pretty good now, aren't you?" She scratched his ears and massaged the shoulder above his missing leg. "Pretty soon you'll be running alongside when I go for a ride." He cocked his head at her with adoring brown eyes and licked her hand.

Her chest expanded. She found herself—like Electra—hoping no one would show up to claim him. The little guy was growing on her. Giving a catlike stretch, she held her face to the sun for a few moments before heading to the corral.

Although the horses had already been fed, they came to the fence to greet her. Even Money, although he stood back, out of reach. "Hoping for more treats, huh?" She gave each a face and neck rub and slipped them a carrot from her pocket.

Holding a large one toward the pony, she spoke to him softly. "C'mon, boy. You'd like this. C'mere, Money."

He snorted and blew, turned sideways, and pawed the dirt. She smirked. *He's trying to ignore me, but he wants his treat.* Continuing to hold out the carrot, she murmured to him. Finally, he stretched his neck as long as he could make it and sniffed. He took a step closer, then another. She kept talking softly to him. One more step, and he grabbed the carrot faster than a rattlesnake strike and trotted away.

"Hey, that's progress." She laughed at him, staring at her from afar, crunching his treat. "First time you've come that close. Good boy, Money, good boy."

She bridled Sugar, swung onto her bare back, and pointed her to the prairie. Loping through the greening pasture, the mare's strong muscles moved beneath her, and tension from the past few days ebbed and released into the wind. She leaned forward on the horse's neck, and her ponytail loosened, her chestnut strands mingling with Sugar's matching mane.

She reined up near the reservoir where the Hereford cows grazed in contentment in the shade of the cottonwoods. Birds twittered and trilled, insects buzzed and ratcheted. She breathed in the fresh spring air. All this—the land, the ranch, her home—was hers now. Despite the hardships and the odds against her, she had achieved that part of her dream. She could be proud of that accomplishment. Tranquility flowed through her like a trickling stream.

Yes, an ache lingered, and questions remained. She missed her companions. Would Brad come back to her? Could they rebuild their relationship, growing it into something meaningful beyond friendship? Was it possible to create the next part of her dream ranch?

She had to believe she could.

After checking the cows and counting the new calves, she urged Sugar homeward.

***

On her next trip to Miles City, Electra came along, chattering as usual about her activities at Clyde's. "I love it there with all the horses and helping him and Mrs. Bruckner and Mom and she's really busy doing their books and she's had several ranchers ask her to help with their taxes and books and stuff and…" She faced her with an earnest look. "But I miss you. And Apache." She glanced back to the horse trailer.

Sam smiled at her young friend. "Well, I miss you too, honey. I'm glad you're coming with me and helping with the vets."

"Yeah." The girl's forehead drew together in a V. "But Brad… I wish he was still here, coming along today."

"Me too." The twinge of missing him stabbed her. "But it's okay. He'll be back." *I hope.*

Electra huffed. "I don't get it. He was doing so good and I know horses heal people and I know he really, really likes you so why did he have to leave?"

She explained his need to get back to work, to feel worthy, and to further heal. "He's doing the honorable thing, and I admire him for that."

"Meh. Well, okay, but…" The teen stared out the window. "Hey. I've been thinking about Apache. I miss him so much, and he was my healing horse… Is there any way I could…take him to Clyde's?"

Jerking her head in a double take, she threw a glance at the girl. "What?"

"Well, I know he's your horse. But what if I bought him from you?" She turned her puppy-dog eyes to Sam.

"And how would you do that? Do you have the money?" Sam's lips twitched.

"No." Electra's voice came as a near-whisper. "But…I'm getting paid a little to help at Clyde's, and maybe… Could I work for you to earn enough to buy him?"

"Oh, gosh." Her mind whirled. This had come out of left field. Although…the girl and that horse had been bonded and meant for each other from the beginning. When they first found him, emaciated and near death, Electra had been immediately overcome by his situation. By caring about and for him, she had transformed herself from Goth-girl to cowgirl.

"Well, honey. I'll have to think about that. And talk to your mom. I assume you haven't asked her."

The dark head slowly wagged side to side. "No," came the little-girl voice. "She probably won't let me."

"Let's not jump to conclusions. I'll talk to her and think about this some more, okay?"

"Okay."

At the ag college, Electra helped her unload Trixi and Apache. They met Nick inside the arena, where he'd brought in several horses. "I thought there might be a few vets—those who don't need the kneeling—who'd want to try some of ours."

"Great idea." Sam waved at the group coming toward them. "Hi, guys."

Garrett scanned the arena behind her. "Brad already gone to see Higgins?"

Her heart lurched. *Here come the questions.* "No, he's gone back to Billings to work. He thought he needed to get back in the saddle, so to speak."

"Oh. Okay." He passed a hand over his sandy crewcut.

Del wheeled up beside him. "Well, we miss seeing him."

She nodded, not trusting her voice, and gestured to the horses, clearing her throat. "As you can see, Nick's brought in some more horses, so each of you will have a mount today. Go ahead, pick one, grab some treats and brushes, and get to know your horse."

Del and Garrett went for Trixi and Apache, and the rest enthusiastically acquainted themselves with their choices. After helping each saddle up, Sam directed them through several turns around the arena.

Afterward, Linc pumped her hand, a big grin on his face. "This was fun."

"Yeah." Del wheeled closer. "Do you s'pose we could take them outside for a ride next time?"

"I think that would be a grand idea." Sam patted Trixi's neck. "If you guys are able to during the week, see if Nick will let you work some more with these horses. Simply groom them and saddle them and get to know them better before we tackle the next step."

"All right!" Garrett joined the group. "We'll do our homework. See you next week."

101

CHAPTER TWELVE

On their way home from the ag center, she received a call. Electra clicked the cell and put it on speaker for Sam to answer.

"Hi, Ms. Moser, this is Bob from JB Construction."

Surprised, she flashed a look toward her young friend. She hadn't heard a word from them since the lumber had been delivered. "Hi, Bob. Long time, no hear."

"Yeah, um, sorry I didn't get back to you. Been busy. But we can come out tomorrow and start preparing for the foundation, if that works for you."

"Tomorrow?" She grimaced. Tomorrow, she had to take Electra back and work at Clyde's. But she didn't want to delay the process any longer. "Yes. That'll be fine. I have to be gone, but you guys come on out and get started."

"Okay. We'll be there about eight."

"Sounds good. I'll see you before I have to leave."

Disconnecting, the teen let out a whoop. "Yay! They're going to start on the barn. Awesome! Oh, I can't wait."

A ray of hope lifted Sam. "Yeah, me too. Wow. I was beginning to wonder…"

The next morning, she was up early and met Electra at the door to do chores, taking a few minutes to pat, scratch, and give the horses an extra treat.

Brad's suggestion came to mind, and she broached the idea. "How would you like to start training Toby to kneel?"

Electra's face glowed. "Really? Could I? Yes, yes, yes! I want to." She strode to the bay and ran her fingers through his black

102

mane. "Hey, Toby. Did you hear that? We get to train you to kneel so you can help the vets too. Isn't that awesome?"

She came back to Sam's side. "When can I start—now?"

"I think we'd better wait till next week. I'll have you come over a day before we go to Miles, and you can get started, and then maybe you could stay another day after. But we have to talk to your mom about it first, okay?"

The teen's head bobbed like a woodpecker. "Okay! I'm excited. Oh, I can't wait."

At 8:00 sharp, a green truck with the JB Construction logo on the doors, pulling a trailer with a small backhoe, roared up the drive. Joe got out and shook hands with the women. Then he flicked his gaze to the pile of lumber and the now-leveled spot where the new barn would rise. "Good. Looks like things are ready to go. Bob will be here shortly, and we'll dig the trenches and get the rebar put in." He took the plans from the truck and spread them out on the hood.

As she reviewed the blueprints with Joe and then with tape measure and plumb lines began marking the floorplan, another truck arrived. Bob hopped down from the truck, followed by another young man. "Mornin'. This is Ted." The brown-haired man nodded, his gaze lingering on her for a moment.

Joe touched a finger to his hat. "Ready for a new barn?"

"You bet I am." Sam beamed at them. "Okay, gentlemen. Looks like everything is in order. I have to go to the Bruckner Dude Ranch to work today. So, I'm leaving this in your capable hands. Any problems, questions, you have my number."

"Sure thing." Joe shook her hand again and strode back to the site.

She drove away, her old tennis-playing butterflies starting up a match inside. *Is this really happening?* Could she trust them to do the work while she was gone?

"Electra, hit Horace's number and put it on speaker."

Her neighbor's gravelly voice answered.

"Good morning, Horace. It's Sam. Hey, guess what? The construction guys are at the ranch getting the foundation ready."

"Fantastic."

"Electra and I are on our way to work at Clyde's. I didn't want to delay them getting started, so I told them to go ahead. But I'm a little concerned about not being around."

"Say no more," the older man rumbled over the speaker. "I'll drop by after a bit, make sure they stick to the plan and do the work."

She blew out a breath of relief. "Thank you so much, Horace. I owe you supper tonight, okay?"

"Sounds good to me. You gals have a good day now, hear?"

At the Bruckners', the two made their way to the house, where Irene poured cups of coffee. Alberta joined them at one end of the big, wooden kitchen table. "Did you girls have a good session with the vets?"

"Yeah, Mom, we really did. We got horses for everybody to get used to and next time we're going to take them outside for ride, and oh, they're all doing *so* good!" She glanced at Sam. "And the construction guys showed up this morning and they're gonna start on the foundation for the barn and ohmygosh it's gonna be so cool."

Her mother brushed back a strand of the girl's hair, now growing out from its short spike. "That *is* great news. Wow. But you're here today?"

Sam explained her reasoning and that Horace would be overseeing the project. "And how is *your* work going here?"

Alberta made a wry face at Irene and Clyde. "Good. I'm slowly getting up to speed, and we're going to whip these books into shape pretty quickly."

Mrs. Bruckner chuckled. "I don't know how quickly, after the mess I made of them."

"Pfft. I've seen worse, believe me."

Sam drained her coffee. "Well, Clyde, what are we up to today?"

After he told her his plans, she addressed Alberta. "Electra has a couple of things to discuss with you." She headed for the door. "I'll be back in at lunchtime."

Over roast beef sandwiches, the conversation turned to the teen's proposals. "First of all, Electra spending a couple of days with you and training the horse is fine with me, if it's okay with you."

"Absolutely. I'd love to have another horse to use with the disabled and save the wear on Trixi's and Apache's joints." Sam patted the girl's arm. "Besides, I like having her around more."

"All right. That issue is settled." Then Alberta's brow furrowed. "Sam, do you really want to sell Apache? I can't see us coughing up enough money to buy him."

"But Mom, I told you I can work and earn the money—"

"Yeah, in how many years? You'll be grown up, and the horse will be long dead by that time."

"Mo-om!" The teen's cry of shock reverberated through the kitchen.

Her mother shook her head. "Sorry. I don't mean to be negative, but we have to think about this logically."

Conflicting ideas of wanting to keep Apache and knowing he was really Electra's horse warred in Sam's mind. What was the right thing to do? On one hand, she loved the horse she had rescued and gone to court to keep. On the other hand, it seemed that the girl and the buckskin were meant for each other from the first moment they'd met.

"Well… I think we can probably work something out." She could hardly believe the words coming from her mouth. "Electra has been helping me with the vets' program, and I'm getting paid for that. And if she comes to work a couple of days a week training Toby, I think she should be earning some money for that too." She inhaled deeply. "I originally paid five hundred for Apache, so I'm willing to give him to her for that amount."

"Really? For real?" The teen jumped up, knocking her chair over, and squeezed Sam's shoulders in a tight hug. Then she glanced at her mom. "Is that...okay...with you?"

Alberta thinned her lips and stared back at her daughter for a moment. Then the corners of her mouth turned upward. "Sam, that is a very generous offer. Yes. I'm okay with that."

A high-pitched squeal made everyone jump. "Ohmygosh! Apache is going to be *my* horse. Ohmygosh, ohmygosh, ohmygosh! I can't believe it. Thank you, thank you, thank you, thank you." She squeezed again until Sam could barely breathe.

Now what have I done?

As Sam drove home that evening, thoughts dust-deviled through her mind and anticipation hummed like a buzz saw. Feeling a bit like her giddy teen friend, she could hardly wait to see what the construction crew had accomplished. Her new barn would be rising from the ashes. She would have more stalls, a nice tack room, and more room to care for the animals and the people she worked with.

Then a crush of loneliness settled on her shoulders. Brad should be there to see this new beginning. To share it with her. She hadn't heard from him in the couple of weeks since he went back to Billings, leaving a persistent ache gnawing at the hole in her heart. *Lord, I hope he is doing well. Please help him heal.*

With her silent prayer offered, when she turned up the drive to her home, the anticipatory thrill coursed through her again. She parked beside Horace's truck. Her neighbor rose from a seat on the porch and followed by Lucky, stepped down to greet her. "Welcome home."

Her glance flickered toward the corrals.

He chuckled. "C'mon, let's take a look."

She had to force herself to keep from skipping down the slope, and for a split second her heart suspended itself in her chest. There it was—the rectangular outline of her new barn. She covered her mouth with her hands. "Oh, Horace. It's real. It's really happening!"

"Yup. The guys worked hard all day. I made sure of that." His weathered face split with a wide grin. "Joe said they'd be back tomorrow to pour the foundation."

"Yeehaw!" She raised her hand to high-five her elderly friend. "Thanks so much for being here today. Let me do chores, and then I'll fix you supper."

Together, they gave the horses their supplemental feed, along with hugs and pats and finger-combing. Money, as usual, stayed out of arm's reach but eagerly ate the treats left in a bucket. "One of these days…" Sam shook her head.

"He'll come around. He's already getting a little closer to you when you feed him."

"Yes. A tiny, tiny bit of progress. But gee, this has been the most challenging animal I've ever worked with." She bent to pat Lucky's head. "But you, young fellow, you're healing up so well. Look how he's been following us around out here."

"I know. He spent quite a bit of time with me today. Gettin' around purty good." He scratched the black and white ears.

"All right. C'mon up to the house. I have steaks to broil."

"Ya don't have to twist my arm twice." Laughing, the two headed to the house.

The next morning the cement mixer ground its way to their location, and the three men worked hard, mixing, pouring, and smoothing the concrete in the footings. By the end of the day, charcoal-gray cement was hardening in the footings. "We'll let 'er set up good and be back in a couple of days to get started on the next phase," Joe told Sam before the men drove off.

CHAPTER THIRTEEN

The following Wednesday, Alberta brought her daughter over so she could begin work with Toby. Lucky danced around Electra on his three legs, she ruffled the dog's fur, and they trotted to the corral, while the women sat over a second cup of coffee.

"She's been so excited to start this, I could barely keep her at home. I thought she might take off walking here."

Sam giggled. "Well, I hope Toby will be cooperative. He's really a nice horse, but he certainly was traumatized by the accident. Took me a long time to ride him again, and just when we got him to go into the barn, it burned down. So I don't know how he'll do when we get the new one built."

"Between the two of you 'horse whisperers', I have every confidence he will turn out very nicely."

After visiting a while longer, Alberta left, and Sam went to the corral where Electra brushed Toby, taking special care with his legs, to get him used to handling. The gelding stood calmly, one hind leg cocked, his eyes half-closed.

Sam leaned against the fence. "I think he's enjoying this."

"Yeah. He's a good boy, aren't you, Toby." The teen's face glowed.

"Well, I'm going to attempt to work again with Money." She shrugged.

"Good luck."

"Yeah. I'll need it." She swiveled on her bootheel, scanning the small pasture where Money stood near the fence. Her breath caught, and she stopped in mid-step. Lucky sat on his haunches next to the pony, his muzzle pointed upward.

She bit her lip. *Oh dear, what's going to happen—will Money bite or kick him?*

But the Shetland bent his shaggy head to the dog, and they touched noses. Then Lucky licked the horse's face.

Sam closed her gaping mouth. *They're bonding!* She gestured to Electra and pointed.

"Ohmygosh," the teen whispered as she drew closer to the fence. "Ohmygosh. I can't believe it. That is so cool."

The two stood, simply observing the animals get acquainted. A hushed breeze stirred the dust, and the sun darted through wispy clouds, warming the earth. After several minutes, Lucky limped to a grassy spot by the fence, turned around three times, and lay down. Money stood still.

Pressing her hands to her mouth, Sam moved in slow motion and squatted next to Lucky.

The pony quietly watched her and the dog for several long minutes, eyes wary but bright. His stance seemed more relaxed, less defiant than usual. Then he took one step closer. And another. Hardly daring to breathe, she reached into her pocket for a cake pellet and held it out as he approached. One more step, and then another. He gradually stretched out his neck as he came closer to the treat.

She murmured to him, holding her palm flat. He took another step toward her, softly lipped the pellet from her hand, and stayed within reach, crunching, with calm eyes on her.

Taking in a slow draught of air, she whispered a reverent "Ohhh." Extending her arm, she rose from her crouch, rubbed his velvety nose, and caressed his face upward to his ears. The pony stayed where he was, allowing the contact. "Good boy, Money, good boy." She kept speaking in a soft voice while stroking his neck. She almost expected a chorus of angels to break into song. This was a miracle!

***

The next day, Sam and Electra loaded Trixi and Apache for the drive to Miles City to work with the veterans. The teen kept up a running patter about what had happened the day before. "Toby is just so, so gentle now and I think he's going to be easy enough to train to kneel and oh, Sam—Money and Lucky—wow! Wasn't that awesome? I was scared, were you scared?"

"Yes, I was. I was picturing Money taking a big bite out of Lucky or turning around and kicking him...like he acted with me at first." She shifted to climb a hill.

"I never would've thought a dog and horse would be friends."

"Oh yeah. I've heard of racehorses having special friends, like a dog or a goat, even, that would live with them in their stalls and keep them calm."

Electra's eyes glittered. "Well, he sure seemed a lot calmer. Maybe he knows that Lucky was broken, and poor Money is broken too and maybe they can heal together. Maybe that's why."

What insight from this young girl. Her chest filled with words she couldn't express. She cut a quick glance at Electra, face aglow, enthusiasm radiating from her entire body. Blinking rapidly to keep the road in focus, she moved her hand across the seat to squeeze the teen's arm. "Yes. I think you're right."

Nick, Del, and Garrett met them outside the ag center to help unload the horses. "Everybody is chomping at the bit, so to speak, to get out and take a ride." The ag instructor led Apache from the trailer.

"Yeah. We can't wait." Leading the way, Del wheeled through the dust, escorting them into the arena. "We've been working with the horses all week."

"That's great." Sam followed with Trixi.

Garrett fell in step beside her. "So, Brad's still not back?"

"Nope. Haven't heard a word."

"I'm sorry. I hope he's…um…doing okay." He ran a hand over his sandy crewcut.

She forced a smile through her empty ache. "Thanks. I hope he is too."

Inside the arena, the rest of the group met them, each already leading the horse they'd chosen last week.

"Looks like you guys are ready to go." She relinquished Trixi's reins to Garrett. "Go ahead and get her saddled up, and Del, you can take Apache. Do you know the signal?"

"Yup." When Electra had Apache tacked up, the veteran wheeled himself next to the horse and gave him the hand gesture. The gelding kneeled, and he eased himself onto the saddle.

Sam surveyed her group. "Okay, everybody. Hop on. Let's take a couple turns around the track first."

After everyone had mounted successfully, she, Electra, and Nick trotted beside them as they took several laps. Then she brought them to the doors leading outside. "Are you ready?"

"Oorah!" Del shouted.

"Yeah." The guys all expressed their approval. Even Sondra gave her a thumbs-up.

Nick opened the doors into the small pasture area behind the arena and mounted his horse. Sam and Electra grabbed two more and led the vets on a short ride over the flat prairie. Rimrocks surrounded the town in the distance and fluffy clouds scampered across the blue sky. A light breeze made the day's temperature perfect. Each instructor rode near two of the students, with Sondra and Garrett gravitating to Sam.

"This is fun." The woman's face shone with her pleasure.

"Yeah," Garrett agreed. "Gives us a better view than inside, going 'round and 'round. Thanks for this."

"Great. I'm glad you're enjoying yourselves. You've all come a good distance since you first started, and you needed a little reward for that." Her own spirits soared with their success and pleasure. *Now if Elliot will come back and join them...* Her heart lurched. *And Brad.*

Too quickly the time came to an end, and the group found its way back to the arena, everyone's conversation buzzing with excitement about being out of doors and the pleasure of the ride.

A small thrill of pride rippled through Sam's core. "You all did an awesome job today. I think you'll be ready to wrangle cattle pretty soon." She grinned at their chorus of "Yeehaws," "oorahs," and "cools."

As she and Electra led their horses to the trailer, Garrett joined them again. "Thanks. That was...great. I...um..." His Adam's apple bobbed as he stumbled over his words. "I'd like...to...um... Can I buy you two lunch?" He finally blurted it out, his face turning as ginger as his hair.

"Oh. Well, gosh." *This was certainly out of the blue.* "You don't have to do that."

The teenager hovered beside her, nodding rapidly.

"I...I'd like to." Garrett swung his gaze from one to the other. "You...you both have helped me so much."

"That's very nice of you." She hesitated. *Would this be crossing a line—teacher and student?* No, this was a different kind of situation. "Sure. We'd like that. I know Electra's starving. She's always hungry."

"Oh, ha ha." The teen pretended to be offended but then burst into giggles.

The veteran joined the laughter. "Let's meet at the 600 Café then."

"All right. See you there."

At the café, the three settled into a red vinyl booth, Garrett burying his face in the menu. Electra grinned beside her. Sam chuckled inwardly at his painful shyness, glad the teen was there to diffuse the awkwardness.

A cheery middle-aged waitress approached. "What'll ya have? Our soup of the day is beef barley."

"I'll have the soup and half-turkey sandwich." She placed her order, while the other two opted for burgers and fries.

"So, I thought you all did really well today," she ventured.

The teen spoke up before the man could comment. "Yeah, wasn't that awesome to ride outside, huh, Garrett? You're a good rider. Did you like it?"

A smile slowly lit his face. "Yeah, I did. A lot. Thanks. It reminded me of my grandparents' place…where I got bucked off." He gave a little chuckle-snort. "I'm glad Trixi is so gentle. She's a great horse to learn…or re-learn on."

The waitress returned with their plates, and attention diverted to the food. Electra told Garrett about Money and Lucky and Toby. "Pretty soon, you guys'll have another horse that kneels! Isn't that cool?"

"Yeah. That'll be great."

"Have you heard anything about or from Elliot?" Sam sipped her Coke.

"He's still coming to classes and seeing Higgins. Hasn't said anything about coming back to ride though. I hope he will."

"I hope so too. Maybe you could tell him how much it's helped you."

"Oh, I have. That's why he came that first time. But he's…" He shrugged.

She sighed. "I know."

After lunch, she and her young friend headed for home. "Well, that was nice."

"Yeah." Electra snickered. "I think he likes you."

"What?" Sam scrunched her nose. *Where did that come from?* "Well…yeah, I hope he does. I hope they all do. I've been trying to help them overcome…things in their lives. I'd hate to think they *didn't* like me."

A huge grin split Electra's face. "Yeah, I know. But Garrett *like*-likes you. I can tell."

She sent the teen a glare. "Now look here. Don't be conjuring up ideas. There is still Brad, you know. I'm not looking for another relationship."

"But what if Brad doesn't come back? You might want some options." Her young friend cocked her head.

Sam's stomach recoiled as if she'd swallowed acid. *How can she say that?* "Forget about it. Brad will come back. Besides, Garrett is not my type. So…" she pierced a look across the truck cab, "no more of that kind of talk, okay?"

Her pulse thumped hard. What if Electra was right—that Brad was gone for good? And if Garrett had an interest in her… No way. She might have to nip that in the bud. *Keep it on a professional basis only.* No. She couldn't…wouldn't think about those things.

***

At home, horses unloaded, and chores done, the two trudged up the incline to the house. The light blinked on the answering machine.

"Ms. Moser, Joe here from JB Construction. Sorry, but we won't be able to come out this week to start the barn. We're…um…tied up with finishing a project right now."

"Phhhtt." She blew her frustration through her lips. "Fine and dandy. Hurry up and wait." She punched the erase button and sent the machine scooting across the counter.

"Geez, what's up with those guys?" Electra slouched in the doorway. "Are we *ever* going to get the barn built?"

"My question exactly." Sam pushed out a forceful breath and squared her shoulders. "Oh well. It is what it is, as they say." She couldn't let a minor setback ruin her day. "What do you want for supper?"

After a quick meal of hotdogs diced into pork and beans, the two washed dishes, and then settled in the living room to read. But Garrett's red face and nervous hair-scrubbing kept popping into her mind. She'd been amused by his embarrassed shyness, but was he really coming on to her? He was a nice guy, yes, but no, she was definitely not interested in a romance with a troubled, broken veteran. She'd already been through that with Brad, had invested time, care, and support for the man who still made her lips tingle with the memory of his kisses. She ached to feel his arms around her again.

The words swam on the page. She caught a sob before it erupted, coughing to cover, and stood to pace to the window, and then to the kitchen. "Want some hot chocolate?"

"Yeah. With marshmallows?"

"Okay." She poured milk into a saucepan to heat and gathered the cocoa, sugar, and marshmallows.

When the phone rang, she nearly dropped the mug she reached for in the cupboard. "Hello?"

"Hey, how's my favorite rescuer today?" Brad's rich baritone flowed through the line.

Goose bumps climbed up her arm. "Hi. Doing great." She leaned her hip against the cupboard and twined her fingers in the phone cord. "I was just thinking about you. How are you?"

"Great minds, huh? I've been missing you a lot." He cleared his throat. "I've been really busy at the station. Even though they said it would be part-time, I haven't seen that yet. They're short-handed, and it seems like there's always something to run off to and video."

He misses me. Her knees dissolved, and she slid down the wall to sit on the floor. "Wow." Her voice quavered. "Well, that's good, I guess. As long as you're not overdoing it. Are you feeling okay?"

"Yeah. I am, actually. I think work is helping a lot. I'm going to the gym, seeing a counselor here, and also talking to Higgins on the phone once a week."

"Great. I'm glad." She told him about the barn foundation, the progress with the veterans, about Electra working with Toby, and Money and Lucky's new-found friendship.

"Super! Congratulations. I can't wait to come back out and witness all that first-hand. Um, it might be next weekend, if things slow down here a bit, and...if you want me to come visit...?" His voice trailed off.

She swallowed, hardly daring to hope. "Yes, of course I do. I...we would love to see you."

"Well, it's a date then. I'll call and let you know how things are going." He pushed out a soft breath. "I *am* really looking forward to seeing you."

As he clicked off, Sam glanced up to the stove to see the milk boiling over. "Yikes!" She scrambled to her feet and grabbed the pan off the burner. "Dang!"

Electra trotted into the kitchen. "What happened?"

"I scorched the milk. I'll have to start over."

"That's okay. I'll help." The girl put the pan in the sink and ran hot water in to soak. "Was that *Braad* on the phone?"

Sam's face heated like the burner on the stove. "Yes, it was. He's doing good, working hard, going to the gym and counseling, and he might come out next weekend." She blurted it out—*just like Electra*—she realized with a tiny giggle.

CHAPTER FOURTEEN

Morning sunshine brought rays of a new day's possibilities as Sam and Electra headed to the corrals. After short rides to stretch the horses' legs and extra grooming and treats for Apache, Electra attached a lead rope to Toby's halter.

Speaking softly as she stood in front of him, she pulled the rope gently toward the saddle. The gelding tucked his head toward his chest and took a step backward. "Good boy." Electra kept talking to him and backing him. Then she brought the rope along her side and around to the saddle horn. She stood next to the stirrup and pulled back on the lead. Toby kept his head tucked and after a moment's hesitation, backed again easily. She released the pressure and repeated the exercise several times, each time rewarding him with praise and a treat.

Sam's lungs expanded, and she couldn't keep from smiling, remembering the sullen, angry Goth-girl she had first met. What a horsewoman Electra was turning into. She had such a gentle touch, and even Toby, who'd been so skittish after the accident, responded to her as a kindred spirit.

Grabbing a brush and curry comb, she loaded her pockets with pellets, and ambled to the pen where Lucky sat near Money. She bent to stroke the dog's ears, and he grinned up at her, his tongue hanging from one side of his mouth. The pony stepped closer and pushed his nose against her pocket, snuffling.

"Ah, so you'd like a treat, huh?" She took one out and offered it. He lipped it from her palm and stood calmly crunching, not backing or running away to eat from a safe distance as he'd done in the past. "Good boy, Money, good boy." She patted Lucky's head again. "And you're a good boy too. Look what you've accomplished." The dog gave a soft woof and licked her hand.

Giving the little horse a couple more treats, she slowly caressed his face up to his ears. They twitched back and then forward, and the muscles in his withers tensed slightly. She kept up a low, soothing patter as she touched an ear lightly while smoothing his forehead with her other hand. A gentle massage at the base of the ears and then down along his neck calmed the quiver. She gave him another pellet and took the brush from her back pocket.

"Your mane is so tangled I might have to work on that with the scissors." With smooth strokes, she brushed his neck to his withers. The pony leaned his head against her side. "You like this, don't you? Good boy. I'll bet that mean ol' lady never did that for you, did she?"

He nuzzled her pocket again, so she rewarded him with more treats, and continued to brush, moving toward his back a little at a time. Money gave a great sigh, and his stance relaxed even more.

"Ahhh, doesn't that feel good, huh, boy? We all like a massage and somebody brushing our hair." Time and surroundings faded into the background as Sam combed and brushed the matted winter hair from his coat, a fluffy pile forming around their feet.

Finally, as she reached his rump, he awoke from his trance and moved away. Not far, but enough to put space between them. "Had enough for today, huh? Okay. That's fine. You did so well. You're such a good boy." She offered him the rest of the pellets and then gathered up the tools and horsehair and headed to the makeshift storage shed, Lucky following.

Electra mounted Toby and rode him around the corral a couple of times before untacking him and joining Sam.

118

"Ohmygosh, look at what you did today. That's as close as you've ever gotten to Money. That is *so* awesome!"

Pent-up air released in a whoosh. "Yeah. I am amazed. It's like night and day from when he first arrived. And I owe it all to our three-legged friend here." She scratched the dog's ears and under his chin. "*You* are the 'horse whisperer' in this family."

The teen giggled. "See? You rescued him, and he helped you with that poor pony. I'm so glad nobody came to claim him. It was meant to be."

Sam put an arm around her and squeezed. "I think you're right, my dear, I think you're right." That vet bill was worth it, after all.

***

At the ag center the next day, Nick handed Sam an envelope. "Your paycheck."

"Ooh, thank you." She still had a hard time wrapping her head around the fact that she was helping these veterans with her horses, enjoying it—and getting paid for it. Her pulse jumped a notch.

"Yes. You're doing such a great job with these guys. I think it's time for you to go to one of the PATH training classes to get your CPR certification, check the equine management skills requirements, and review for your standards exam."

She gulped. Oh dear. She'd known this would be coming up. Even though she'd done well in the online courses, she wondered if she really had the skills to become certified. "Okay. I guess it is time."

"I'll get you a list of possible courses and email it to you. You'll do fine." He patted her arm. "Oh, by the way, a heads-up, Elliot is coming today."

Like a boxer taking one blow after another, her solar plexus squeezed protectively in on itself. She took a deep inhale and blew it out. "All right." She glanced around the arena where the

119

group already gathered with Electra and the horses. "I guess I'll have to modify the program a little. I'm sure everyone will want to take another outdoor ride, but I'll have to start from the beginning with Elliot."

"Yeah. You do what you need to with him. I'll help Electra."

As she strode to the group, in her peripheral vision she saw the veteran enter. "Okay, everybody. Get your horses brushed and tacked up. Nick and Electra will take you through your warmups and for a ride later. I'll be keeping Trixi inside to work with Elliot today." She waved him over.

He approached with hesitant steps, his gaze lowered to the ground in front of him.

"Good morning, Elliot. I'm glad you're back." She put on her brightest, friendliest smile.

"Mornin', ma'am." He lifted his eyes to hers for a moment. "Thanks."

"We'll go at your pace. There's no pressure at all." She kept her voice soft. "Can I introduce Trixi to you?"

His face granite-hard, he stared at the mare.

Oh dear. Is he going to refuse? What is he doing here? She'd never seen someone quite so reluctant, so contrary. Dipping her hand into her pocket, she brought out the favored cake pellets. "Trixi is extremely gentle. She was a trick horse for Montana's well-known Miss Ellie, so she's used to all kinds of handling."

She held out her palm with the pellet. "Keep your hand flat. She won't bite you. She really likes these treats, so if you feed her, she'll like you too." Caressing Trixi's face, she murmured, "Good girl. This is Elliot. Treat him kindly."

The mare bobbed her head and rubbed it against Sam's shoulder.

Facing the vet, she offered a handful of pellets. "Would you like to try?"

He stood silent, as if carved from stone. Moments stretched into seconds into a minute or more. *C'mon, Elliot. What are you going to do?*

She spoke again, weaving her words softly into the tension. "If you don't want to, that's all right, but I think she'd love another treat."

His shoulders lifted almost imperceptibly, and he swallowed. He took the pellets.

Trixi stretched her neck toward him.

Elliot's chest expanded with an audible puff, and he held out his hand.

Trixi's lips brushed his palm gently as she accepted the treat. Sam smiled. *Good girl.*

One corner of his mouth moved slightly upward. He cut a quick glance at Sam, then back to the mare. Again, he held out his palm, and she took the morsel. Crunching, she nudged his hand. He gave her another and then smoothed a touch over her nose and up her face, as Sam had demonstrated.

Trixi stood calmly, her liquid chocolate eyes searching the man as he petted her head. He moved his hand to her neck, caressing the soft hair, speaking in a low tone barely above a whisper.

Sam didn't dare move, but simply watched the slow, gentle process. Elliot's shoulders relaxed, his breathing calmed as he combed his fingers through the mane. Then he leaned his forehead against her neck, and the mare curved hers around his shoulder.

A clump of emotion rose in Sam's throat, and she squeezed back tears. She would have thought she'd be used to this by now, but no. *It gets me every time.* There was something about a horse that reached the most troubled soul and tamed the ferocious inner beast. Every time she witnessed a troubled human bonding with a horse, new hope erupted inside. This was validation. This is what she was meant to do.

Elliot stood for long minutes, leaning against Trixi, simply breathing, slowly, in and out. Finally, he lifted his head and stepped back, his hands still resting on the mare's neck. He continued to caress and talk to her. Then he swung his gaze to Sam. His rock-hard face had softened, and moisture glistened in his eyes.

He nodded and whispered, "Thank you, ma'am." Turning, he walked toward the arena door.

Clasping her hands over her chest, Sam could only stand, as if rooted to the spot. What she had just witnessed was so moving she didn't want it to be over. A wave of compassion and love washed through her. She stepped to her horse and encircled the neck with her arms. "Oh, Trixi, you are such a good, good girl." She buried her nose in the mane and inhaled the pungent, horsey smell of healing.

Gradually, Sam became aware of voices around her. She raised her head to see the group, huge grins on their faces.

Nick gave her a thumbs-up. "Well done."

She puffed through her lips. "Well, it wasn't a total success, but it was a first step."

"Hey." Garrett stepped forward. "Remember how long it took me to get acquainted with Trixi, let alone get on her back?"

"I do." She grimaced, remembering his tentative steps, and then his fall when he did mount.

"And me too, ma'am." Sondra's eyes shone bright.

"You've made a huge difference in all our lives, Miss Sam." Jimmy ran a hand over his short blond hair.

A pleasant ray of hope and satisfaction filled her. She tried to speak but had to clamp her quivering lips together. Clearing her throat, she said, "Thanks, everybody. Okay, I seem to be free. Want to go for a ride?"

The vets all shouted in affirmative and went for their mounts.

The afterglow of Elliot's small success lifted Sam like a hot air balloon through the trip home. Electra, as usual, was full of bouncy chatter and praise. "I was watching, but I could *feel* him relax and give in to Trixi. I remember that feeling. It's awesome!"

"Yes, it is, isn't it? I hope he'll come back next week and do it again." A tender warmth flooded her once more.

"He will." The teen bobbed her head emphatically.

At home, after unloading Trixi and Apache, Electra went to work with Toby for a while, and Sam brushed and petted Money. After doing chores, the two headed for the house. The answering machine light blinked.

"Hello, Miss Moser. Um… Ted from JB Construction. Joe called me and um…wanted me to call you…um…to tell you he's still tied up with a project over in Colstrip. He said he'd get back to you soon."

With the ending click, Sam's happiness balloon deflated. "Dang it! When somebody says they're going to do something, why can't they follow through? Especially since I gave them that advance on the work." And the boss hadn't even bothered to tell her—had his hired hand deliver the news. *Chicken!*

The next message brought Brad's rich baritone. "Hey there. Sorry to miss you. I'm not going to be able to come out this weekend after all. Got a story we're working on. Hope you two are doing okay. See you soon."

She sat hard on a kitchen chair, clamping her eyes shut, clenching her hands into hard balls on her thighs. Her heart that had felt so full all day shrank like a pond in a drought.

Electra's hand rested softly on her shoulder.

She covered the girl's hand with hers, simply sitting, neither speaking. Just when things seemed to be going well…

Disappointment reared up inside, threatening to unseat her from her life perch.

Her young friend's fingers kneaded her tense shoulders. She forced herself to take deep, calming breaths. *Okay, time to cowgirl up! This isn't the end of the world. Just a couple of minor setbacks. Nothing to lose your cool over.*

She opened her eyes, set her shoulders, and swung her gaze upward.

The teen's mouth turned down. "Bummer."

"Well, I guess plans are made to be changed, right?" She stood and inserted a cheerful note into her voice. "Let's get Sugar and Toby and go for a ride."

The canter over the prairie in the cooling evening breeze helped blow the gray cloud from her mind. She concentrated on Sugar's even stride, drawing strength from the horse's great muscles as she ran. Her hair came loose from her ponytail, and she felt as one with the mare.

Back at the corrals, they unsaddled and stowed the tack in the shed. She glanced at the concrete foundation, shaking her head. "Hope I can get that barn built before next winter."

"Yeah, I hope so too. I'm sure they'll be back soon." Electra lifted a hopeful face toward her. "Shall I heat up some of that chili for supper?"

"Okay. Sounds good. Thanks."

"You sit and rest. I'll take care of it," her young friend offered.

After they'd eaten, and Electra washed the dishes, the two found their comfy chairs and books in the living room. Sam had no sooner become engrossed in Ivan Doig's *Last Bus to Wisdom* when she heard the sound of a big diesel engine approach the house.

"Sounds like Horace." The teen jumped up to peer out the window. "Yup. Here he comes."

The tall, older man filled the kitchen door with his grandfatherly presence. "Hey there, how are my two favorite gals today?"

She gave him a hug, and Electra followed suit, squealing with delight. "I've missed you, Horace. I'm so glad to see you!"

His guffaw rumbled as he held the teen at arm's length. "I've missed you too. That's why I thought I'd better come for a little visit." He grinned at Sam. "So, what've you been up to?"

"Come in the living room and sit." She gestured toward the door. "Electra, would you put on the coffee and get out some of those oatmeal raisin cookies you baked?"

Over cookies dunked in steaming cups, they filled him in on their activities, Electra first with her running monologue of working with Toby: "…and he's really calm and gentle and he's easy to work with and I think he's going to be another good kneeling horse for the vets. They're gonna love him!"

Horace gave her a thumbs-up. "Sounds like you're doing a great job with him, little gal. Keep up the good work. Speaking of work, how's the algebra going?"

She flashed him a pleased look. "Better, thanks to you. Mom's been helping me, and I'm keeping up with home school really good. Pretty soon we'll be done for the summer, and then I can concentrate on my job, and guess what? I'm buying Apache!"

"Wow. That's great."

With Horace's nod of approval, she leaned forward, her face settled in earnest seriousness. "And, Sam, tell him about Elliot. You're doing good things there too."

At her neighbor's raised eyebrow, she related the small step of progress the vet had made that day. "I have to admit, it did make me feel pretty good."

"Well, as it should. You may not realize how much good you're doing them, but I know, from talking to Del and

Garrett, how much being around horses—and you—have helped them."

"Thanks. I guess I needed to hear that." She huffed. "Especially after the phone messages I had when I got home." She shared her frustration.

"Well, dadgummit! I can't believe those construction guys. Whatever happened to the 'handshake is a deal' policy we've always had around here. Besides, you *do* have a written contract." He shook his head. "By golly, I oughta go find them fellers and give 'em a little lecture on keepin' their word."

The picture of Horace towering over Joe and Bob made her chuckle and eased her irritation. "Yeah, maybe so. Well, enough about us. How have you been?"

"Still wakin' up on the right side of the sod." Taking another cookie from the plate, he took a bite. "But I was just over t' the Jersey Lilly for supper, and Billy told me something that made my hackles set up straight."

Sam cocked her head. *What could it be, to rile Horace like that?*

"He said there's been a guy from New York in, asking questions, kinda like them fellers from the Big Open a coupla years ago. I sure as heck hope they're not gonna try that exotic game refuge idea again. I thought we run 'em off for good."

CHAPTER FIFTEEN

After Horace left, Sam stared out the window, her face scrunched, as she recalled that Roberts guy who'd teamed up with Murdock, trying to buy up land in their area to create a game preserve. The ranchers were all skeptical, and no one had been willing to sell. After warning the men not to come back, the locals had lined the street in Ingomar, all armed with long guns. That's the last they'd seen of the New Yorker.

She huffed a snort. That's when she'd first met Brad who'd been hired to film a documentary for this Big Open group. To say they had not hit it off right away was an understatement. A lot had changed since then, thankfully, and Brad was definitely one of the "good guys." Yes, his personality had been affected for a while by his head injury and coma after the accident, but he seemed to be progressing back to the old Brad. At least that's what she hoped. She remembered how his smile made her knees go weak, and his kiss had promised so much more.

Rising from her chair, she wandered to the kitchen to tidy up. But now, what was going on? Was this Roberts, or someone else, back to try again? Didn't he get the hint the first time?

"I'm going up to bed. G'night," Electra called from the stairway.

"See you in the morning. Sleep well." Sam absently ran the dishcloth over the already-clean counter. *I need to talk to Brad about this.*

***

Morning brought the clatter of boots on the stairs and clanging in the kitchen. Sam sat up in bed and stretched. Always-eager Electra—couldn't wait to get out to work with Toby. Well, bless her enthusiasm. Her mind flashed to the construction guys. *Wish they were more like her.*

She padded to the kitchen, where her young friend had the coffee brewing. Cinnamon rolls warming in the oven filled the air with a sugary scent.

"Hey, good morning! I woke up with the sun shining and the horses whinnying, and I just couldn't stay in bed any longer and I have to get out there and work with Toby some more. I'm so excited to get him trained." The teen took a mug from the cupboard and filled it for Sam. "How about you? Are you going to work with Money some more?"

Chuckling, she cleared the morning frog from her throat and took a sip. "Yeah, I think I will. And yes, it's a beautiful day for working with the horses."

When the two wended their way to the corrals and pasture, Lucky was already nose to nose with Money. He woofed and hopped away, then turned and woofed again. The pony followed in a mock chase along the fence and came to a stop where Sam stood. He stretched his neck over the wire, sniffing in the direction of her pockets.

"You make me laugh. You're just as hooked on treats as the rest of them, now that you know I'm not going to hurt you." She fed him the desired pellets, and he and Lucky took off again in playful pursuit of each other.

Electra giggled beside her. "That's *so* cute. Wow. I can't believe the difference our little doggie made with Money. That's so awesome, Sam, isn't that just *so* awesome?"

Sunshine flooded her soul. "Yes, it is, my dear. It *is* awesome." She gathered her grooming tools and scissors and opened the gate into the corral. Enticed by more treats, the little black horse trotted right in. As she brushed him, a calm energy radiated between them. He seemed to actually enjoy the attention and didn't shy away when she snipped the tangles and mats from his mane. But again, when she reached his rump, he'd had enough and moved away to nuzzle Lucky sitting nearby observing the process.

"Good boy. We'll get to that tail eventually." She picked up her tools and the pile of hair and headed to the shed.

Electra continued her work with backing Toby, each time prompting him to bend his head lower. She murmured to him and fed him treats to reward his progress.

Over lunch, the teen extolled the gelding's virtues. "Hasn't he calmed down so much since Brad worked with him and overcame his fear of going into the barn? I'd like to try the hobbles soon to see if he'll kneel…or maybe he'll do it without."

"That would be the preferable outcome." Sam took a bite of her sandwich. "I'm really pleased with his progress too. And I really hope we don't have to start over with him when we get the barn built."

"Naw. I don't think we will." Electra nodded emphatically. "I think he's past that. But…" she sipped her milk, "I think Brad needs to come out and ride him and bond with him some more."

"Yup. I agree. He does." *He needs to come out here for more than one reason. I miss him.* Her heart tripped a beat.

***

The next day, Sam drove Electra to Clyde's, and over the weekend they worked with the kids from the group home in Billings. When the van pulled up, Sapphire and Wendy spilled out almost before the vehicle came to a complete stop. Squealing and shrieking, they grabbed Electra in an exuberant hug.

129

The counselors, Robin and Jim, exchanged a bemused glance as they exited. "Well, are you ready for the 'wild bunch'?" Robin hugged Sam.

"Oh, always." She chortled. "Good to see their enthusiasm. I remember the first few times they came out here. Lots different now."

"Oh yeah. The healing power of horses." Robin gestured to a pre-teen girl Sam hadn't seen before. "This is Heather. She's new to our group, but she's been around horses a little bit before."

"Nice to meet you, Heather. Where did you have horses?"

The girl ducked her head, her brown curls falling over her face. "Grampa's," she mumbled.

"All right, that's super." Gesturing to Electra, she introduced her. "Electra and I will help you get reacquainted. We have a nice, gentle horse named Ginger I think you'll really like." To the group, she said, "Okay, kids, let's head for the corrals. Get your tools out—you know what to do." They sprinted away, boys jostling each other, girls giggling.

Electra put a gentle arm around Heather. "Hi. I'm glad you came today. Sapphire and Wendy probably already told you how much fun we have here. Come and meet Ginger." She led the younger girl to the corral, where she gave her a handful of pellets and showed her how to feed the mare.

Heather flattened her palm, held it out without hesitation, and then smoothed her hand over the horse's nose and up her cinnamon brown face. Ginger nuzzled the girl's arm. She ran her fingers through the mane and then wrapped her arms around the mare's neck.

Sam's spirits flew as she witnessed yet another kid and horse bond. Electra let out a long exhale beside her. "Awesome," she whispered.

On her way home from Clyde's, thoughts niggled about Horace's story of someone nosing around the area again. Surely, the ranchers' "not welcome" message had been received, and surely the Big Open people weren't going to try to run them off their land to establish a preserve again. At least she didn't have to worry about Murdock selling the place out from under her this time. There was no way she would sell now that the ranch was hers. "They couldn't pay me a million dollars in cash." She spoke out loud and hit the steering wheel with her fist.

At Ingomar, she turned into town and angle-parked in front of the Jersey Lilly. Inside, the familiar bar smells of beer and fried meat wafted over her. Ranchers enjoying supper occupied several tables.

She sat at the huge cherrywood bar, where the proprietor greeted her with friendly enthusiasm. "Hey there, Sam, long time-no see. What can I get you?"

"I'll have a burger and a cup of coffee, please."

He grabbed a cup.

"Say, Billy, what's this I hear about somebody asking odd questions about land around here?" As a bartender he'd certainly be in a position to hear any gossip about this issue.

He poured the coffee and set it in front of her. "Well, a guy came in a coupla days ago, said he was with—what was it called?—oh yeah, the American Prairie Reserve. It sounded so much like the Big Open guys. I told him in no uncertain terms that we'd been there, done that, and run them fellers off, and nobody 'round here was interested in anything like that."

"Hmm. How odd. I hadn't heard about that group." She scrunched her forehead. "I hope he got the message."

Billy shrugged as he headed toward the kitchen to cook her burger. "I dunno. Hope so too."

Jim Gardiner, a neighbor she'd met at Clyde's, sauntered up beside her. "Sorry, I overheard you and Billy. I was here that day too. Guy had an odd manner about him, like he was some undercover spy or something. Askin' strange questions, like how many ranches in the county, how many acres each owned, stuff like that."

"Things he could've found out at the county courthouse." The back of her neck tingled. "We better not have another fight on our hands."

"Naw. I doubt he'll be back. Nobody would tell 'im nothin', and we did talk about the armed standoff within his hearing." Jim chuckled. "He left shortly after."

After downing her burger, she headed home to feed the horses. Lucky hopped from Money's side as they all met her over the pasture fence. She scratched the dog's ears, and his black tail wagged his whole back end. Giving each horse a few pellets and a petting, she checked the water tank to make sure it was full, gathered a few eggs, and trudged up to the house.

Inside, she punched in Brad's number. His warm voice vibrated over the line, sending goose bumps up her spine. "Hi Brad. Hope you're doing good."

"Yeah, I'm good, doing fine. Just got home from work, scrambling some eggs for supper. What's up?"

"Something's been bothering me, and I wondered if you'd heard anything about this." She filled him in on Horace's report and her visit with Billy and Jim.

"American Prairie Reserve? Hmm." A silence, and she heard a pen tapping. "It kind of rings a faint bell, but I can't remember where or why. Maybe the Big Open guys I worked with in Wyoming mentioned it. I can do some research, get back to you."

"That would be great. I'm worried they are going to try again out here."

"I can't imagine they would, after their great 'send-off,' but you never know. They were persistent in Wyoming, but nothing came of that either. There are private game preserves for hunting there, but as far as I know, that particular group went back to New York, tail between their legs."

Sam snorted. "As well they should."

"Yeah. I was working on kind of an exposé about all that when I…had the…accident. That's all been on the back burner, with not much activity to go on." His voice rasped and faded.

Her breath hitched. *Yeah, that really threw a wrench in the works.*

He cleared his throat. "But maybe I should look into that again, especially with your new development."

"Thanks. I appreciate it."

"No problem. It'll be interesting. I'm going to come out next week to see you, come hell or high water. I want to go to the vets' group with you, talk to Higgins again, and…I just want to see you. I miss my horse rescuer."

A tide of joy swelled through her. "That would be great. I've missed you." She giggled. "And I think Toby—and Electra—do too."

The following week, Alberta brought her daughter for her work days with Sam and stayed for supper. "Oh, I can't tell you how much more relaxed I am since moving here."

"I'm so happy for you." Sam smiled. The woman's worry lines had softened and the aura of tension she had shown on her visits from New York was gone. "Are you getting enough work to keep you in the manner to which you'd like to become accustomed?"

Electra giggled, and her mom laughed too. "Well, with room and board taken care of, doing Clyde's bookkeeping and a few late tax returns for other ranchers, I think we're going to be all right."

The teen's face lit in eager anticipation. "And Clyde's paying me a little and so are you and I'm saving up and I'm going to buy Apache—soon!"

"Yes, you will." Sam patted the girl's arm. "You're doing a fantastic job of training and helping me with the vets. I couldn't do it without you."

Electra's face pinked, and she focused on her plate.

"There's a training class for my PATH certification in Billings in a couple weeks. I'll have to be gone over a long weekend, so maybe I can hire you to stay here and take care of the horses?" She swung her gaze from the girl to her mother.

"Yeah! Can I, Mom, huh? Can I?"

"Okay, I don't see why not. Maybe I can come stay too and help."

Sam nodded. "That would be great. Thanks, both of you. And of course, Horace is just a phone call away."

The next morning, when Sam got up, she found Electra already in the corral, working with Toby, backing and bowing his head.

"He's getting ready to kneel, I can tell." The teen patted the horse's neck and fed him a treat.

"Wonderful." She grabbed the grooming gear from the shed and joined Lucky with Money. To her surprise and satisfaction, the pony allowed her to brush his tail and snip out the matted knots. "Good boy," she murmured as she brushed and patted him, feeding him a pellet reward with each step. Lucky sat close by, wagging his tail, and keeping his eyes on her as she worked.

She paused to scratch his ears and give him a dog biscuit. "Good puppy-dog. Good boy."

After an afternoon ride, the two returned to see a black pickup parked at the house. Brad leaned against the hood and waved as they rode up. "Howdy," he called.

Sam's heartbeat fluttered, and her face heated.

Electra prodded Apache into a short gallop, slid out of the saddle, and encircled him in a bear hug in one smooth motion. "I'm so glad to see you," she squealed, bouncing on her tiptoes.

"I'm happy to see you too." He swiveled from the girl's embrace as Sam made a calmer dismount and approached.

His firm hug sent a pleasant ripple through her body, and her stomach tightened into delicious prickles as he lowered his face to kiss her. They stood, swaying together until a throat clearing from Electra startled them both back to the here and now.

She gave an embarrassed chuckle.

Brad ran his hand through his dark hair. "Well now, that was a fine welcome. I'll help you ladies unsaddle, and I expect to hear all about your latest adventures."

Toby hung his head over the fence and whickered as the trio approached the corral. Brad moved forward, hand outstretched, and smoothed his palm up the gelding's face. Then he climbed over the fence to hug the horse. The bay rubbed his head against the man's arm. "Aww, Toby, old boy, I've missed this."

Electra sniffled beside her. "Isn't that sweet?" she whispered.

"Yes, it is." A surge of happiness coursed through Sam. *They need each other. Like I need him.*

After untacking Apache and Sugar, Electra had to show Brad the progress she'd made in teaching Toby to kneel.

His face beamed. "I'm impressed. You're doing great."

Supper and dishes finished, they retired to the living room with coffee, hot chocolate, and cookies. Brad stretched his long legs out from his seat on the couch, and she curled hers under her next to him.

Electra took Sam's usual seat in her rocker. "So, Brad, what you been up to?"

He told them about his workouts at the gym and a couple of stories he'd been working on for the TV station. "I've done a little digging on that American Prairie Reserve group."

Sam scrunched her forehead and leaned toward him. "What is it? Another name for the Big Open?"

"No, I think this is a different group. They've actually bought up quite a lot of land in the Lewistown-Malta area, but it sounds like they are similar to those New York guys in setting up a game preserve, for 'conservation' purposes and for people to come to hike, birdwatch, or hunt."

She pursed her lips. "So, in other words, drive the ranchers off their land and replace the cattle with wild animals."

"Yup. Sounds like it. I haven't gotten too far into it, but I'm going to pursue a story."

"Good. I hope you will. This nonsense has got to be stopped." She huffed and straightened her legs. "They'd better not come back around here, that's for sure!"

"Yeah." Electra's face tightened into a determined scowl. "We'll have to get everybody together for another stand-off, like they did in Ingomar."

A chortle bubbled up from Sam's mid-section, Brad guffawed, and after a moment of startled silence, the teen joined in with giggles. "You shoulda seen them," she crowed, "all lined up along the street, holding rifles and shotguns."

"That would have been something to see." He glanced at Sam. "So, you two were there to witness this event?"

"From the side of the post office, out of the way." She grimaced. "It *was* a little scary."

"But effective, apparently." He chuckled again. "You've gotta be the bravest woman I know."

"Nah, just curious mostly, and a little bit stupid." She flashed him a wry smile.

***

The next morning as Sam, Electra, and Brad loaded Trixi and Apache for the trip to Miles City, a green truck roared up the driveway.

"Who can that be?" She walked around the horse trailer to approach.

A young, brown-haired man got out of the driver's door and called out, "Mornin'."

Ted from JB Construction. She frowned.

"Good morning. What are you doing here? I didn't know we had an appointment today. I thought Joe and Bob were still tied up with other jobs."

He studied the ground by his feet. "Well…" He cleared his throat. "I'm afraid I have some bad news."

A fist squeezed her insides. "What?"

"Uh, when I came to work yesterday, the trailer headquarters was gone." His gaze met hers. "No Joe and no Bob… And um…when I tried to call, their numbers are disconnected."

CHAPTER SIXTEEN

Air locked in her chest. She could only gape at Ted, mind as empty as her open mouth.

"I'm so sorry, ma'am."

"G-gone?" Her voice rasped like unoiled hinges. "Wha... I don't understand..."

"I don't know where they went." The young man studied the dirt clod he nudged with his boot. "I know they were having some trouble with a project over in Colstrip. Joe told me not to come to work last week, and then I didn't get my paycheck. Went to get it yesterday, and that's when I found out."

Brad's arm steadied her on one side, and Electra leaned against her on the other.

"B-but I paid them an advance to start the work." White-hot bile rose into her throat. "Those lily-livered lowlifes! How could they?"

"The s-snakes...th-the oily, slimy slithering *snakes*!" Electra's words hissed from her lips.

Ted swiped a hand over his hangdog face. "Yes, ma'am, I know. It's not right."

"We need to call the sheriff." Brad's voice was taut as barbed wire. "This is a breach of contract. It's out and out theft."

"That's a good idea." The young construction worker gazed into her face. "And they were in the process of making me a partner, so my name is on the business documents. I feel really bad about this, and...and I...want to do something to help." He gestured to the lumber pile. "You have the materials, and I

138

have some experience. If we can get a crew together, I'll oversee this project."

Her mouth gaped again. *What did he just say? He's going to help?*

"I'll work without pay…maybe just a meal or two…"

"Ohmygosh, Sam, ohmygosh!" Electra's body hummed with electricity beside her.

She squeezed the girl's arm with hers. "Ted. That is an extremely kind and generous offer. But how can you afford to do that?"

"I was raised to do a job to the best of my ability. It's not in me to walk away. I…feel like it's my responsibility to see this project through." Ted's face was crimson, and he scuffed his workboot in the dirt.

Giving herself a mental shake like Lucky after a bath, she met Brad's gaze and then swung it back to the young man. "This is a lot to take in right now. We're on our way to work with the veterans' program in Miles City and have to get going. Let me digest all this, and I'll get back to you."

Ted took a pad and pen from his shirt pocket and scribbled something. "Here's my number. I'm serious. I want to help, to make up somehow for this mess Joe and Bob left."

"Thank you. I really appreciate you coming here to tell me and for your offer." She took the paper. "I will get in touch with you." She swiveled her head to Brad. "We can stop in Forsyth on our way home and talk to Sheriff McCollum."

"Yes. Let's do that. We can't let them get away with this." His brown eyes smoldered like ashes.

"All right. I'll go talk to him too." Ted touched the brim of his ball cap and strode back to his truck. "Again… I'm so very sorry."

"It's not your fault, but thanks." She mustered a weak smile as he got in and drove away. "Whew." She drew in a shaky wheeze. "This is all too much." Taking a step toward her pickup, her knees jellied, and she stumbled.

Brad caught her in his strong arms and guided her to the big rock next to the corral fence. "Sit for a minute. You've had quite a blow. Do you want me to get you a cup of coffee or anything?"

"No, thanks. I'll be okay. I've got water in the truck, and I'll have a drink in a minute."

Electra dashed to the vehicle and returned in a flash with a water bottle.

"You're so sweet. Thank you." The girl's care calmed the angry fire in her veins. "We do need to get on the road. We'll be late, and they'll all be chomping at the bit."

The teen giggled, and Brad guffawed. "That they will. I can see it, veterans and horses alike."

The moment of levity eased her shakiness. She stood and straightened herself to her full 5'6" height. "Okay. Those guys are not going to get the best of me. We have places to go, things to do. Let's go!"

***

The vets were indeed waiting outside the corral when Sam drove up. "You're late," was Garrett's anxious greeting.

"We were getting a bit worried." Nick shook her hand and then Brad's. "Good to see you, man."

"Yeah." Del wheeled toward the group. "We didn't want to miss our time with you."

"Is everything okay?" Sondra asked.

Their concern sent ripples of sunshine through her core. "It's a long story, but the short version is the construction company I paid to start work on my barn has left the country."

"Oh no!" The woman vet's eyes grew large.

"That's terrible." Nick leaned against the hood. "What are you going to do?"

"She's going to talk to the sheriff, for one thing," Brad answered for her. "We're not letting this go. They've stolen money from her."

140

Electra rocked back and forth on her heels. "But that nice Ted guy—he's going to help."

Sam explained what had happened that morning. "There's a lot to figure out, and it'll take some time. Meanwhile, we have horses to groom and ride."

"Let's roll," Del boomed.

She strode to the trailer, followed by Brad, Nick, and Garrett.

Once inside the arena, Brad left for his session with Higgins, and she got the veterans brushing and saddling their horses. After several turns to practice mounting and riding at various gaits around the arena, Jimmy spoke up. "Are we going outside today?"

Since Nick had told her Elliot was out of town, she saw no reason not to get out. "You bet we are."

The May sunshine highlighted the clear sapphire sky, with cottony cloud wisps floating lazily above. The spicy, pungent scent of the new grass and sage wafted through her nostrils, and she settled into the rhythm of the horses' hoofbeats on the earth. The fire and ice of the morning's shock gradually ebbed, and calm overtook her.

Garrett rode up beside her. "How are you doing?"

"Better now." She was able to respond with a genuine smile.

"You know what? One of the classes I've been taking is carpentry. Linc and Jimmy are too. I'd like to help you build your barn."

A double-take. "W-why, Garrett, I-I...don't know what to say."

"Say yes." The other two men flanked her, along with Al. "We're in too."

Sondra joined the group. "Count me in. I can swing a hammer."

"Oh, you guys! You're too much." Her eyes stung, and she blinked away the rising emotion. "Thank you. You don't know what your offer means to me."

She glanced from one grinning face to the other. "When I get everything sorted out, I'll let you know if I need your help."

Nick swiveled in his saddle to give her an "okay" gesture.

Gratitude rolled over her like one tumbleweed after another in a summer wind.

When the group returned to the center, Brad stood by the corral with his hand-held camera, filming.

"What are you up to?" Sam cocked her head.

"I thought maybe I'd get some shots, possibly do a little piece on this program, if it's okay with everyone."

Whoa! That sure came out of the blue. She flashed back to her "debut" when he did a documentary on her horse rescues with Apache and Trixi and how nervous and tongue-tied she'd been. Gulping a frog of fear, she forced a smile. "Well…I guess so. Nick? Would that be all right?"

The ag instructor slid from his horse. "It's fine with me." He glanced around the group. "How about you guys—are you ready for your fifteen minutes of fame?"

"Sure, why not." Del urged Trixi forward.

Garrett scrubbed his hand over his sandy brushcut. "Good with me."

"Yeah." Linc raised his one good arm in a salute, and Jimmy flashed a thumbs-up, his face pink up to his blond hairline.

Sondra ducked her head and then swung her gaze to Sam. "If I can see what I look like before it goes on TV." She gave a shy smile. "I don't want to look stupid."

Tenderness flowered inside. She put a hand on the woman's arm. "I understand. You won't, I promise. Brad does a great job of interviewing and showing our best sides." She winked at him. "Thanks."

"Would it be okay if I interview at least a couple of you today before we all head out?" He balanced the camera on his shoulder.

"How about Garrett and Del," Nick suggested, "since they were the first ones to benefit from Sam's instruction."

"Sounds good. Let's go inside, and Del, I'll get a shot of how you dismount with the horse kneeling."

A glimmer of hope flowed through Sam. Brad really did seem to be getting back to normal with his work. This was the first sign of enthusiasm she'd seen in a long time.

While Brad worked and talked with the two veterans, Nick took her aside. "Have you looked over the PATH classes and made a decision yet?"

Nerves fluttered. "Yeah. The one in Billings at the Horses Spirits Healing center looks good. It's the closest, and they do work with veterans."

"Great. If you'd like, I'll make the arrangements for any fees and send them the info on our program, the number of hours you've been working, and whatever else they might need."

"Okay." She grimaced. "If you think I'm ready."

"Oh yeah, you're more than ready. I have every confidence in you." He touched her shoulder. "You'll do fine. Just have fun."

In the truck, headed for home, Sam mock-scowled at Brad. "So, why didn't you tell me about this plan to do a show on the vets?"

He cleared his throat. "Well, actually, I didn't think of it until I was talking to Higgins today. And since I don't know how soon I'll be back, I figured I might as well get started."

She recoiled. *What does he mean by that—doesn't know when he'll be back?*

Before she could say anything, Electra giggled. "I didn't even see you put your camera gear in the pickup."

"That was kind of a spur-of-the-moment thing too. I didn't know why when I threw it in, but I do like to have it along, just in case…"

"Always prepared, Mr. Boy Scout journalist," Sam teased.

He chuckled. "Yup, that's me."

"Well, I think this is all *so* exciting." The teen bounced and squirmed on the seat. "Ohmygosh, what a day, huh, Sam? First Ted comes and drops his bomb, then the vets volunteer to help, and now Brad is doing a story on us. I can't wait to see it, Brad, you da man!"

She and Brad laughed at the girl's enthusiasm, but she had to agree. *What a day, indeed!*

"Electra, grab my cell and call Horace. Invite him for supper. We do have a lot to share with him."

***

At Forsyth, Sam turned down 13th Street and pulled up in front of a low, brown-stucco building with a sign reading: "Rosebud County Law Enforcement." The trio piled out of the truck and entered the reception area. After several minutes waiting on the same cracked plastic chairs she remembered from a couple years ago, Sheriff O'Connor ambled out of his office, offering his big, rawboned hand to each. "Howdy, Sam. C'mon in."

He gestured to tan padded chairs in front of his desk and slowly settled his large frame into his own. "What can I do for you today?"

She inhaled fortification. "I have a rather disturbing problem." She related the events with the barn project leading up to this morning's bad news from Ted.

"Hmm." O'Connor scratched his gray-stubbled face and sat in silence for several long moments. "You gave them an advance, huh?"

She nodded. She'd learned from experience that one did not hurry the sheriff's slow, contemplative manner.

144

The secretary stuck her head in the door. "Sorry to interrupt, but a Ted Doyle is here to see you. Says it's related to these folks here."

At the sheriff's raised brow, Sam explained. "Yes, that's the employee with JB Construction who came to see us."

"Ahh." He cocked his head. "Okay. Send 'im in."

Ted ducked a nod toward the group, stuck out his hand to O'Connor, and introduced himself. "I'm sure Ms. Moser has already told you what happened, but I wanted to talk to you as well." He glanced at Sam. "With your permission?"

"Of course. Go ahead."

He told his side of the story, the sheriff nodding, pursing his lips, and squinting as he listened. After another interminable silence, he steepled his fingers. "And you don't know where they went."

Ted shook his head. "The trailer that was their headquarters is gone, so I'm assuming they've left the area. I left a message with the client in Colstrip but haven't heard anything back yet."

The big man leaned back in his chair. "You have a contract, Sam?"

"Yes. And a copy of the cancelled check."

"Okay." He shuffled through papers on his desk and, apparently not finding what he was looking for, glanced toward the reception area. "Go ahead and file a complaint with Betsy, but this is more of a civil procedure...a breach of contract. What you will need to do is contact a lawyer, and he'll send them a letter to get things started."

"Meh." Electra squeaked beside her.

Brad put a gentle hand on her arm.

A large clod sank to the pit of her stomach. *Oh no. Not another court procedure.* When she'd rescued Apache from starvation and near-death, the owner had taken him back even though she'd paid his nephew for the horse, and she had to go through small claims court to reclaim him. The nervous butterflies she'd experienced then came back to brush against the inside of her chest.

As though a large sandstone boulder had been lowered onto her shoulders, she struggled to right herself from her chair. "Thanks, Sheriff." She plodded into the outer room, where Betsy gave her and Ted complaint forms.

Back in the pickup, Brad leaned across Electra and squeezed Sam's thigh. "It'll work out. I have every confidence in you, and whatever I can do to help..."

"Yeah. We did it once, when we got Apache back." The teen swung an eager gaze toward her. "You were awesome. We can do it again."

"Well, somebody has to find them first." She huffed. "Good luck with that."

The other two had no comeback, and a heavy silence settled in the cab. Her nostrils flared, and she ground her teeth. *What next?*

She flashed a glare at Brad. "And what's this about 'I don't know when I'm coming back'?"

"Um. Well..." He cleared his throat. "You know I have this job now, right? I'd love to come back out every week, but I'm never sure what story I'll be assigned or where I'll be sent from one to the next."

"Hmmph." Heat flushed through her body. Yes, she knew that, and his work was probably exactly what he needed to get back his self-esteem. *But what about us? Can we develop a relationship by long-distance?* She knew she was reacting irrationally, but *dadgummit. Just when things were starting to improve...*

CHAPTER SEVENTEEN

Horace gladly accepted the invitation to supper, and over chicken casserole, Sam told her story once again. Tears threatened to disrupt her narrative, but she fought them back with the tide of anger rising. *Every time I think of Joe and Bob...* Her jaw tightened.

Her elderly neighbor alternately frowned, grimaced, and harrumphed while she spoke.

"And here I am, looking at another civil court procedure, which I absolutely hate...providing I can even find those...those..."

"Snakes—slimy snakes!" Electra provided the words she searched for.

He set his fork down with a clank. "Yup. Snakes, indeed." He blew through clenched teeth. "Boy, when I get my hands on them..." His fist thudded on the table. "Lord, give me patience, cuz if you give me strength, I'm gonna need bail money too."

The look of indignation and his struggle for composure almost made Sam laugh. *Dear Horace. He's so like my grandpa.* The knowledge that this tough old cowpoke had such a tender heart toward her melted her anger and frustration.

She put a hand over his gnarled one. "Thank you. I'll help ya when we find them." She smiled. "I'm so grateful for your support."

Brad sipped his iced tea and set down the glass. "Well, the good news is that Ted has volunteered to oversee the project, and the vets said they want to come help with the construction."

Horace's face brightened. "So, there *are* good people in this story after all. Wonderful. I'm available to do whatever you need—crack the whip or pound nails—anything you want me to do."

"Oh, Horace, what would I do without you?" She gestured to his plate. "More casserole or are you ready for dessert?"

He patted his belly. "I think I have just enough room for a big slice o' that carrot cake I see settin' over there on the counter."

After their neighbor left, Electra excused herself to go say goodnight to Apache and the others. Sam sat in her rocking chair, while Brad reclined on the couch.

"That Horace is a real gem, such a good neighbor. I'm glad you have him close by." He finger-combed the dark lock off his forehead.

"He is. I'm lucky. He reminds me a lot of Grandpa Neil— usually very stoic and calm, but get his back up..." she chuckled, "and well, you saw his reaction tonight."

"Yeah, a little like my dad too."

She pinched her lips together and released an audible breath through her nose. "Brad. I...need to know something."

He cocked his head. "Okay?"

"Where do we stand? What's going on? You're living in Billings, and I'm here, and you can't or won't come visit. Are we a 'we' or are we just friends?"

Drawing his head back sharply, he widened his eyes. His mouth opened, but he didn't speak for a long moment.

She chewed her lower lip. *That surprised him? Is he that clueless?*

"I...Sam...I...don't know what to say. I thought we'd had this conversation about 'just friends'—I thought you knew I want more than that." He sat bolt upright. "But you know how hard it's been, coming back from that accident. I *am* getting better. I can feel it."

"Yes, I can see that too. And I'm glad." *Yes, he is healing. But he sure isn't showing he wants "more" than friendship. Is that what I want—more?*

He scooted to the edge of the sofa and clasped her hand in his. "You've been so patient with me, and I can't express how thankful I am for you. This distance between Billings and Ingomar doesn't change anything. I want to be with you, and I promise I will make every effort to come out whenever I can."

She bit harder on her lip to keep the tears at bay.

"C'mere." He drew her out of the chair to sit beside him and pulled her close. "I really miss you when we're apart."

She melted into him, her head against his chest. A tear escaped down her cheek, wetting his green plaid shirt. "I miss you too." Her words muffled against the fabric. *Does this mean he's "the one"? Will he follow through on his promise, not be like Kenny and Bolt?*

Absorbing the comforting, soft beat of his heart, she wanted to say more, hear more.

With a slam of the screen door, Electra returned from the barn, interrupting their quiet moment.

"Your timing is impeccable." Sam snorted a laugh as they broke apart.

"Oops, sorry. Going to bed now." The teen scooted out of the room, giggling softly as she tip-toed up the stairs.

They sat silent for a moment, mood broken. When she tilted her chin to look into his face, his gaze searched her eyes.

Nerves rippled through her. She wanted to linger and yet to escape. "I guess I'll go too. Morning comes early."

He touched her chin and brought her face close, giving her a deepening kiss. A shiver ran the length of her body, tingling up her arms and down her legs until her toes twitched. Moments passed exquisitely as her heart floated past the moon.

When at last their lips parted, he whispered, "Sleep well." His chocolate eyes crinkled at the corners.

"Um, sure…" She cleared her throat. *After this? I don't think so.* "You too." She rose, spun on her heel, and ran up the stairs.

***

The full moon sent silvery rays through the window, lighting Sam in her bed like daylight. Her head spun with the images and emotions of the day, like an ethereal presence, both light and dark, golden and gray. From gut-wrenching disappointment to the uplifting offers of friends, from the dark fear of court and lawsuits to that toe-tingling kiss from Brad.

She rolled away from the window and plumped her pillow. After long minutes with her eyes wide open, she turned toward the moonlight, bathing in its soft glow. Something began to flower inside her, something like hope… maybe?

The tantalizing aroma of bacon and coffee woke her. She untangled herself from damp, dream-twisted sheets, pulled on her robe, and glided downstairs, the kiss still seared on her lips.

Brad's wide smile greeted her as he offered a steaming cup. His fingers brushed hers lightly as she took it, leaving an electric trail.

Her face burned, and she flicked her glance from his to the cup. "Thanks."

Electra plated the bacon and cracked eggs into the skillet. "Good morning. Hope you're hungry. I thought we'd better fortify ourselves. We have a lot of work to do with the horses today." Her face beamed as she swung her gaze from Sam to Brad. "Hope you guys slept good."

Brad coughed and hid a grin. "Some. You?" His eyes searched hers.

The corner of her mouth twitched. "Not a lot." She averted her eyes again, the fast flush rising up her neck.

The teen smirked knowingly as she put breakfast on the table but mercifully didn't comment.

150

Silence reigned as forks clinked on plates. Sam barely tasted her food. She glanced from her plate to catch Brad observing her and just as quickly swinging his gaze away.

When they were finished, he pushed his plate aside. "Well, ladies, I'll stay and watch you two work for a little while, but then I need to get back to town. I have some things to finish for a deadline next week, and I want to do more digging on that American Prairie Reserve group."

"Oh. Okay." Disappointment sent a shot of gloom through her. *So much for a long weekend together.* "Good. I'll be curious to know what you find out." To cover her fluster, she rose and took plates to the sink. "All right, Electra. We can leave these to soak. Let's go get busy."

Brad leaned against the corral fence while the teen put Toby through his paces, backing and bowing, repeating with pellet rewards and soft murmurs of encouragement. "Good boy. You're doing so good."

Sam enticed Money to her with treats and brushed him, his formerly matted coat now beginning to show a glossy sheen. When he seemed relaxed, almost to the point of dozing, she picked up a halter and rubbed it against his neck, keeping up a soft patter. He opened his eyes wide and turned his head to sniff. "It's okay, Money, it's okay. I won't hurt you." She held it to his nose, and he snuffled and snorted. Caressing his face and ears, she continued to rub the halter against the pony.

At last, tiring of the game, he wheeled away, kicking up his heels as he ran to the far end of the corral. Lucky followed with his three-legged hop-trot and sat next to him with a soft "woof." The two touched noses, and then Money lowered his head to graze.

She returned to where Brad had his eye on Electra and Toby. "I saw that," he said. "You've come a long way with him."

"Yeah. A bit. It's been really slow. But I think we'll get there eventually."

"Yup. You will." He leaned a shoulder into hers. "And Electra is training Toby very well. I can see he's almost ready to kneel."

He swiveled on his heel to face her. "Okay. Gotta go." His mouth turned down. "Sorry."

"I know." She moved away, shyness nearly paralyzing her.

He clasped her arms, bringing her close, and gave her a quick, hard kiss. "I'll be thinking of you the whole time." He waved at Electra. "Doing good, kiddo. See ya next time."

"Bye." She waved back. "Don't be a stranger, Bra-ad!"

"Yeah, what she said." Sam tried to lighten her mood with a flip tone. "See you soon."

He trailed his fingers lightly on her cheek, leaving an electric tingle, and strode away. She gave him what she hoped was a cheery smile and swiveled her hand at him as he climbed into his pickup.

Good-byes. She bit her lip to hold back tears. *I'm always waving good-bye...*

CHAPTER EIGHTEEN

The next couple of weeks progressed with agonizing slowness, May warming into June, spring rains bringing splashes of pink, yellow, orange, and blue wildflowers to polka dot the green prairie.

Some days Money allowed more contact, even to the point of accepting the halter, but on others he snorted and ran away as soon as she approached. With a great sigh, Sam held out her arms in resignation. "Okay, Lucky, you do your magic with this pony. Maybe tomorrow will be better." The little black and white dog stuck close to the persnickety horse, playing with him, and calming his agitation.

Brad called every few days, with cheery reports of stories he was working on. Her emotions alternately soared when the phone rang and plunged when he offered no mention of coming out to visit nor any words about their passionate kiss. *Does he regret that? Is he embarrassed?* Her thoughts drew parallels between him and Money. *Up and down. Hot and cold. Will it ever even out?* She stared at the infinite horizon. He'd never been married. She'd been close to it with Kenny. *Maybe I intimidate him and his timidity stems from that. He doesn't know how to talk to me.* Well, at least he was calling. That was progress.

Electra continued to stay at the ranch three days a week to train Toby and help her with the veterans' program.

The vets enjoyed their weekly outings, venturing a little farther and riding a little faster each time. Even Elliot had progressed to mounting Trixi or Apache and riding tentatively around the arena. He seemed to be keeping his bouts with alcohol at bay, with no more violent outbursts, although he sometimes exhibited impatience with the horse or her teaching tactics.

She fought to take a hands-off approach and give him room to vent and then calm himself. "Sorry, Miss Sam." He came to her after one such outburst with downcast eyes, scuffing his boot in the dirt. "I'll try to do better next time."

"You will," she encouraged. "You have already improved by leaps and bounds. Give yourself permission to let the horse help you heal."

With a noncommittal grunt, he left the arena. *Is Elliot going to be my first failure in this program?*

***

Sam leaned against the rails, observing Electra stroking and murmuring to Toby. The teen showed such patience— uncommon to teenagers—in the weeks she'd spent riding, grooming, backing, and bowing the gelding. *I could probably learn something from her, for working with Elliot.* The damaged veteran had a lot in common with the horse who had been so traumatized by the accident he had refused to enter any enclosed space for months afterward.

Maybe this upcoming PATH training the next weekend would offer some suggestions too. Nerves skittered through her body, and her fingers went icy. She both looked forward to and dreaded the class. Would she pass muster? Or was she simply a rank amateur who would be sent to the "dunce corner." She snorted a laugh, picturing herself with a pointy hat, facing away from the group.

Toby bowed his head as the teen pulled back on his lead rope. His knees bent, and he touched his nose close to the ground. Electra tapped a spot on his forearm. He bent a tiny bit more. She tapped again, and then he lowered his front legs to kneel on the dirt.

Sam stifled a gasp.

Electra flashed her a wide-eyed glance but kept talking softly to the horse. "Good boy, Toby. You did it. Good boy." She stroked his leg and patted his withers. "Okay, you can get up now." She tapped again, and he rose.

Sam swore he had a grin on his face.

"He did it, Sam, he did it!" Joy radiated from her young friend's face, and she gave him a handful of pellets.

"*You* did it!" She climbed over the fence and enveloped the girl in a strong hug. "I'm so proud of you." Releasing her embrace, she squeezed Electra's shoulders and peered into her face. "All your patience and hard work paid off." Her lungs filled to bursting. How her young friend had grown! She wanted to shout it to the world.

"Yeah. We did it." Wonder lit the teen's eyes, and she shook her head, as if she couldn't believe it was true.

"You *are* such a good boy." Sam stroked the bay's face and ears. "I think this calls for a celebration. Let's call Horace and Teresa and your mom and invite them for steaks tonight."

"Yes!" Electra squealed. "Can I bake some brownies?"

What a far cry from Goth-girl. Sam couldn't help but chuckle. "Of course you can. Let's go do that right now."

The evening temperature remained pleasant enough for an outdoor barbecue, and after Electra had demonstrated Toby's new trick, the five friends gathered around a table set up on the porch.

Teresa poured wine for the adults and sparkling cider for Electra. She raised her glass. "Here's to your success, young lady. You are turning into a first-class horse trainer."

"Hear, hear!" Horace's deep voice boomed.

"I'm very proud of you." Her mother's grin rivaled the Cheshire cat's.

The teen's face pinked as she clinked her glass with theirs. "Thanks." She lifted her gaze to Sam. "I couldn't have done it without you. Thank you for helping me heal and teaching me and being my mentor…my friend." A tear rolled from the corner of her eye.

Sam's eyes misted over, and she had to take a breath before she could speak. "I'm proud of you too. You have a natural talent in bonding with horses and understanding them. That's not something I could ever teach you." Her mouth quivered as she raised her glass. "Thank you for being my helper, *my* friend, and my teacher. I've learned a lot from you."

**

On Monday, Ted called. "Is it okay to come out today and take another look at your blueprints and supplies? Maybe get started with plans for building the barn."

Hope soared with eagle's wings. "Yeah, that would be great. I'll call Horace to meet with us too."

Mid-morning, her neighbor roared up the driveway, followed shortly by Ted's green pickup. The two men got out and shook hands.

When they greeted her, she barely restrained herself from skipping down the slope from the house. "Hi, guys. Thanks for coming. I'm so excited."

Horace beamed. "Yeah, little gal. You're gonna get yourself a barn. We're gonna see to that."

"Thank you." She turned her smile to Ted. "I want to pay you something for overseeing this project. It's not right that you work for nothing, especially when those…" she cleared her throat, "*snakes*, as Electra calls them, stiffed you as well."

The young man shrugged. "Well, we can work something out later. But since they were in the process of making me a partner, I do feel responsible for this project. Let's see how it goes."

She handed them her copies of the blueprints, and Ted spread them out on the hood of his truck.

He and Horace pored over them, running thick, calloused fingers over the diagrams, glancing at the foundation around

156

the burn spot, now with new sprigs of grass showing through the blackened earth.

"At least you've got the materials," her neighbor remarked. "Now we need the manpower and a work plan."

Ted ambled over to the lumber pile, covered with tarps for protection from rain. Peering beneath, he nodded, mumbled to himself, and scratched his head, spiking his brown hair in all directions. He took a tape measure from his pocket and motioned to Horace. They walked the site, measuring and taking notes.

"Ya know what?" The older man pushed his hat back from his forehead. "I know we already have the foundation, but what would you think of building a pole barn?"

Ted scrunched his eyebrows together and pursed his lips. "Hmm." He paced the length of the proposed structure, stopping to study the corners, tapping on the concrete, chewing on his pencil.

"Yeah. Yeah, we could do that. Use heavy drill-set brackets to anchor them." He nodded at Horace. "Good idea, man. Yeah. That way we don't need load-bearing interior walls, and it'll be quicker to put up."

She listened with growing excitement. The men sounded like they knew what they were talking about. *Oh my. Is this really happening?* She put both hands over her mouth as she shifted her gaze from one to the other.

"Great!" Her neighbor's voice boomed. "How soon can we get started?"

"I'll take an inventory of what we've got here and what we'll need yet, and we'll have to chart out the steps, how many guys and on what days." Ted swiveled his head toward Sam. "Can you talk to your vets, see if they're still up to helping, and if they could be available, maybe as early as next week?"

Exhilaration spiraled from the bottom of her feet, electrifying the length of her body to the top of her head.

"Yes!" She nearly squealed like Electra but modulated her voice. "Yes, I'll call Nick today."

Her face warmed, and she wanted to grab both men and swing them into a jig. "Hey. C'mon up to the house and do your plans, and I'll fix us some lunch."

"Lunch sounds great." Horace rubbed his belly, and Ted nodded his agreement.

While the men scribbled and figured and muttered and discussed, she fried potatoes and onions and put burgers on the grill. After refilling the coffee pot with water and grounds, she set plates on the table, her movements gliding her across the kitchen floor on a bubble of joy.

The three continued their discussion and plans over the meal, topping it off with Electra's leftover brownies and cups of steaming coffee.

Ted left, with a promise to call later in the week.

Horace flashed his huge grin at her. "Well, little gal. It's comin' together. I'll give Clyde a holler and see if we can rustle up a few more hands."

"Oh, Horace. I can't believe this is really happening. I'm so excited, I feel like Electra when she goes off the rails with her shrieking and squealing."

He guffawed. "I can see the two of you now, when you tell her." He left shortly after, chuckling all the way out the door.

She couldn't wait. First, she called Nick, who assured her the group would be there "with bells on." Next, she called Alberta and Electra with the news, then Teresa, and then Robin from the group home. Each of her friends laughed and whooped with words of encouragement and "I told you so's."

That evening, when Brad called, she barely let him say "hello" before launching into her news. "You're not going to believe this." With the giddiness of a young girl, she related the day's events.

"Awesome!" Brad chortled. "Fantastic news. I'm so happy for you. You're going to get your barn. I'm proud of you."

A bright glow of happiness suffused her core, and she curled into a comfortable ball on the floor beneath the wall phone.

"Let me know when the work party begins, and I'll come out and join in, as much as I can. I want to do some more filming and interviews with the vets too."

"That'd be great. Oh, and I'll be in Billings this weekend for my training class. Maybe I'll see you then?"

She was greeted with a momentary silence. "Oh. I'd forgotten about that. Darn. I have to go out of town for a story the station assigned me weeks ago." His voice dropped. "But I *will* make it a point to come out the end of next week, okay?"

Disappointment cooled her excitement like a dash of cold water. "Okay. I'll probably be too busy anyway." Her words came out subdued. "I guess I'll see you when I see you, then."

"Wait, Sa—"

"'Bye." She slammed the phone down.

She remained on the floor, curling her knees to her torso, and squeezing her eyelids tight to keep the hot tears at bay. Had she read him wrong? *Why is he acting so cool toward me? He never sounds as needy for me as I am for him.* After that *kiss,* she thought surely he must feel the same about her as she felt for him.

When the phone rang again, she ignored it. Her chest tight, she shuffled into the living room and stared out of the window at the lengthening evening shadows. It rang several more times, the shrill sound piercing her heart. She crawled onto the couch and covered her ear with a pillow. *Was I so easily fooled by one kiss? He doesn't care. He doesn't want to be with me.* She pounded her fist into the back of the couch. Why did she always choose guys who were unavailable? *Why do I even bother with hope? It's useless.*

For a moment she wished she hadn't sworn off her vodka crutch. She could almost taste the bitter, cool liquid as the fire and ice slid down her throat and brought welcome oblivion.

Swallowing the saliva that rose, she put it out of her mind, visualizing her symbolic dumping of the bottle two years ago. No, she didn't need that anymore.

When she woke, the room was pitch dark, and her neck screamed at its kinked position. She struggled for breath until she threw the pillow off her face and sat upright. The wall clock read 3:00. She stood and staggered toward her room, catching a glimpse of her answering machine blinking in the darkness. *Phht. Who cares?* Ignoring the pulsing light, she threw herself on the bed without undressing and pulled the coverlet over her.

A tiny voice niggled in her ear. *You hung up on him. You're not totally in the clear here.* She snorted and turned onto her side. No, she *was* in the right. Shouldn't she expect more from a relationship? *Yeah, but you didn't give him a chance to explain.*

"Explain what?" She spoke aloud, her angry words echoing in the dark. "He's known for weeks when I would be in Billings."

This is his job, after all. Do you expect him to ignore his assignments to see you for a few minutes or maybe a lunch, if at all?

Her righteous indignation deflated. Her conscience was right. *Dang!* Maybe she did expect too much of him. There were two sides to a relationship, and after all, she hadn't said the "L" word to him either…

She sat up and dangled her feet over the side of the bed. A shaft of moonlight shone through a gap in the curtains. She couldn't face this alone. "Hey, Lord, it's me again." Her shoulders slumped. "I know I haven't talked to you in a while, and I only seem to call on you when I have troubles. Sorry 'bout that. I am truly grateful for all the good things that are happening in my life." She moved to the window and looked out at the inky sky, dotted with pinpoint stars. "Help me be more patient with Brad and please help me know what to say to him."

She undressed and crawled back in bed. "Thank you, Lord. G'night." Curling into a fetal position, she fell asleep.

CHAPTER NINETEEN

In the morning over coffee, Sam listened to five messages from Brad, each one more entreating than the last, explaining his job and his assignment. "I'm so sorry I upset you. I feel awful that I can't be in town when you're here. I *do* want to spend time with you. I *will* be there for the barn raising next week, I promise."

Even though she'd had that heart-to-heart talk with herself last night and realized she was also culpable, her self-righteous side couldn't bring her to call him back right away, and she preoccupied herself with chores. Apprehension tickled her gut. Would their next meeting be awkward? *Should I call him back? Yeah, I probably should. That would be the courteous thing to do. But not right now.* Part of her was afraid there was no hope for a close relationship. She blew out a long sigh and saddled her horse.

Checking her small herd of cows, she chuckled at the white-faced calves frolicking in the grass. Then she gasped. They were big enough to brand. Oh dear, that had completely slipped her mind, with everything else going on. And with her class this weekend and the building project coming up, it could be at least a couple of weeks, maybe more, until she could get it done. *Oh crap!* She dug her heels into Sugar's side and raced home. *Maybe Brad's schedule is just as crazy as mine. Maybe that's the explanation, and I'm seeing mountains where there are only molehills.*

Back at the house she phoned Horace and Clyde to see if she could enlist their help on short notice. They both responded with an enthusiastic "Sure," and she set up branding

162

for Thursday. A weight lifted from her shoulders, and she was able to smile. *What good and faithful friends I have!*

As she slathered mayo and mustard on whole wheat bread, she stopped short. The vets. Thursday was her day to go to Miles City. Exasperation fluttered her lips. How could she forget? She punched in Nick's number. "Hey," she jumped in when he answered, "I have a conflict at the ranch this week, but I have an idea. The group is doing so well with riding, I wonder if we could have the session here at the ranch this week, and they could ride and help with branding."

A momentary silence. "Yeah. Sure. That's a great idea. I bet they'd love it. Let me run it by them. I'll leave it up to each one, if they're comfortable doing that. I'll call you back."

"Great." Two birds with one stone. Her day was looking up.

Nick called back later with an affirmative. "Everybody except Elliot wants to ride. But he said he'd come along to watch and help out in other ways."

"All right! See you bright and early Thursday."

***

Branding day awakened with pastel washes of gold and pink across the sky as Sam met the neighbor men and Electra at the corral. Shortly after, a van pulling a large horse trailer with extra horses pulled up, and the veterans piled out, waving and laughing. "We're gonna be 'real' cowboys today," Garrett shouted.

"Yeehaw!" Linc and Jimmy chorused. Al sported a huge grin, and even Sondra's face shone with excitement.

She shook hands all around and gave each one a task. Nick would oversee Del and Elliot in building the branding fire and setting up the vaccine gun, castrating knives, and BloodSTOP. The rest of the group, along with her, Clyde and Horace, would ride out to the pasture to gather the small band of cows and calves. She mounted Sugar and set out.

163

The vets bantered back and forth as they trotted through the gullies and over the rolling prairie. A red-tailed hawk soared lazily in the clear aquamarine sky, and meadowlarks trilled their happy greeting from fenceposts. The spicy scent of sage filled Sam's nostrils, and the tension of the past days melted in the warming sunshine.

Most of the cows and their babies were gathered around the reservoir. She counted, missing half a dozen. "Okay, guys," she instructed, "you go with Clyde and start this main bunch toward home. Horace and I will ride up on the butte and see where the rest are."

"Yes, ma'am." Garrett's face beamed as he reined his horse to follow the rest to the reservoir.

"Can I go with you two?" Electra raised her eyebrows.

"Sure. C'mon."

The three cantered toward the flat-topped hill and climbed to the top. From there they could see for miles into the undulating distance. "There." She pointed. "A little group in that corner."

Horace spotted another cow and calf a ways from the rest. "Let's get those two and drive them to the others, bring 'em all in at once."

Nodding, she touched her heels to ·Sugar's sides and descended. As they approached, the Hereford cow raised her head, watching with quick, suspicious eye-movements. She swung her gaze to the calf beside her and back to the riders.

"Hey, bossy, bossy," Sam crooned. "C'mon now, girl, let's go home. C'mon." She clicked her tongue.

The cow gave a guttural bellow, wheeled around, and ran. The calf followed for a few paces and then veered off in the opposite direction. Electra on Apache galloped after the calf, zig-zagging across the prairie. Horace went after the cow, and Sam urged Sugar to circle around, hoping to head the calf off before it reached the fence.

164

Her hair blew loose from its ponytail. Out of the corner of her eye she glimpsed the teen leaning forward in the saddle, racing the little animal, trying to get even with it. The calf was gaining. Sam dug her heels into the mare's sides, urging her faster.

Her horse grunting and panting, she reached the fence just in time to ride in front of the calf, Electra right behind, whooping. Together they sandwiched the runaway and turned it back in the direction of its mother. Horace trotted over a rise with the cow who mooed when she saw her baby. The calf gave a bleat and ran to mama, nuzzling her teat.

"Whew!" Electra's short hair stood out in every direction, and her face glowed. "Wow. That was *fun.*"

Sam tucked her loose strands back into the scrunchy band and chuckled. "Yeah, that's always a rush. You never know if you're gonna catch 'em."

"Them little guys can flat-out *run.*" Horace chortled. "I've seen many a horse bested by a tiny critter."

"W-e-l-l… Sugar *is* a racehorse, after all." She winked at him.

"Yup." He gave Electra a thumbs-up. "And Apache did you proud too."

She giggled. "Yeah. Wasn't he something? Ohmygosh." She patted her mount's neck. "Good boy, Apache."

The short ride to join the other two cows who were "babysitting" several calves was much more sedate, and they were soon on their way home. Catching up to the rest just as they approached the corral, Sam and her group joined the other riders, flanking the herd to drive them into the corral. Nick had the gate open and stood at the far end, rattling a cake bucket. The red and white cows trotted in eagerly.

Elliot tended the fire in a barrel, and Del sat in his chair next to the chute. Irene and Alberta came from the house to observe as Sam, Electra, Horace, and Clyde separated the calves from their mothers and turned the cows back out into the pasture. The cacophony of bleats and bawls rose, along with dust churned by miniature hooves.

"We have coffee and cinnamon rolls ready if you guys want to take a break." Irene gestured to the tailgate of her SUV.

"Yeah. Rolls and coffee sound great." Jimmy headed over first, followed by the rest of the veterans.

"How did it go?" Sam walked alongside Sondra who flashed her a wide grin.

"That was fun. I was really scared a cow or calf would get away from me, like I heard happened with you. Wish I coulda seen that." Her eyes widened. "But we managed to keep the animals together, with Clyde coaching us the whole way."

Sam patted her shoulder. "That's great. I'm so glad you came to help and get some real-life practice working cattle. Good job."

As everyone lined up for steaming coffee and warm rolls slathered with butter, she went to help Irene and Alberta. "Thanks for doing this on such short notice."

Her motherly neighbor shrugged. "Aw, don't even think about it. No problem for us to rustle up some grub in a jiffy."

"We brought potato salad, coleslaw, and baked beans to go with the pot roast you have simmering." Alberta gestured toward the house. "I baked a couple of pies, Irene made a sheet cake, and Electra made oatmeal raisin cookies."

"I think we'll be well-fed." She poured coffee for Clyde. "Thank you all."

The branding process went like clockwork, able-bodied vets pushing calves to the chute, Clyde working the levers to enclose the calf and lay the mechanism on its side. Horace applied the running "M" with a hanging "S" brand, while Elliot gave the vaccinations and Del kept the medications refilled.

Clyde did the castration. "Are we saving for Rocky Mountain Oysters?" He cast a glance at Sam.

"Not on my behalf." She wrinkled her nose. She'd tried the so-called delicacy when she was younger and found it bland and mealy-tasting, like liver. Not to her liking. But many people did. In fact, there was a "Rocky Mountain Oyster Festival" near Missoula every year that drew people from all over.

Electra, who kept the tally, cocked her head. "Rocky Mountain Oysters?"

The rancher grinned and held up the surgically removed tissue. "Yup. Delicious."

"Eeeww, *no!*" She stuck out her tongue and grimaced.

Sondra had a horrified look on her face too. "Yuk. Really?"

Horace and Clyde guffawed.

"Guess not then." Clyde threw the "oyster" into a bucket. "Horace, let's divvy 'em up. I'll be over later to enjoy."

They finished the chore by noontime and reunited the calves with their mothers, babies suckling happily while the cows grazed, once again content to have their offspring returned.

***

That evening, after everyone had gone, Sam punched in Brad's number and settled in a kitchen chair. "Hey," she said when he answered.

"Sam!" His voice rose in pitch. "I…I—"

"Listen," she jumped in before he could go further, "I apologize for hanging up on you the other night and not calling you back. I over-reacted. I know you have a job to do, and you can't tell your boss 'No, I can't go out of town because I might be able to see my…friend…for a few minutes.'"

Her heartbeat rat-a-tatted in her chest as she heard a long sigh on the other end. *Oh dear. Now he's mad.*

"Oh, Sam, it's good to hear from you, and I'm so glad you're not angry at me. I wish I could see you more often, but this is an important story—and there could be more—we're working on, and—"

"Of course it is. And you'll be here next week when we start work on the barn, right?"

"Yes. Wouldn't miss it."

A huge, dark weight lifted from her back. *I did it—I called. It was all just a tangled web of miscommunication. Why didn't I believe him?*

Almost giddy with relief, she related the day of branding, with her crew of veterans and neighbors. "It was a great experience for the vets—they all really got into cowboying, even Elliot. It did me good to see that. I think maybe I *have* made a difference in their lives."

"You sure have. I can see that. And I'm glad you're getting further training. Remember, you're my Number One Rescuer!"

She giggled, and when they disconnected the call, the glow of the day spread through her body like liquid gold.

CHAPTER TWENTY

Friday morning before Sam left for the PATH training, Alberta and Electra hauled in their overnight bags. Sam went over the instructions for caring for the horses, checking the cattle—"Be sure to watch for any calves that might be acting sick after castration; they might have an infection"—ticking off the chores on her fingers, repeating directions, spinning in one direction then another on her bootheel. "Oh, and Lucky's food is in the bag in the pantry..." At Electra's cocked head and bemused expression, she stopped and laughed. "Oh! Here I am babbling on and on. You know all this stuff." She cuffed her young friend's shoulder. "And Horace is just a few miles away."

"I know you're nervous about leaving the place, but we will be just fine." Alberta encircled her shoulders with one arm. "I may still be a greenhorn, but I have the 'old hand' here to show me the way."

The teen tittered behind her palm, and her mom flashed her a mock-serious look. "This is one time you'll get to tell *me* what to do."

Sam threw her bag into the truck, climbed in, and gripped the steering wheel with tight, cold fingers. "Okay. You two have fun. Call me if—"

"We won't need to." Alberta tapped the window frame. "*You* go have fun. Don't worry about anything here and don't worry about the training. You'll ace it."

Electra gave her a high-five. "Yeah! You go get 'em, Sam."

169

The familiar prairie-scape rolled outside her window in varying shades of spring greens mingling with leftover golds of winter grasses. Wildflowers blanketed the hillsides in Indian Paintbrush orange or Bitterroot pale pinks.

She willed herself to relax, but anxious thoughts insinuated themselves into the calm surroundings. What if she wasn't prepared? Maybe she hadn't had enough experience yet. They'd all laugh at her and tell her to forget about being a PATH instructor. After all, she didn't have any formal training before this. *I just fell into it. They came to me. I'm only flying by the seat of my pants.* Her methods could be way off base.

But you've taken the online courses, her inner sane voice interjected. *You know what they expect, and you've been doing that.*

What if she'd missed something though?

Look at those vets. Look at what they did yesterday and compare that to the first time you met any of them.

"I know, I know." She spoke aloud, banging a fist on the steering wheel. "Okay, Sam. Stop this incessant worrying. Right. Now!" She laughed, flipped on the oldies country station and sang along with Waylon and Willie and the Boys as the two-hour trip flew by.

Pulling into Billings, she passed the MetraPark convention center downtown and took Highway 3 to drive another thirteen miles northwest of town. The equestrian center beckoned, with large, well-maintained red barns and metal-roofed arenas. She drove in and parked. Getting out of the truck, she stretched and cast an admiring glance around. *Ahh, this is the kind of facility I'd love to have.*

A young woman with short, dark hair, appearing to be in her early to mid-thirties, strode her direction, leading a bay mare. She put out a hand to shake. "Hi. You must be Sam. I'm Paula, the program director here." She gestured to a young man, clad in jeans and a blue western shirt, who came up beside her. "This is Jeremy, my assistant."

Sam shook. "What a lovely place you have. I'm envious."

The woman smiled. "Thank you. It's taken a long time to develop, but we're proud of it. C'mon, I'll introduce you to the rest of the staff and the other students."

New names and faces became a blur as she took the tour. She admired the large barns and the huge, covered riding arena, making note of some of the amenities. Paula showed her where she'd be bunking, with two other women, Linda and Amy. A serious-faced, brown-ponytailed Linda was there to take her final exam, while Amy, a bouncy blonde, was a newer student, like Sam. One other student, Eli, mid-twenties and dressed in brown plaid and denim, joined them to meet all the horses, and Paula instructed them to pick a mount to work with.

Standing at the corral fence, she gazed over the horse bunch that ranged from blacks to chestnuts, paints to bays. The animals milled around, some ignoring the newcomers while others ambled to check out the group at the fence. A black with a white diamond on his forehead walked right up to her and thrust his nose against her hand.

"Well, hello there. And who might you be?" She stroked his soft muzzle and scratched his ears, feeling in her pocket with the other hand to see if she'd left a cake pellet or two there. "Yes. You're in luck. Here you go." He gently licked the treat from her hand and nuzzled her arm.

"Looks like Milkshake has chosen you." Paula chortled. "Why don't you tack him up and go for a short ride, get acquainted."

Amy picked Dawn, a luminescent gray appaloosa. Linda was already saddling Alec, another black with a star on his forehead, and Eli chose a paint. Paula mounted her bay, Bella, and led them into the brush and grass-covered fields beyond the barns.

As always, on the back of a horse, she allowed her guard to fall, her shoulders to relax, and her mind to empty of everything except the crunch of hooves on vegetation, birdsong from the cottonwoods, and the tangy scent of wheatgrass and sage. The shadows lengthened as dusk approached. Milkshake had a gentle, rolling gate, and Sam felt as though they'd always known each other.

After supper and get-acquainted time over coffee and dessert, Sam and the other women retired to their beds in the long, one-room bunkhouse. She lay awake, listening to her roommates' breathing and gentle snores. She mulled over the evening, a shiver of nervous anticipation running through her core she wondered how she would measure up the next day. Everyone was so friendly—except maybe Linda, who seemed a little standoffish. But then, she was more advanced in the program and perhaps she had her own worries and doubts on her mind. Amy was nice, though, more like Sam, still learning…

Sunrise brought Sam out of a sound sleep, her tennis-playing butterflies in full final-round competition. She gathered her chestnut hair into a ponytail and dressed in her nicest dark-washed jeans and a blue chambray shirt, turning this way and that in front of the small mirror in the bathroom. Maybe she should've brought something fancier to wear, like barrel racers' costumes. She huffed a laugh. *The horse won't care. I'm not here to impress with my looks, only my skills.* She joined the other students and staff at a hearty breakfast buffet in a roomy mess hall next to the bunkhouse. Not knowing if she could swallow pancakes or eggs and bacon, she chose a cup of yogurt and coffee, and sat next to Amy at the long, rough-hewn table.

The other woman had a similar breakfast in front of her. "Nervous?" she asked.

"Yeah, a little." Sam nodded. "Where are you doing your volunteer work?"

"My husband and I have a ranch near Hardin, and we want to expand the work we've been doing with some local veterans."

"Oh, that's great." She told her more about her program through the ag college in Miles City. Eli joined them, and soon they were comparing notes.

Paula and a man who looked to be in his forties sat across from them. "Good morning. This is Matt, one of the veterans we've worked with in the past. He's graduated to volunteering with us now."

Matt bobbed his ballcap-clad head, his mouth crinkling under his gray-streaked mustache. "Mornin', ladies. Welcome."

She returned his smile. "How did you get involved in this program?"

"Well, after I came back from Iraq, I had a hard time adjusting. I couldn't engage in 'normal' activities or connect with friends and family." He sipped his coffee. "Then my doctor told me about Horses Spirits Healing. I took a few riding lessons, and one day I realized I was looking forward to something for the first time in a long time."

"That's wonderful." *Another testimony to the healing power of horses.*

"I've really started to enjoy life again." Matt glanced at Paula. "I can't find the words to express my gratitude for what this program has given back to me."

The director patted his arm. "We're thankful we could help and now for you helping us." She swung her gaze to Sam and Amy. "I know that's what you gals are looking to do too, and I'm only too happy to assist. I don't know if you know this, but Montana has the second highest number of veterans per capita in the nation. Yellowstone County alone has 22,000 vets."

Sam raised her brow. "Wow. I knew there were a lot, but…"

"Too often, vets struggle through their pain, feeling hopeless and frustrated," Paula went on. "Our goal here is to help them heal through interacting with our horses."

Matt nodded. "Ask anyone who's spent time on a horse—there's an undeniable bond, and healing follows. Like the oldtimers say, 'The outside of a horse is good for the inside of a man.'"

Her heart stirred. "Yes. That's so true. I've seen it first-hand with the kids and the vets I've worked with so far." This man's story only served to underscore what she wanted to accomplish.

"Well, ladies and Eli, let's go out and gather our mounts." Paula rose. "We'll be going through your riding component first, and then this afternoon, we'll have a group of veterans come in for you to work with."

She gulped and exchanged a wide-eyed glance with Amy. They followed the instructor to the corral, where her assistant Jeremy waited.

"I'll be working with Linda, since she is testing for her certification," Paula informed them, "and Jeremy will take you three through your paces."

Sam reacquainted herself with Milkshake, giving him a treat and caressing his face and ears. Then she saddled him, led him around the corral and checked his cinch. Mounted, she awaited instructions.

"You'll take turns in this arena." Jeremy gestured to a small rectangular paddock. "First, I want you to take your horse to the starting corner, halt, and proceed at a walk to the half-way point. That blue post there." He pointed. "Then you'll post a trot to the orange marker."

Eli went first, then Amy, and finally, Sam. She'd never done much equestrian style training, but Milkshake proved an old hand, and she relaxed into the rhythm of his trot as they negotiated the lead changes, posting, and sitting diagonal trots. *All right, Sam, you can do this!*

They cantered, loped, jogged in a circle, walked into the center of the arena, halted, backed a few steps, then moved forward, and dismounted.

Okay, that wasn't quite as bad as I thought. She whooshed a breath.

Jeremy held a clipboard, making notes as each student went through their paces. When Amy finished, she flashed Sam a "made-it" gesture and bowed. Everyone laughed and applauded.

"You all did very well." The instructor took each one separately to a shade-covered picnic table outside the arena to go over their patterns and scores. "You demonstrated excellent control of the horse," he told her, "and you have a keen sense of what the horse needed in all the phases."

Her face flushed with the positive comments.

"It's clear you haven't had the experience in this type of riding, with a couple of awkward transitions, but I think you adapted very nicely and worked in tandem with your mount, learning and improving as you went."

"Thank you. Milkshake is a dream to work with."

Jeremy grinned. "Yeah, he's a good horse."

Lunch was a picnic under a canopy of cottonwoods, and by that time, Sam was famished. Her jitters had subsided with the morning phase out of the way.

"Whew! That part is over." Amy plunked on a bench across from her. "You looked good out there."

"Thanks. I'm a little green when it comes to that kind of riding." She shook her head. "I've only ridden western-style, out on the prairie."

"Me too, although I did take some riding lessons when I was a kid." Amy bit into her sandwich. "How'd you do, Eli?"

175

The young man set his plate down and sat on the bench next to her and shrugged. "It was tough. I have a ways to go. I need to learn to relax and relate to the horse better, I guess." His shoulders slumped. "According to Jeremy, anyway."

"Well, you'll get there," Sam offered. "Plus, I don't really know how doing all this 'proper' reining and trotting stuff is going to help us work with veterans. But there must be a 'method to the madness' in this program."

"I guess so. Probably to demonstrate how well we relate to the horses ourselves, so we can pass that along to them." Amy slurped her iced tea.

"That makes sense, I suppose."

That afternoon, Paula introduced the students to several veterans with a variety of disabilities, visible and unseen. "In this phase of your training evaluation, you will instruct a twenty-minute group riding lesson. I will oversee Linda again. Sam, you'll be with Jeremy, Amy with Craig, and Eli with Matt."

Sam swallowed hard, her lunch sitting like a lump of lead. *Oh my. What am I supposed to do?* Her mind blanked. *C'mon, Sam, think!* Ideas ghosted through like wisps of smoke. *Help me, Lord.*

She inhaled and exhaled slowly, trying to calm the jumping, jittering nerves in her body. "Okay." She faced her group of two men and one woman. "I'm Sam." She told them briefly what she'd been doing on her ranch and in Miles City. The vets introduced themselves, and she asked them to choose a mount.

Holding out her hand flat with a cake pellet, she rubbed Milkshake's face, ears, and neck, all the while talking softly to him. "Now, you guys try it." The vets followed suit. They'd been to the center before and were familiar with the program, but she didn't want to take that for granted and gauged their fear.

When one of the guys drew back, she spoke to him in what she hoped was a calm voice. "You're doing well. She won't bite you. She just wants her treat." He snickered and tried again.

After they led their animals back to her, she picked up her brush and curry comb and showed how to groom the horse. "You want to keep talking to them all the while, get to know them and them to know you. Don't be afraid. They love this. It's like you getting a massage."

Her hesitant vet chuckled.

Good. I must be getting through. The next step, tacking up, she demonstrated first with Milkshake and then helped each saddle his horse. She repeatedly reassured the vets, telling them to do only what they were comfortable with. "Now, I'm going to mount and ride around the arena, and then if… and only *if* you are ready, I will assist you."

When Jim, with a prosthetic leg, came forward, she found herself wishing for Trixi or Apache. "Have you done a full mount before?" She held a gulp of air.

"Once. It was kinda hard, cuz of this." He pointed to his left leg prosthesis.

She fluttered a breath through her lips. "Let's see how McMillan deals with a right-side mount." Murmuring softly, she worked her way around to the opposite side. "Good boy. Are you okay with this, huh, boy? Will you let Jim get on this side?" She stuck her boot into the stirrup and paused with her weight resting there a moment. The horse didn't so much as flinch, so she swung her leg over the saddle. "Good boy, McMillan. Good boy."

She slid off. "All right. It looks like he's okay with a non-traditional mount. Ready to give it a try?"

While everyone leaned forward with eager looks of anticipation, she walked Jim through each step, helping him distribute his weight on the stirrup and then swing his prosthetic leg over the saddle into the stirrup on the other side.

177

He wiggled in the seat and flashed a huge smile. "That was a lot easier than last time. Thanks!"

The other vets gave him thumbs-up or a slow hand-clap. "Way to go, Jim."

Her shoulders let down a notch. *Whew! One down, two to go.*

The rest of her lesson went smoothly, with the vets expressing enthusiasm for her teaching style. "Thank you, Ms. Moser." Jim shook her hand. "That was the easiest time I've had of it so far."

"I wish you could come to my ranch and meet my two horses who kneel," Sam told him. "Maybe one of these days I'll have my barn and arena set up for lessons."

"Awesome. I look forward to it." He touched the brim of his cap and left the arena.

Yay, you! her inner voice cheered. Her chest puffed out a bit. *I did it. Thank you, Lord.*

In the evening, the staff, vets, and students gathered for a barbecue, celebrating a successful day. One of the staff brought out a guitar, and a veteran stroked a bow over the strings of his fiddle, providing a lively background to friendly chatter. Sam and Amy exchanged numbers and promised to keep in touch.

The next morning, she met with Jeremy to go over her training scores. "We've already talked about your riding skills, and you know your strengths and weaknesses," he said. "Now, your lesson…"

She tried to swallow past the sandstone boulder in her throat. What would he say? She thought she'd done okay, and the vets all said so. Biting her lower lip, she waited for the verdict.

"I talked with your students, and they were quite enthusiastic about your demonstration and how you helped them, especially Jim. I don't know why we didn't help him

178

mount from the other side to begin with. Good remedy. Not all horses will allow that, but you tested him out first, and that was good thinking."

He glanced at the papers on his clipboard. "Overall, I would say you did an excellent job working with the vets. Nick Seward, your mentor at the college, has been quite enthusiastic about how well you've done with their program." He raised his gaze to hers and grinned. "And I'm happy to second that."

Her audible breath came out like a cross between a kitten's mew and a whirling dervish. She allowed herself to relax. "Oh, thank you so much. I'm very relieved."

"Keep up the good work, get your hours in, and the next step is back here for certification." Jeremy stood, gave her copies of the score sheets, and headed for the office.

As she floated on the pillow of praise toward the bunkhouse, Paula called out to her. "We usually all gather for a farewell lunch downtown at Jakers, if you want to join us before you go home."

"Sure. That sounds like fun. I'll grab my stuff and meet you there." She could hardly keep herself from skipping the rest of the way. Inside, Amy was already packing up. Sam grabbed her duffel bag. "How did your evaluation go?"

"Pretty well. Some room for improvement in a few areas, and I need to get over my nervousness when working with the vets. I'm usually not this bad at home, but here…" The young woman gave a short chuckle, "I guess I knew my every move was being watched and graded."

"Yeah, it was nerve-wracking, that's for sure. Are you going to Jakers?"

"Absolutely! One more outing in the 'big city' before heading home to work."

The group met in a nearby parking lot and filed into the popular restaurant, already bustling with customers at 11:00. Sam's gaze took in the rich wood columns and area dividers that gleamed under a pressed copper ceiling. The hostess took the group to a small meeting room in the back, where they ordered and continued a spirited conversation about horses and working with the veterans.

"How did this PATH program get started?" Sam asked.

"Actually, back in 1969, a group in Virginia got together and formed the North American Riding for the Handicapped Association, which later became PATH International in the mid-nineties. And it began to offer three levels of instructor certification—'registered,' 'certified,' and 'master.'"

Paula leaned back in her chair. "After years of success in working with people with disabilities, studies began involving veterans with PTSD. It showed amazing results, that PTSD scores dropped by eighty-seven percent after just six weeks of therapeutic horsemanship sessions."

"Wow." Amy's eyes grew wide.

"Horses for Heroes was added to PATH in the mid-2000s as a supplemental program for veterans, and it's been growing ever since," Paula added.

"I've felt that healing power since I was a little girl." Sam thought back to all the times a horse had mended her hurts.

"Yeah," Jeremy chimed in. "They respond to emotions, and they have no ulterior motives. One session in the barn is worth about five sessions on the psychiatrist's couch. I call a horse 'twelve hundred pounds of lie detector'."

Everyone laughed, and then the group began to gather their belongings and head up front. Sam shook Paula's and Jeremy's hands. "Thanks for a great weekend. This has been so helpful and really validated my dream."

Jeremy nodded. "You're a natural. See you soon for your qualification."

Her boots barely skimming the floor, she followed Amy toward the exit. As they walked through the crowded restaurant, dark hair with a wayward lock over the forehead registered in Sam's periphery. A gasp locked in her throat as she swung her gaze to a booth in the corner. A blonde, curly head leaned close as the couple studied something on the surface of the table.

Brad!

CHAPTER TWENTY-ONE

A glacial ice flow overtook Sam's body. Rooted to the floor, she could only stare at the two heads bent toward each other. What was Brad doing in town? And what was he doing with that woman? A pulse of hot anger pushed against the ice lump, hard and electric. She fought for clarity, one moment wanting to run, and the next to grab the carafe from a passing waitress and dump hot coffee over Brad's head.

The heat of anger thawed her frozen limbs, making her skin clammy. The room swirled. A horse-sized weight crushed her chest. She couldn't breathe. Time stopped.

"Sam, are you coming…?" Amy's voice echoed through the fog.

She swiveled her head toward the sound, saw herself as if from above, only able to observe. The earthbound Sam moved one foot and then the other through the viscous atmosphere, like an ancient turtle, slow and deliberate.

Moving toward the voice, she somehow stayed upright, and footslogged her way to the door.

"Sam? Sam, are you all right?" Amy's voice again. "You're as white as a ghost. What's wrong?"

Then, as though a dam had burst, she moved, rushing out of the restaurant, her friend behind, calling her name. She stopped on the sidewalk and leaned against a lamp post, gasping. Turning her gaze to Amy, she blurted, "Brad. My boyfr—I thought he was… I'll kill him. He's with… He lied…" She shook her head like a dog after a swim. "I need to go. 'Bye."

She sprinted through the parking lot, fumbled her keys in the lock, yanked the door open, and slid inside. The engine roared to life, and tires squealed as she gunned out of the lot.

Miles slid beneath the truck. Questions bounced in her head. Anger burned red in her vision and then turned to icy fear that trickled through her body. Shock froze her fingers to the steering wheel.

When her cell phone rang, she jumped at the shrill sound penetrating the cloud in her mind. She glanced at the screen and bit her lip, hard. Brad.

Jamming on the brakes, she pulled off on the side of the road and clicked to answer. "Don't even bother," she yelled before he could say a word. "I saw you in Jakers just now, with…with…that blonde. That tears it, Brad. You liar. Don't come to the ranch this week. I don't want to see you again. It's *over.*"

She disconnected, switched the phone to vibrate, and threw it on the passenger side floor. Shifting into gear, she popped the clutch, and the engine stalled. She shoved her foot against the gas pedal and ground the ignition. The engine turned over but wouldn't start.

"Crap! I've flooded it." She flung the door open, her boots hitting the asphalt with a jarring thud. Stomping around the vehicle, she paused to kick the already-dented blue fender, again and again, each kick punctuated with her anguished howls. "Brad, you liar! You two-timer! You low-life pond scum!" She stopped, moaning with the pain in her toe and the bloody rip in her heart.

A couple of cars sped by, paying her no attention. At first, relief she wouldn't have to explain herself buoyed her but quickly changed to indignation. "You didn't even stop to see if I needed help," she yelled after the last disappearing vehicle and slammed her fist on the side of the truck.

Scooting back in, she tried the ignition again. This time the engine started, and she peeled back onto the road, pushing the accelerator as high as the old pickup would go. From the floor, the phone vibrated intermittently, insistently. She set her face in stone and drove onward through her new reality.

Electra and her mom were in the corral, the teen untacking Toby, when Sam pulled in at the ranch. She sat a moment, steeling herself against the questions, and pasted on a smile.

Alberta strode to her side and gave her a hug. "Welcome home."

Her young friend let Toby go, scrambled over the rails, and ran to her side. "Hey, Sam. I'm glad you're back. I hope you had a good time, and ohmygosh I've been working more with Toby and he's doing so great and I think he's ready for the vets!" Her eyes were moon-sized, her face eager and shining.

Sam couldn't help but chuckle as she hugged the girl. *Always a bright light in the midst of my darkness.* "That's wonderful! We can try him out while they're here helping on the barn."

"Yay!" Electra scurried to the pickup, yanked open the door, and grabbed Sam's bag. Her mother took it from her and guided Sam toward the house. "Did you have a good training session?"

"Yeah, it was great. I learned a lot, and the trainer gave me quite a positive review." She forced herself to focus on the good.

"Oh, that's great. I knew you'd do well." Alberta squeezed her shoulder.

She peered into her friend's face. "I assume you were fine here by yourself since I didn't get any panicked phone calls."

Alberta grinned. "Nope, no problems. Electra is a trouper, knew exactly what to do, and ran a tight ship."

They both chortled.

Electra clumped up beside them, with the rest of Sam's things.

"Hey, you have fifteen messages from Brad." She held the phone out. "Sorry. It was vibrating on the floor, and I thought maybe you'd want to take the call."

Sam pressed her lips together, took the cell, and shoved it into her pocket.

Alberta shot her a puzzled glance, her forehead pinched. "You look pale. What's wrong?"

She shook her head in tight, quick movements and stalked into the house. In the kitchen, she slumped on a chair, burying her face in her hands. In a flash, Electra was beside her, an arm over her shoulder.

The girl's mom sat next to her. "Honey, tell me what happened."

Her eyes grew hot, and a tear sliced her cheek. Fingers of pain clutched her throat, shutting off her voice. The women stroked her back and arms, issuing soft murmurs.

"Why did I hope?" The words came out strangled. "Why did I think I could have a relationship?"

"Brad?" Alberta peered into her face.

She nodded. "He lied to me, told me he couldn't see me this weekend, 'cause he was…" she drew air quotes, "…out of town… And then I saw him in Jakers…sitting so cozy-like with his head close to a blonde woman." The last words squeaked out of a narrow passageway in her throat.

Electra gasped. "No!"

"Oh, honey." Her friend embraced her tightly, smoothing her hair away from her face. "I'm so sorry."

A sob as hard as a stone rose in her throat, and her tears wet Alberta's shoulder. They sat, rocking each other, until the waves of disappointment and loneliness washed through her and left her on an empty shore.

Electra set a cup of steaming chocolate in front of her.

She gave the girl a wan smile. "Th-thank you."

"I'm going to dump a ton of horse apples over that guy's head when I see him." The teen's rigid face flushed. "He's got a lot of 'splainin' to do!"

"Well, yes, he does," her mother agreed. "And maybe there *is* a simple explanation."

"No." She hardened her face again. "He's had his chance. Many chances, in fact. I've been patient with him, put up with his moods, his reserved actions toward me. No. I'm done. I can't do this anymore."

***

Sam deleted all of Brad's messages without listening. With this betrayal, she cemented a brick into the wall around her heart to repair the chink opened by allowing him into her life. Donning her "all's-well" mask, she moved through the next few days robotically. She refused to think, didn't answer the phone, refused to give in to tears, to anger, or any emotion. Someone did her chores; someone cooked a meal and did dishes; someone brushed the horses. She startled herself awake at times to see what had been done. *It must have been me.* No one else was around.

***

Thursday morning, the June sun slanting through the gap in the curtains woke her early. Today was the day. The vets, Horace, Clyde, and their crews would be there to start work on the barn. A fleeting charge of excitement lifted her out of bed. Then the image of a dark head next to a blonde one slammed her in the gut. *No!* She bit hard on the inside of her cheek until the pain and coppery taste of blood washed away the memory.

She tugged on worn jeans, a short-sleeved plaid shirt, and her boots. After brewing an extra-strong cup of ebony coffee, she filled her travel cup, grabbed a handful of carrots, and hoofed it toward the pasture next to the corral. Sugar and Trixi waited for her, heads reaching over the fence, whickering softly

186

as she approached, treats in hand. As the mares crunched, she pulled their heads close to hers, sandwiching her face between them. Their manes tickled her neck, the heat from their necks warmed her, and she drew from them all the strength they had to offer.

Before long, Apache and Toby appeared, interrupting the peaceful moment, snorting, and nosing at her arms for their treats. "Oh, you rascals." Snickering, she offered the rest of the carrots from her pocket.

As she contemplated taking a quick ride before the crew appeared, Horace's big diesel engine signaled his arrival, Ted's green truck following. Like a caravan, more pickups pulled in, men spilling out, buckling tool belts, and grabbing toolboxes out of the back of their trucks. On their heels came the van from the college, the veterans bounding out almost before it came to a complete stop.

"Mornin', little gal," Horace boomed. "Are you ready for this?"

Pasting on her best grin, she nodded. "You bet I am."

Ted touched fingers to the brim of his cap. "Hi, Ms. Moser. We're here, ready, willing, and able."

"G'morning, Ted." Gratitude welled up, nearly spilling into tears, as everyone gathered around, nodding at her, shaking her hand, and offering friendly greetings.

Rounding up her thoughts, she coaxed the words past the lump in her throat. "Th-thank you all for coming today." She cleared away the raspiness. "I know you're all giving up your time to do this, and I can't even begin to express..." Clamping her lips tightly, she held back the spillage.

"Aw, think nothin' of it." Clyde put a fatherly arm around her shoulder.

"We're happy to do this—for you." Garrett thrust his reddened face forward. "You're special to us."

"No place we'd rather be." Sondra gave her a thumbs-up.

"Yeah." Even Elliot looked eager to begin.

"Oorah, let's roll!" Del pounded the arms of his wheelchair, and the rest of the veterans joined in the chant.

"Okay, guys, listen up." Horace broke into the lively chatter and cheers. "Ted here is the foreman in charge. What he says, goes. And I'm here to help keep you all in line."

Laughter greeted his remark, but all eyes turned to the young man.

He tapped his clipboard. "All right, here's what we're gonna do…"

The rest of his instructions were lost in a whirlwind of words and questions, as she could only stand back in awe and gape at the organization as it unfolded.

Before she made sense of it all, groups formed. Some stacked lumber and plywood near the foundation. Others gathered nail guns and hammers, saws and levels, while Ted and Horace measured, once, twice, and marked.

The piercing whine of electric saws and the spicy scent of new-cut wood filled the air. Sawdust flew in spouts, dusting heads and shoulders. Shouts, laughter, and banter punctuated the morning, along with the rat-a-tat of nail guns.

Unable to comprehend fully what was happening, she moved to sit on the boulder by the corral, simply witnessing a miracle unfold. *How do I deserve this? These people, my friends…* A sense of belonging built and crescendoed, filling in the lonely, empty spaces in her soul. The cacophony—a symphony in its own right—comforted her. As they worked, she could be invisible mere yards away.

As if in an expertly choreographed dance, Horace, Nick and a couple of the veterans set poles into place, drilling into the concrete, and mounting them with heavy duty drill-set brackets. A framework materialized, 2x4s and 2x6s crisscrossing the poles. Ted gestured, and men moved lumber into place.

The rhythm of metal thudding and shearing against wood mesmerized her. A wall was forming—the beginning of her barn—before her eyes. Not the wall of brick and mortar around her heart, but a wall made of community and camaraderie and people helping others. The kindness lifted her like an ocean wave and gently rocked her.

Then, as though a magnet drew her, she rose and strode into the midst of the activity, grabbing a hammer and a handful of nails. Someone strapped a tool belt around her waist and gave her gloves, eye and ear protection. Someone else pointed her to the framework.

She centered the nail and swung. A satisfying *thunk* reverberated through her arm. As if the lumber sported Brad's face, she swung again and again, each whack of hammer against steel driving into the meat of the wood. Sweat beaded on her forehead. She took out another nail and another, beating until exhaustion forced her to stop.

Garrett handed her a bottle of water. "Man, you were really going at that." His face held a wide-eyed look of admiration. "You can swing a hammer, girl!"

Laughing out loud, she took a red bandana from her hip pocket and mopped her face. "Yeah. Feels good."

From her periphery, she caught a glimpse of Irene, Alberta, and Electra arriving along with several other neighbor ladies, and setting up folding tables. Soon, the earthy aroma of coffee and cinnamon-sugar mingled with the scents of sweat and sawdust.

"Time for a coffee break." Ted called a halt to the buzzing, whining, pounding staccato noise, and with a welcome lull, the crew headed for the table laden with rolls, doughnuts, and coffee.

Sam grabbed Irene and Alberta in a long, hard hug. "Thank you, thank you. I should've been on the ball, getting stuff ready, helping you. I'm sorry."

"Phht!" Irene pecked her cheek. "You were having a blast down there. I could see the satisfaction in your face. You need to be a part of your new barn."

Alberta gave her a knowing look. "Taking out your frustrations on the nails and the wood, maybe?"

She giggled. "Maybe."

At lunch, Ted stood across the picnic table from Sam and ducked his head. "Mind if I sit here?"

"Of course not." She waved her fork toward the barn structure. "You and the crew are making great progress. I'm impressed."

"Thanks." He dipped his roast beef sandwich into the *au jus*. "You've been a big help too, really pitched in this morning."

"It's been…a bit cathartic, I guess. And I feel like I need to contribute to this project too, not just sit back and watch."

He finished chewing his bite. "Well, I admire a woman who works alongside." His face pinked.

She averted her face to hide a smirk. *I think he's trying to flirt with me.* "I intend to do my share."

Horace joined them, his plate loaded with sandwich and salads. "Mmm, my stomach's been chewin' on my backbone for an hour." He tucked into his food with gusto.

When he came up for air, he leaned forward. "Hey, little gal, you know what I been thinkin'?"

"What?"

"You don't have an office in your plans."

She jerked her head in a double-take. "No. That's right, I don't. I guess I figured I'd continue to use my kitchen table."

"Naw. You need a real office in this brand-new barn o' yours."

Ted nodded. "Yes, you do. And it's a simple add-on."

"But... that's going to add to the cost, isn't it? I'll need a floor and more lumber." She swallowed, seeing dollar signs dance before her eyes.

"W-e-l-l now, not necessarily." Horace shoveled a forkful of potato salad and held it half-way to his mouth. "I got this old outbuilding on my place I need to tear down, but it has a lot of good wood left to salvage."

"Yeah." Ted's eyes shone with eagerness. "And Joe and Bob left a partial load of Quik-Crete sacks back at the office site. They ain't gonna be usin' it. We might as well."

"Say the word, little gal. We can have plans drawn up this afternoon or evening and pour concrete tomorra."

Her mouth felt like a gate hanging loose from its hinges. "Really? You would do that?"

"Yup." Her elderly neighbor exchanged a glance with the young foreman. "And you need a floor in your tack room too."

"You guys!" Wonder and gratitude flowed over her like a pleasant spring rain. "A concrete floor sure would be easier to keep clean. Thank you."

"Settled, then!" Horace rose from his seat. "I'm goin' for some of Irene's chocolate sheet cake over there."

Ted grinned at her, a gleam in his eyes. "Better go get my pencil busy." He reached out a hand tentatively and after a moment's hesitation, patted her arm before bolting for his pickup.

Her mouth quirked. *Such a nice young man. Too young for me though. Besides, I'm done with men.*

Electra stood at the head of the serving table and banged a ladle against a metal pot. When the chit chat subsided, she announced, "I have something to show you. Please come with me."

Amid puzzled murmurs, the veterans and neighbors followed the teen to the corral and climbed on top or leaned against the rails. She led Toby into the center, circling him

191

several times and then backing him. His head bowed. She tapped his forearm, and he bent his front legs, going down on his knees.

The crowd gave a collective gasp.

Electra slid onto the gelding's back, tapped him again, and he rose. She rode him around the corral to the spectators' applause.

"Whoa!" Garrett's exclamation came from beside Sam. "Another kneeling horse. You two are somethin'!"

She shook her head. "It's all Electra. She's the trainer in all this." Her chest cavity expanded until she thought her buttons would burst. *That's my girl. She has done amazing things since I first met her.*

The girl slid from Toby's back and beckoned. "Del, you want to come give him a try?"

"Heck yeah, I do." He wheeled and bumped his way over dirt clods into the arena.

Electra signaled the bay to kneel. The vet eased himself out of the chair and into the saddle, lifting his right stump over with his hands. When he had a firm seat, he nodded, the teen strapped him on, signaled, and horse and rider were off, circling the corral. She walked close alongside, ensuring Del wouldn't fall.

A loud cheer rose, hands beating on the rails in thunderous approval. With a cheek-splitting grin, he waved at the crowd, his pleasure shining in his face.

After several of the vets took their turns on Toby, Horace's voice boomed. "Ain't that somethin'? Good job, little gal. I'm prouda ya." He pushed his hat back on his forehead. "But as much fun as we're havin', we need to get back t' business now."

"Aw, you spoilsport!" yelled one of the men, and with laughter and banter, the crew headed back to work.

As Sam pivoted to join them, she froze. Brad stood inside the corral, his camera trained on Electra and Toby. She fought for a breath, and her pulse ratcheted. Marching to the fence near where he stood, she shouted, "What the heck are you doing here? I told you I didn't want to see you again!"

He lowered the camera. "Now wait, Sam, let me ex—"

"Get out! I mean it!" She spun on her heel and stormed to the barn site, each step a killing stomp. Stopping in front of Horace, she thrust her hot face close to his and gestured over her shoulder. "I want him off my property. Get rid of him."

The older man's face paled under his tan, and his bushy brows pushed toward each other. "Wha—what's wrong?"

"Please." Her words strangled her. "Please tell him to leave."

She sprinted to the pasture, where Sugar grazed, grabbing a halter hanging on the fence. The mare lifted her face and whickered. Sam slipped on the halter and then flung herself onto the horse's bare back. Touching her heels to Sugar's flanks, she urged her into a gallop, riding as though the demons of hell were on their heels.

CHAPTER TWENTY-TWO

Screaming into the wind that whipped her hair loose, she goaded the horse faster, through scratchy sage bushes, into dry gullies, up and over hills. Her thighs clutched her mount, the great, rippling muscles carrying her away. Away from Brad. Away from prying eyes and minds. Away from her problems. The lie. The disappointment. The betrayal. The accumulated anger and hurt and abandonment of a lifetime lashed her like the lacerating strands of hair in her face.

Sweat foamed on Sugar's neck. The mare's breath came in snorts and grunts. Sam panted too. As they came in sight of the reservoir, with its emerald copse of cottonwoods, she drew back on the halter reins, slowing to a trot, then a walk. In the shade of the trees, she slid off the horse's back. Her jeans were sodden with sweat and her legs wobbly, as though she'd just done the gallop.

"Oh, Sugar, baby. I'm sorry. I shouldn't have run you so hard." She took off her outer shirt and wiped her pal down. Draping the garment from a branch, she slumped to the ground. The heat of her anger gradually cooled under the cottonwood.

Why do you feel so angry, so betrayed? her conscience prodded.

"Because he said one thing and did another." Her words came out loud, defensive. Sugar's head jerked up from the grass. "He could've told me he was in town but working. Why did he lie to me?"

But do you really know that? You haven't given him a chance to explain.

194

"I saw what I saw."

Maybe you're over-reacting. You could be mistaken. Things aren't always as they seem.

"Bull tinkles! They sure looked chummy to me."

You only caught a glimpse of them before you stormed out.

"Pffft." She blew, fluttering her lips like her horse. "I've given up so much for him. I committed to him during his months of recovery from his accident, but I'm not getting much of anything back. He's a self-centered jerk!" She pounded her fists on her thighs.

At her outburst, the mare swung her head toward Sam, her liquid brown eyes searching.

"Oh, Sugar. I'm not yelling at you." She rose and leaned her face near the horse's nose, breathing in and out along with her, calm returning to her body.

"Are you cooled down enough for some water?" She led the mare to the reservoir and allowed a short drink, then back to the shade, where she sat again.

Staring at the calm water, listening to the music of cottonwood leaves rustling in the breeze, she tracked the movement of a beetle climbing a weed stalk only to fall when it nearly reached the top. *I'm like that beetle. I'm almost there, and then my precarious hold sways and bends and dumps me in a cow patty.* She huffed. The beetle began its ascent again. "I think you've chosen the wrong stalk to climb, Mr. or Mrs. Beetle."

Heaviness weighed on her. *Have I done that? Do I need to rethink things?*

"Don't let yesterday use up too much of today." One of Horace's sayings echoed in her mind.

The beetle reached the top, the stalk swayed toward the tree trunk, and the insect crawled over and up the bark.

She squared her shoulders. *I need to keep trying until I reach a sturdy branch.*

195

Changing light and shadows brought her back to reality. The day was waning, dusk on its way. She donned her now-dry shirt and pulled herself onto Sugar's back for a calmer, more leisurely pace back. Focusing her mind on the persistent beetle, she strived to think more optimistically. *You can achieve your dream, Sam Moser, with or without love. You have cowgirl-strong blood in you.*

As she neared home, she heard no sounds of construction. The crew must have finished for the day. *Oh dear. I abandoned them. What must they think of me, falling apart over some dumb guy?*

She took off Sugar's halter, turned her out into the pasture, and headed to the house.

Hearing voices in the kitchen, she plodded in, embarrassment scorching her face when she saw Horace and Ted huddled over the table. "Hi, guys." Her voice croaked like an old toad.

"Hey, little gal." Her neighbor's gentle smile soothed her flustered emotions. "Hope you had a good ride."

She pushed air through pursed lips and sat across from the men. "I'm sorry I flaked out on you. There's no excuse—I'm better than that."

"It's okay, Ms. Moser." The younger man's forehead creased. "We did get a lot done today, and we're going over our plans for your office and tack room. Hope you don't mind we commandeered your table."

"Oh, no, no. That's fine." She stood. "How about I fix you supper?"

"You don't need to do that." Ted's protest sounded half-hearted.

"It's the least I can do for you. It'll be simple. I have eggs…" she rose and opened the refrigerator door, "…and leftovers from lunch."

Horace guffawed. "You know me and food. Anything sounds great."

Within fifteen minutes, she served scrambled eggs with roast beef and cheese chopped in, toast, a tossed salad, and coffee. The men fell to as if they hadn't eaten in a week. She allowed herself an inward chuckle.

Forking a bite of eggs, she paused half-way to her mouth. Did she dare ask? She set her fork down and cleared her throat. "So, uh… Did Brad leave when you asked him to?"

Horace finished chewing, all the while peering intently into her face. "After a time, yes. He *is* working on that documentary about the veterans and your program, and would like to continue…"

She pressed her lips together and exhaled audibly through her nose. "Yeah. I guess that's okay… As long as he stays away from me."

The older man ran a hand over his steel-bristle hair. "W-e-l-l, little gal. I think you need to talk to him."

"I'm done talking." She set her face in stone. "I've given him several second chances. I don't even want—"

Horace put up a palm. "Wait just a minute. I'm not getting in the middle of this, but you really *do* need to clear the air. What's it gonna hurt to hear him out?"

What's it gonna hurt, indeed. Pain seared through her heart. Would the scar tissue harden that agony after a while? Should she talk to him? Should she give him another chance? Probably. But not yet…

"Whatever…" She knuckled the threatening tears from her eyes and shrugged.

Desperate to change the tone, she addressed Ted. "So, what plans have you two concocted?"

Beaming, he grabbed the papers they'd been working on. "Take a look." He pointed to a rough diagram. "We'll pour the cement first thing in the morning, and since we haven't put up trusses for the roof yet, it'll be simple to build out from the larger structure and add your office."

197

Horace pushed his plate to the side. "And since you have a loft in the main barn, we were thinking of that upstairs area over the office for a small apartment, maybe? You have a lot of company and a small house, and I know you're always giving up your bedroom for someone."

"Oh, wow." She threw a hand to her neck. "What a great idea. That would help a lot until I'm able to build the bunkhouses I want."

"Yeah, and it'll give you access to a bathroom when you're working in the office," Ted added.

She slipped her hand down and over her chest. "You guys. You're too much…too good to me." Thankfulness sent a tingling glow through her limbs. "How will I ever repay you?"

"No need." Horace patted her arm. "Seeing you fulfill your dream and being happy will be repayment enough for me."

She nodded, unable to speak for a long moment.

"I feel responsible for JB running out on you. And, I'm getting the experience of heading up a project on my own. That'll be good for my resume." Ted's eyes were earnest and round. "Besides, I like working with you. You are an admirable woman with everything you've done on your own." His face reddened.

Her cheeks heated as well. "Thank you, Ted. I appreciate that so much. But I will see that you do get paid something for your efforts, I promise you that."

He waved a hand through the air as if to dismiss the idea. "Anyway, we'll be here bright and early in the morning to pour cement. The vets and others will be back too, but they'll work on putting up poles and building roof trusses for your arena cover, since we can't do that for the barn until the concrete sets."

"Oh my! Yes, the arena. I'd almost forgotten about that. Thank you." She steepled her hands. "Thank you so much." *Is this all really happening?*

After the men left, she called Alberta to tell her about their plans.

"I saw what they were working on. That's a wonderful idea. And Electra and I will help you decorate it." Her friend's voice gushed happily. "It's all coming together, Sam. You're getting your barn and your arena, and who knows what will happen next?"

"Your dream is coming true!" Electra's voice squealed in the background.

The women both laughed.

"Are you feeling okay after…?" Alberta's voice softened.

"Yeah. I'm fine. Embarrassed. But I'll be okay. Just need time."

"You've got us. Don't forget that."

After disconnecting, Sam sat in her darkening kitchen, watching the violet shadows play on the distant hills. *Dreams coming true… Well, maybe some of them.*

***

Sam rose as the first glimmer of dawn lit the horizon with a golden glow. Setting up a crockpot with chili, she mixed a large batch of cornbread and put it in the oven. She didn't want the neighbor ladies to have to provide all the food again. This was her project, after all.

Over coffee and toast with peanut butter and strawberry jam, she riffled through the mail Irene had picked up for her yesterday. A hand-addressed envelope caught her eye—return address *Fred Robbins, Bozeman MT*. Frowning, she slit the seal. *I don't know a Fred Robbins.* She extracted a slick, color brochure showing pronghorn antelope and buffalo grazing a green rolling prairie-scape. The letter read:

Hello Ms. Moser,

My name is Fred Robbins, and I'm a Realtor in Bozeman. I would love to chat with you about purchasing your property in the Ingomar area.

We are offering top dollar for the preservation of our Montana heritage and restoration of a fully-functioning prairie ecosystem.

"Phht!" She wadded the papers into a ball and tossed it toward the waste basket. "Another Big Open attempt. Well, you're not getting *my* prairie!" Her boot heels echoed off the linoleum as she slammed out the door and headed for the corral.

Petting her horses, she blew away memories of the New York-based group who had tried to force her off her ranch a couple years ago. She'd hoped to see the last of that nonsense—repopulating the prairie with exotic game animals, indeed!

Hearing vehicles approach, she strode to the barn structure to meet the crew. Soon, the air filled with laughter and back-and-forth banter among the neighbors and veterans as they strapped on tool belts and grabbed shovels, posthole diggers, and poles.

Ted reviewed the office addition sketch with her. "So, if that looks good to you, we'll start pouring the concrete right away."

"Yeah. Go for it." She aimed a happy smile at him.

Horace touched his hat. "Well, in that case, I'll go supervise the arena crew, and we'll get those holes dug and posts planted in concrete."

She executed a jig-step. "Yippee-kiyi-yo! Let's do this."

Ted and his group first built forms for the addition. Then they unloaded sacks of Quikrete. Del manned the hose from the well in the corral as Ted mixed wheelbarrow loads of cement. One man poured while other men shoveled the wet sludge into the forms and still others smoothed the top.

Sam roamed from the cement-pouring site to the arena, where several crew members dug holes. Nick ran the wheelbarrow of concrete there, and pole-setters completed each step. Bouncing on the balls of her feet, she caught Horace's eye. "It's taking shape. I can see it already."

He chortled. "Yup. Won't be long now."

She swung her head around as a black SUV pulled up the drive and parked near the other vehicles. She slitted her gaze. *Now who can this be?* A man in a dark, western-cut jacket, black jeans, and shiny black boots got out, holding a leather portfolio.

Glowering, she strode to meet him.

With a big grin, he stuck out a hand. "Good morning. Ms. Moser? I'm Fred Robbins."

Stopping in mid-stride, she didn't take his hand. "Mr. Robbins, I got your letter, but before you even begin, let me tell you right here and now, I am *not* interested in selling my ranch."

His smile grew even bigger. "But, Ms. Moser, we are offering twice the going rate for this kind of arid land. You—"

"Enough!" She shot mental daggers at the man's leering face. "I told you, I. Am. Not. Interested. Now, please leave my property."

The man wouldn't give up. "J-just hear me out—"

"There a problem here?" Horace's booming baritone cut him off. "I heard the lady ask you to leave. I suggest you do that. Right now."

Robbins scuttled backward, his shiny boots now covered in dust. Opening his car door, he tossed the portfolio onto the seat and stepped in. "Well, you have my brochure, if you change your mind…"

"I won't!" she shouted as she swiveled on her heel and stomped back to the construction site. She glanced at Horace beside her. "Thanks."

"What was that all about?"

"Oh, it's that new group, I think, like the Big Open guys, trying to buy up prairie 'reserves.' Well, they can go do it somewhere else." She ground her boot heel into the dirt.

"Yeah. Well, we can always have a repeat of the 'showdown at the Jersey Lilly.'" He guffawed.

Her anger melted, and she laughed along with him. "Right. Let's get back to work." Horace always knew the right thing to say to lift her out of a funk.

CHAPTER TWENTY-THREE

At noon, the women arrived, and Sam helped them set up tables and bring out the food. After a quick hug, Electra bounded to the corral to check on Toby and Apache and the other horses. Irene and Alberta exchanged a bemused glance.

"She couldn't wait to get here," the girl's mom said, "and she was miffed with me that I wouldn't let her come with Clyde this morning. But I needed her help first."

Sam chuckled. "She's resilient. She'll be okay now that she's with the horses. I have to tell you how proud I am of her and what she's accomplished, first with Apache and now with Toby."

"Oh, I know. I am too. She has blossomed here." Alberta dabbed at her eyes with her fingertips. "And no more signs of cutting. I'm so relieved. That seems like a lifetime ago now. I'm grateful to you for being such a fantastic mentor."

"Pshaw." Sam waved a hand through the air. "It's really the horses that healed her. And it's been my pleasure and to my advantage to have a helper here. And I'm going to need even more help, once I get this barn and arena set up and..." she took a fortifying breath, "maybe expand my services from here." *My dear horses. How amazing they've been in helping so many heal.* Yearning swelled in waves. This is what she wanted...needed to do.

"You will. I have faith in you. You have the determination and perseverance to accomplish whatever you set out to do."

Her friend hugged her. "And I'm here to help in any way you need."

Irene rang a cowbell, and the crew took a break for lunch, their good-natured repartee continuing as they loaded bowls with chili and slathered cornbread with butter.

"Good eats!" someone called out.

"Yeah, thanks, Sam!" The veterans raised their spoons or drinks in a salute.

"Thank YOU!" she called back.

The noisy, yet somehow comforting, sounds of shovels thumping dirt and men shouting and laughing resumed. Sam observed the progress, at times pitching in, and others, simply staring in awe. By the end of the afternoon, poles surrounded the arena, the cement floors for her office and tack room lay smooth and glistening, and the posts for the addition walls had been sunk into the concrete.

As the crew gathered their tools and cleaned up the site, Ted sought her out. "Tomorrow we should be able to get the roof trusses built and put up for the barn and with luck, also the arena."

Sam crossed her arms and hugged herself to contain her rush of anticipation. "That's great, Ted. You're doing a fantastic job as foreman on this project. If you need a reference for future jobs, I'll be more than happy to write you one."

The young man ducked his head as a flush rose from his neck. "Thank you, Ms. Mo—Sam. I appreciate that."

She hid a grin at his shy embarrassment as he kicked one boot toe against the instep of the other foot.

"Um… Okay then. See you in the morning." He whirled away and nearly sprinted toward his truck, running a hand through his wavy brown hair and shaking his head.

She tittered softly to herself.

Garrett limped up beside her. "We're going to head on home now, but I want to thank you for this opportunity to help you build your barn."

Her face probably reflected the shock she felt. "No, thank *you*. This wouldn't be happening without all of you." Her voice choked. "Volunteering your time, giving up your days, and working out here in the heat and dust…"

He waved the words away with a swipe of his hand. "It's nothin'. It's giving us great experience."

Del wheeled alongside. "Yes, ma'am. Between our work with the horses and this project, we—at least I do—feel we're contributing to society again."

Garrett gazed into the distant horizon. "When we came back, as veterans we had nothing to offer other than fighting and killing." His voice fell soft, almost inaudible. "I've been afraid to go out in public. People intimidate me. Loud noises set me off. I've had nightmares, flashbacks."

She pressed her lips together. That was one of the longer speeches she'd ever heard from this impassive man.

"A feeling of being disconnected," Del added.

"Yeah." The other man stood in silence.

She shifted her vision to the prairie grasses moving like a sigh in the afternoon breeze. Tears whispered past her lashes. What these guys had gone through, she couldn't begin to imagine. The horror of war, seeing your friends die in front of you, and then returning home to—what? Nothing was the same, nothing could be the same. A breath waved through her lungs, her own pain passing through her lips like smoke. Her heart filled with words her mouth couldn't say.

"Oh," she whispered and placed one gentle hand on Garrett's arm and her other on Del's shoulder.

"But…" Garrett switched his gaze to hers, "you, your horses, and your barn have given us a purpose." He took her hand in his. "And for that, I thank you."

"Me too. From the bottom of my heart." Del's eyes glistened.

"And me." Sondra's voice came from behind.

"Us too." Jimmy, Linc and Al joined the group and gave Sam a salute. Elliot hung back, rubbing his neck scar, but nodded.

The young woman vet hugged her, and then the others gathered around her, hugging, clapping her back, and shaking her hand.

"Sorry to break up the love-fest." Nick's mirth-filled words interrupted. "But we'd better get on back to Miles. Another early morning's coming up."

Levity returned in shades of a rainbow as everyone laughed and headed toward the van. "See you tomorrow," and "Thanks, Sam," echoed with the fading sound of the engine.

Horace stopped by his truck to throw his tools into the back. "I heard some o' that, little gal. You have given these guys a gift."

She swallowed hard, trying to compose herself. "And they're giving it back...in huge measures." Taking a step closer, she clasped the older man in a tight hug. "And so are you."

"My pleasure." His voice rasped by her ear. "You're family. You're the granddaughter I would've wanted."

She held him at arm's length. "And you don't know how much you remind me of my grandpa Neil. You two would've liked each other."

"If you inherited any of your traits from him, then I know we would." He touched a finger to his hat. "Well, I better get t' goin'. See you in the mornin'."

Silence settled with the dusk, bringing a gray haze of loneliness over her. The roller-coaster emotions of the day made her feel both large and small at the same time. The veterans' revelations and gratitude raised her up, while the encounters with Robbins and Brad diminished her. An unsettled feeling came over her like an unfinished sentence.

She wandered up the slope to the house and picked up the phone. "Teresa?" she said as her friend answered. "Do you have any Rocky Road ice cream?"

"I just bought a carton today," came the answer. "I can be there in forty-five minutes."

When her friend roared up the driveway in her red sportscar, Sam had coffee ready and waved two large spoons as she sat waiting on the porch.

Teresa bounded up the steps. She took the ice cream from her cooler and set it on the small patio table between them. "So… what's up?" She gestured to the construction site. "Looks like a barn, for one thing."

"Yeah. It is becoming one, very quickly." Sam scooped a spoonful of the sweet, icy concoction into her mouth. "Mmm. Thanks for this."

"You bet. Anytime." Teresa took a bite and then a sip of coffee. "Fabulous combo…" She swung her gaze to Sam. "So, spill."

"Where to begin…" she huffed a laugh. "I'm overwhelmed. I'm happy and grateful, and I'm sad and angry too." She told the story of seeing Brad and the blonde woman.

Her friend's brows lifted and scrunched, she scooped and sipped, her face turning from puzzlement to darkness.

"Horace hinted that Brad has an explanation, but I can't bring myself to talk to him. I don't know if I can go through the ups and downs of this relationship anymore—if it ever really was one." Her voice faltered. "I don't know if I can trust him—or anyone—anymore. Everybody I ever loved—my parents left, Jace left, Kenny left. But then I found Brad, and I had such hopes. And when hope fails, it breaks you. If you can't trust hope, what can you trust?"

"Oh, my dear. My heart hurts because yours is broken." Teresa made tiny murmurs of sympathy. "Are you sure about all this?"

Sam studied the ice cream in her spoon, the chocolate swirl with clumps of walnuts, drops melting over the side. "No. I'm not sure of anything. I thought he might be the perfect guy, but it's been such a struggle to get him to commit, to say anything, even to kiss me!"

"Well, there's no such thing as a perfect guy." Her friend tittered. "But parts of them are pretty nice."

Sam had to giggle. She licked her spoon. "When they're good, they're very, very good, but when they're bad, they're very, very bad—to paraphrase Longfellow."

Teresa spewed her mouthful of coffee, and they collapsed into helpless laughter, then tears as the darkening evening closed its warm arms around the two friends.

Her friend stayed the night again. Sam awakened in the dark to thunder and then the sound of rain pounding on the window. *Oh dear. The men won't be able to work on the barn in the rain.* But the June rains had been late this year and the moisture would be needed for the grass and hay to flourish and survive the summer heat. She went back to sleep, the drumming on the roof a pleasant, soothing beat.

At first light, she was up, and donning a raincoat, she pulled the hood up and raced to the building site. The floors had been covered by tarps. That's right, the clouds had been gathering last night. She'd been too distracted to really notice.

Ted called to say he wouldn't be out that day. "I'm sure the concrete was set up enough anyway that the rain wouldn't hurt it, but we thought we'd cover it, just in case," he reassured her. "And the framed structure will dry out fine."

"Good thinking. Thanks."

She phoned Nick, Horace, and Clyde, telling them she'd see them in a day or two, when it was dry enough to work.

Over coffee and French toast, she and Teresa resumed their conversation. "I simply can't seem to let go of my anger and disappointment with Brad. I was patient with him while he recovered. I feel like I gave him so much, but he's keeping me in limbo, not giving me anything back. I know I'm over-reacting, but I feel like I'm treading water, and I'm exhausted."

Her friend poured more maple syrup over her toast. "I can see that. But he did go through a huge trauma after the accident."

"I understood the trauma—probably even the PTSD—he suffered...maybe still does, but..." she stared into the murky depths of her coffee cup, "why can't he talk to me, tell me what he feels? I think he cares for me. One time he'll say or do something that shows me that, but then the next time he says or does something totally the opposite. Like not leveling with me that he would be in town but couldn't see me. That is, if it really was work. I'm so confused."

"Some men have a difficult time expressing their feelings. Even though Brad is of the 'modern' generation where it's okay to do that, perhaps he was raised by a stoic father, or he is simply wired that way." Teresa speared a chunk of her breakfast. "My dad is like that. He wouldn't say 'Ow' if a rattlesnake bit him on the nose."

Sam chuckled. "Yeah, my dad's that way too. Men! How simple yet complex, how frustrating, how *maddening* they are!" She jolted her cup onto the table, sloshing coffee over the side.

"Can't live with 'em, can't live without 'em," Teresa joked, then peered into her face. "Do you love him?"

Love. Her throat closed. *Do I?* Thoughts of him consumed her when he was away, she ached for him to hold her, to kiss her until her toes tingled, to tell her—yes, *tell* her that he loved her. But, on the other hand, she hadn't told him that either.

"I…I don't know… I think so…" Her face felt hot, and she couldn't look her friend in the eyes.

"Well, I know this is hard for you, but I really do think you need to sit him down and have a heart-to-heart with him."

She rested her head on the table. "Oh, man. I don't know if I want to…to open myself up for more hurt." Raising her face slightly, she squinted at Teresa from the corner of one eye. "What if he tells me he's found somebody else?"

"Then you'll face that with the strength and courage that you know, deep down, you have." She leaned forward. "Life begins at the end of your comfort zone. When you're afraid, simply take one step forward. That's all you need—one step."

Her lips and chin trembled. Her pulse raced. Could she do this? All she wanted to do was run and hide.

CHAPTER TWENTY-FOUR

When the earth absorbed the life-giving moisture from the rain, and the building site had dried out, the crews returned to resume the joyous pounding, buzzing, shrieking sounds of construction.

Horace and Clyde approached Sam, travel cups in hand. "Mornin', little gal."

"Good to have you all back again." She gestured toward the table set up with coffee and sweet rolls. "Can I top off your cups?"

"Sure." Clyde swiped a cinnamon roll. "We wanted to let you know that Robbins fellow stopped by our place the other day."

"Yeah." Horace scrunched his face into a scowl. "He came sniffin' around mine too. I told him to get lost, nobody 'round here was goin' to give him the time o' day."

She curled her lip. "Why? Why are those 'reserve' people persisting? What part of 'NO' don't they understand?"

Clyde pushed his hat back from his forehead. "They claim they're on our side, that they want to help manage the prairie grasses and wildlife in the remote areas of the state, so it doesn't die out."

Horace snorted, spewing a mouthful of coffee into the air. "Yeah, right. They're tryin' to make whole cloth outa two threads. What do they think we've been doin' out here all our lives? We are the original conservationists—before that term became one of their buzzwords."

211

"They *are* offering quite a substantial price in comparison to other prospective buyers," Clyde put in, "and I'm wondering how many of our hard-luck neighbors will be lured by those dollar signs. It *is* a difficult life, and a lot of us aren't gettin' any younger."

"Well, they're not getting an inch of *my* land." She ground her bootheel in the dirt.

"Yeah, they'll have to carry me offa my place, feetfirst." Horace stirred cream into his coffee. "Guess we'd better get back to work or Ted'll be all over us like buzzards on a dead carcass."

Chuckling, she followed them to the barn. The cement floors were dry and smooth, the walls of the addition framed in, and a prickle of excitement ran through her as she pictured her office.

The triangle-shaped roof trusses took shape on the ground, and Ted supervised setting up a method of lifting them to the roof. The crew embedded 2x4s upright into the ground, with "slider poles" angling from there to the top of the wall. Four men lifted a truss onto the slide. A rope between the poles provided support, and he tied additional ropes, which hung from above, onto the truss.

She took in the process with wide-eyed amazement. She'd had no idea how they were going to get the roof supports up so high without a crane.

Men positioned above pulled the truss, inching it up the incline until it reached the top, and then they were able to grab hold of it, move it, and bolt it into place. One went in about every two feet, like puzzle pieces.

"That is ingenious," she told Ted. "I'm quite impressed."

The young man's face flushed, and he ducked his head. "Thanks. It took me all of the last couple of rainy days to figure out how we were gonna do that."

"So the roof goes on before the walls?"

"The trusses anyway. Hopefully we'll get them all up today and maybe get started on putting up plywood and siding on the walls. That is to support the weight of the roof. Plywood and shingles will be next and then the interior finishing."

She clapped him on the back. "Great. It's taking shape. I can hardly wait." She wandered off to observe the crew building trusses for the arena. Pressing fingers to her smiling mouth, she tried to think of how she could repay all these people who had volunteered their time and talents to rebuild her barn.

Horace caught her eye, and she gave him a two-fingered salute. Her eyes welled, but she couldn't find the words to express her gratitude. Heading back to the house, she set about preparing the noon meal of barbecued beef brisket and baked potatoes. Irene, Alberta, and Electra showed up with their daily array of salads and desserts.

"I can't believe how much they've gotten done." Alberta shaded her eyes, squinting to take in the evolving structure.

Electra hovered nearby. "Isn't this exciting? I'm so excited, I'll bet you're so excited you can't stand it! How soon will they be done and when can we decorate your office? Oh, it's going to be so cool!"

Sam put her arm around the girl. "Yes. I am excited and can hardly wait. I don't know how long it'll take yet, but maybe only a few more days. Even with the rain delay, it's going faster than I thought."

"Yeah." The teen whooshed a happy sigh. "I'm gonna run down and visit Apache and Toby…if that's okay with you?"

"Sure, you go ahead. They told me this morning they missed you."

With a grin as big as the outdoors, the girl sprinted toward the pasture.

"Aah, life is good for a teenager and her horses." Alberta winked. "And for a ranchwoman and her new barn."

"Yes." She blinked rapidly. "It sure is."

By the end of the day the roof trusses pointed into the sky, the skeleton of her barn silhouetted against the lavender horizon. Brad had not shown up today, and Sam's thoughts warred between relief and disappointment.

***

Day by day the barn took on more shape. Sam helped the crews nail walls into place and then the wood siding, which would be painted red. Men cut holes for windows and doors, and the plywood went on to form the roof. Nail guns punctuated the song of the saws, and she reveled in the aroma of new wood, the feel of sweat from hard, meaningful work, and yes, even the blisters forming on her hands.

Ted complimented her, Garrett hovered, and Horace teased. "Them boys are sweet on you, little gal."

She scoffed. "No way. We're just having fun, and they're a great help. And so are you, even though you're a bit of an overprotective grandpa."

"Ha!" He guffawed and went back to his work.

The light moment burst its bubble as Brad's truck drove into the yard. Her shoulders slumped. *I know I should, but I don't want to deal with him right now.*

Dragging her feet, she stopped a vehicle's length away as he got out. "Brad. I still don't want to talk to you. You go ahead and do your interviews and your filming, but please, leave me alone."

His hangdog face nearly did her in. Her heart flipped, and she fought the urge to go to him, to comfort him. But she hardened her resolve and spun on her heel.

"Sam, please," he called out. "Please hear me out. I can't eat, I can't sleep…" His voice broke. "I'll be dead in a week if I can't talk to you."

She froze in mid-stride. An overpowering wave of sorrow washed over her, leaving her as weak as a newborn foal. She glanced back over her shoulder. Tears clung to his lashes, making him look like a young boy.

Lifting her palms half-way, she let her hands fall by her sides as she faced him. Claws of deep issues—disappointment, abandonment—scratched at the depths of her soul. She brushed at her face and hair as if to sweep the memories away like debris.

"All right, Brad. We'll talk." Her voice grated, and she steeled herself against all emotion. "But not right now. I have things to deal with. You go ahead and do your filming or whatever, and when I'm ready, I'll let you know."

As she turned away, she heard a sound like air escaping from a deflating balloon. She bit back tears that squeezed from her innermost being, grabbed her hammer, and joined the men building walls.

Sam didn't see Brad again for the next couple of days. She pounded nails into her frustration, she built inner as well as outer walls, she covered her pain like the shingles on the roof.

Her inner voice kept trying to intrude, but she shut it out. "Go away! Leave me alone," she spoke out loud to the voices fighting in her head. The same response stopped Horace, Alberta, and Irene in their well-meaning tracks.

Every evening she rode one of her horses until both were lathered with sweat. But she still wouldn't allow herself to think. When Brad's tearful face came to the surface, it merged into Kenny's. She blotted out the images with harsh words. "Liar! Cheat! Scum! Love 'em and leave 'em. I don't need you. I don't need anyone."

Who are you kidding?

"Be gone, conscience! You don't know anything!"

Adrift in a sea of hopelessness, she rode the swells of anger and self-pity until she thought she would vomit. As she sat on Trixi's back one evening, watching the play of dusky charcoal

215

shadows on the russet hills, Teresa's voice echoed in her mind. "Quit fighting the sails, and let the wind move your boat. Rest. Listen to what God has to say to you. Drift on faith for a while."

The realization hit her with a mule-kick to the solar plexus. In all this turmoil, she had forgotten to talk to God.

She lifted her eyes to the lingering pink wash along the horizon. "I'm sorry, Lord. I know I haven't been a very good daughter. I haven't thanked you for all the wonderful blessings in my life—my friends, my neighbors, my barn…"

Embarrassment blazed up her neck, and she lowered her gaze to the ground. "I seem to only talk to you when I want or need something. But my brain is pickled. I can't think or feel or make decisions. Do I give Brad another chance? Am I being unreasonable? Do I love him? Is he my soulmate? What do I do? Lord, help me. Please."

No voice boomed from the hills. No clap of lightning showed her "the way." Not even a small breeze spoke to give her a clue.

A hot tear trickled over her cheek, and she sighed. "Time to go home, Trixi."

CHAPTER TWENTY-FIVE

Horace, followed by Clyde, arrived at the barn site with news. "A bunch of the ranchers around here are gettin' together at the Jersey Friday evening t' talk about these real estate people and them wantin' to buy up our property."

"Again," Clyde added with a scowl.

"Count me in." Sam's blood boiled, and she clenched her fists at the thought of the slick New Yorkers from the Big Open and now Fred Robbins with this American Prairie group. "What do you think we can do about it?"

"That's what we aim to figger out." Horace took off his hat and scratched at his gray brushcut. "We gotta be united in not selling, not giving in."

"Well, I know *I'm* not selling." She stomped a bootheel into the dirt.

***

Friday found the Jersey Lilly packed with neighbors from miles around who had gathered early to grab a bite to eat before the meeting. Sam joined Horace, Clyde and Irene, Alberta and Electra at a table and ordered a chicken fried steak.

"Good for business, huh?" She teased Billy as he brought their orders.

"Yeah. We oughta have something like this more often." He chuckled. "By the way, there's a TV documentary on at 7 I think you'll all be quite interested in watching."

Sam surveyed the men at the table. "Did you know about this?"

"Just heard a few minutes ago from Billy. Guess it's about this group." Clyde pushed back his plate and stood. Clinking a fork against his glass, he got the room's attention.

"Ladies and gents, thanks for comin' out today. Several of us have had a real estate guy by the name of Fred Robbins, and maybe somebody else, nosin' around and wantin' to buy our ranches for this new 'conservation' project."

"Yeah. I did, and I run 'im off," one man spoke up.

"Me too," another added.

"Well, they *are* offerin' a whole lotta money for these ol' gumbo prairie acres," a stooped, white-haired man said.

"Yeah, I know. It's tempting for some of us." Clyde nodded. "We've worked so hard all our lives, just eking out a living, some years having to borrow to get by. It sure would be nice to get a good price for the land and be able to retire in comfort in our old age."

Horace stood. "I agree with my friend here. But think about it… How many of us would really thrive with nothin' t'do but sit in front of the TV all day in town where your next-door neighbor can pass a cuppa sugar from their window to yours?"

The crowd murmured, heads shaking. "Naw. That's no life." "Wouldn't catch me livin' in a city, cheek and jowl with everybody else."

"Well, I think we need to stick together on this." Horace spoke again. "What they're proposin' doesn't make any sense for this area—lettin' the land go back to grass and putting buffalo—or maybe even elephants like those Big Open guys wanted—in place of our cattle. What tourist in his right mind is gonna come all the way out here to see a buffalo?"

He glanced at Clyde. "No offense, friend. I know you get a few people from back east or California who want to experience the 'western' life on your dude ranch."

"But that's different," Clyde said. "This new reserve wouldn't offer that western lifestyle. It'd just be another glorified zoo."

Billy set a round of drinks on a table nearby. "Well, folks. There is a documentary about this group coming up in a few minutes. Why don't I fire up the television, and we can watch and see what it's all about, then talk some more after."

The program came on, showing film of wide-open prairie dotted with an artist's palette of wildflowers and silver sage, black angus cattle, red and white Herefords, horses and cowboys at roundup.

"Tensions are high over the fate of more than three million acres of public and private land in Montana," a familiar voice spoke over the panorama. "And two groups have very different views on the future of this vast area.

"The American Prairie Reserve, or APR, is a project that has already scooped up more than 450,000 acres of land in Montana, with the aim of creating the largest fully functioning ecosystem in the continental U.S."

The next image showed a map of a remote area between Lewistown and Malta, outlining APR's holdings.

Whistles and exclamations greeted that expanse. "Whoa! That's already happened?"

Sam blinked. "That certainly happened in secret," she whispered to Irene. "I never heard a word about it."

"Us either." Her friend grimaced.

A tall man with sandy hair, dressed in khakis, stood in the midst of knee-high crested wheat grass. "Our mission is to assemble the largest complex of public and private lands devoted to wildlife in the lower forty-eight." He spread his arms wide.

Another man stepped into the picture, brushing a lock of dark brown hair from his forehead. "In comparison, this would be about twenty-five percent larger than Yellowstone National Park."

She gasped. *Brad!* This was his documentary.

"This is Derek Tibbets, APR's CEO," Brad introduced. "And how are you going about accomplishing this land acquisition?"

Tibbets smiled, perfect white teeth glinting in the sun. "We're not asking the federal government for any money. We are engaged in private philanthropy and voluntary exchange by buying ranches from people who want to sell to us."

"And what happens to the ranches and the cattle?"

"This is a wonderful dream to create an 'American Serengeti' of sorts to attract Montanans and people across the world to hike, birdwatch, hunt, or just experience nature."

Brad persisted. "What about the cattle?"

The man's face took on an earnest expression. "Well, this does require removing the livestock that have been overgrazing the land and replacing it with species like elk, antelope, prairie dogs, pronghorn, and bison—animals that once roamed this land naturally."

Clips of a herd of elk and one of buffalo played across the screen.

"Montana's temperate grasslands are just the place for a reserve because of its biodiversity," Tibbets continued. "Grasslands are impeccable carbon sinks because of their ability to absorb carbon dioxide from the atmosphere. Our goal is to restore and preserve the land's ecosystem for years to come."

Sam frowned. *Eco-speak. Trying to confuse us "dumb farmers" with scientific terms.*

Horace scoffed. "Biodiversity. Carbon. Phht."

The film switched to a different location with Brad holding a microphone. "The American Prairie Foundation has raised tens of millions of dollars in recent years, according to tax filings, thanks in large part to foreign and domestic donors, which include well-known Wall Street and Silicon Valley magnates, Mars candy fortune heirs, and a daughter of the founder of the Hewlett-Packard company."

Sam leaned forward. "Oh my gosh! With that kind of backing…"

Clyde's head bobbed slowly. Horace's face had turned a shade of scarlet she had never seen.

Onscreen, Brad continued. "Another group, Save the Cowboy— a grassroots movement of farmers, ranchers, business owners, and families—are working hard to oppose this 'eco-project.' They have the backing of Montana Department of Agriculture Director, Susan Tomey, who says the plan would remove large chunks of land from production agriculture, likely decrease agricultural production revenue, and harm support industries in the area like machinery sales and ranch laborers."

Another panorama of lush wheat fields, rippling in the breeze.

"It's just flatly illegal." Another man came on screen, who Brad introduced as Montana Attorney General Abe Hollowell. "This is federal land that is specifically—by the Taylor Grazing Act of 1934, federal law—set aside for livestock grazing. Bison are not livestock, even under federal law. That's the part everyone seems to be ignoring here."

The image switched to a ranch corral and Brad speaking again. "For third-generation Montana rancher Dede Humes and leader of Save the Cowboy, the reserve is non-negotiable. He held the microphone out to a young, curly-haired blonde woman.

"We don't just 'occupy' this land, and I think that's what a lot of people don't understand. Our life's work is growing food, and this is a hungry world."

Brad interjected. "The U.S. exports a hundred-fifty billion dollars' worth of agricultural products a year."

Something about the woman stirred a sense of deja vu in Sam. Who was this? Did she know her? What she was saying sure made sense.

Dede Hume continued. "This area's grasslands are perfect for cattle ranching and hunting because the grass is high in protein and minerals. It's good for producing beef livestock, and that has been considered the highest purpose of the land for over a hundred years."

Brad stepped in. "As cattle ranchers, there's a lot at stake for Dede's family and land if the reserve goes through. Her family has an operation where they sell calves grown for beef production."

"Wild species such as grizzlies, wolves, and free-roaming bison would be a threat to cattle, and a glut of elk and deer would compete for grass or forage." The young woman's voice rose. "Plus, bison can infect surrounding livestock with brucellosis, a highly infectious disease, and would be extremely costly for us ranchers if it spread to our cattle. We've seen it happen before."

She waved her arm toward a pasture with red and white calves frolicking. "APR's three and a half million-acre goal will wipe out the surrounding vibrant, healthy communities of family ranches and the local cowboy culture.

"We're here to educate the public about the reality of who is 'saving' the prairie and who is exploiting it. This area is viewed as pristine today because of a hundred years of agriculture conservation caring for it and cooperating with the Bureau of Land Management to improve and protect it."

Her face tightened. "And, because APR is a non-profit group, money from taxes and rancher leases of this BLM-owned land would cease and would provide nothing to improve monetary income to the state."

Brad spoke up. "It is already recognized as a world class hunting, fishing, and hiking area while also providing forage for production livestock that helps feed our nation and beyond. Being a cowboy, to Ms. Hume, fosters an independent, entrepreneurial spirit."

"And this was all accomplished long before American Prairie Reserve ever cast their eyes upon it." The sun caught the glint of a tear in the corner of the woman's eye. "And I'm very proud to be a part of that culture."

When the program ended, no one uttered a sound. Sam sat frozen, her mouth agape. She'd had no idea this was going on in her state nor that Brad had been working on a documentary.

Someone scraped a chair in the back of the room and a stir rippled through the crowd as Brad and Dede Hume came forward.

Sam drew in a sharp, audible breath. The blonde woman. That's who she'd seen with Brad at Jakers!

CHAPTER TWENTY-SIX

A blowtorch lit Sam's cheeks aflame. Icy sweat trickled from her armpits.

Brad and Dede stood at the bar with Clyde. "Folks, what you've seen here is just the tip of the iceberg." Brad motioned toward the young woman. "Ms. Hume is struggling mightily to fight this encroaching takeover, and she needs your help."

The room tilted and swirled. *I was wrong!* A strangling band tightened around her mid-section. She shot a glance toward the door. *I've got to get out of here.*

Alberta put a gentle hand on her arm. "It's okay," she mouthed.

"I realize our area is two hundred miles from you," Dede's voice penetrated the fog, "but I've been told that the real estate company involved with APR has been here, putting out feelers."

Heart thumping, brain disconnected, face and neck impossibly hot, Sam struggled to hear.

"...you're not immune to this insidious, secret movement." Dede ran fingers through her curls. "I...we—the Save the Cowboy group—are so grateful to Mr. Ashton for working on this documentary. We need to get the word out to all the farmers and ranchers in the state, and this is going to help a lot."

Sam crossed her arms over her chest and hugged herself tight to contain the screams, the sobs, the compulsion to flee.

He was merely trying to help her group…and me too, because of the Big Open experience.

Brad, Dede, and Clyde brought out more statistics and reasons to fight the APR, repeating loss of livelihood, meat and grain production, and income loss to the state. The information overloaded Sam's brain like a pack mule, and thoughts as tattered and frayed as an old rope fluttered and flapped.

"So, one of the things—besides warning you folks—I would like to do is ask for your support, whether in donations or time or simply getting the word out in any way you can." The young blonde summed up her plea.

Ranchers shouted out questions, and while the trio at the front was engaged, she eased from her chair and slipped out the door. Her whole body shaking, she leaned against the hitchin' post rail in front of the Jersey Lilly, fighting the urge to vomit.

Oh, Lord, I don't know what to do now. I'm so absolutely mortified. I've treated Brad like dirt, and it's me who's scum! I jumped to conclusions and over-reacted, painted him with an "all men are evil" brush. A hot tear scalded her cheek. *Forgive me, Lord? I don't know if Brad will… I wouldn't blame him if he didn't.*

She doubled over and leaned her forehead against the rail, fighting tears of shame, nausea of regret, the pain of all the mistakes she'd ever made in her life. Sobs and dry heaves wracked her body.

A gentle touch on her shoulder, and Electra's voice whispered by her ear. "Sam, Sam. Don't cry. Don't be upset. I'm here. I love you. You're going to be okay."

Another arm encircled her shoulders. Alberta now: "Our girl is right. You *are* strong, you *are* resilient. This is just a momentary glitch in the scheme of things."

She straightened and fixed blurry eyes on her friends. "I don't feel like that… I feel two inches tall… like Lucky could step on me and squash me flat."

The two women hugged her tight. "No, no, that's not true. You've had a stressful couple of weeks, believing Brad betrayed you, and now you've had a huge shock." Alberta rubbed her back. "Let's get you home, so you can process and recover from this earthquake."

Sam sat in her rocking chair and allowed her friends to care for her. Alberta covered her with a knitted afghan, Electra made hot chocolate, and both sat with her and talked and listened.

"Horace told me there was more to what I saw and that I should talk to Brad." She hiccupped. "But I was on my high horse, and I knew what I saw, and I wouldn't listen to reason."

A sip of the hot brew soothed her nerves. "I think I made Brad pay the price for Kenny's betrayal. I lumped them together, and they are nowhere near alike." A pain pressed her chest so fierce she thought her ribs would crack. "I messed up. Maybe he'll never speak to me again, after the way I've treated him."

"I think he will." The teen's face shone with hope.

"Okay, you made a mistake, but it's not the end of the world. It's fixable." Alberta peered at her earnestly.

"I hope so."

Her friend nodded. "I agree with Electra. He will. I believe a good talk is in order."

Silence settled over the three as Sam sat and rocked and thought. *Will he? Do I deserve a second chance?*

The sound of an engine broke through the quiet.

Electra leaped from the couch and peered out the window. "It's Brad!" She giggled. "I told you!"

The two women gathered their things and headed for the door. "Forgive him," Electra mouthed.

Alberta winked and turned the knob. "Why, hello, Brad. We're just leaving. Good job on that documentary, by the way.

Wow! That was eye-opening." She stepped onto the porch and held the door open for him.

"See ya later, Bra-ad," Electra sing-songed as she bounced past him and down the steps.

Sam's blood had congealed in a cold mass throughout her body. She stood rooted to the spot in the living room where she had risen from her rocker when the teen yelled her announcement. *Oh, dear Lord, what do I say? What can I do to make this right?* Her fingers trembled, and her legs disappeared from the knees down.

Brad stepped into the room, holding his ballcap in his hands.

She followed him with her gaze as he moved slowly toward the couch.

"Brad." "Sam." They both spoke at once.

Her lip curled upward a tiny fraction. "Please. Sit down." Her voice came out a squeak, as if she'd inhaled from a helium balloon. She collapsed into her chair. Gulping a big draught of air, she released it between pursed lips. "Brad. I owe you a huge apology." Her voice quavered.

He said nothing, his face stony.

Pain slingshot like a rock into her chest. "I saw you with your head close to Dede's at Jaker's, after you'd told me you weren't going to be in town, and I *assumed* you'd found someone else."

He bobbed his head, just a fraction, his gaze riveted on her.

She closed her eyes for a moment. *This is not going well.* "I jumped to conclusions. I wouldn't let you explain. I was wrong, Brad. I'm sorry, so very sorry."

"Yeah." His chest rose and fell. "You hurt me."

A gasp as sharp as a dagger slid through her windpipe. For a split-second her defenses rose. *Who hurt whom? You're not entirely innocent here.* But she forced herself into calm. "I know I did. And I didn't mean to do that. I was hurt too. I thought you'd lied to me. You've been…distant…and I…I didn't know where we stood… If there was a 'we'." Nerves flapped like a sheet in the wind.

His gaze dropped to his boots, and a flush rose up his neck.

Outside, a sudden gust whirled a dust devil through the open window.

She couldn't breathe.

The seconds crawled around the clock on the wall as he finally raised his eyes to face her. "You're right. I know I'm not without blame."

He rose from the couch and moved to stand in front of the window. "I might not be the best man for you, Sam." He swiveled his head toward her. "I don't know if I can give you what you want."

His words raked through her like barbed wire. *No! Is he setting me up for more heartache?*

She stood and made her way to his side. "Brad. Please don't give up on us over my silly, stupid pride. I'm sorry for the way I reacted. Can't you see your way to forgive me?" She placed a tentative hand on his arm.

"The question is, can I forgive myself?" He stared out the window again.

The breeze ruffled the curtains.

"Brad. We need to talk to each other, to communicate. You need to tell me how you feel and what you're thinking." She squeezed his arm. "And I need to do the same."

Silence hovered over them like a specter from the past. He stood, pitchfork-rigid.

Then, he whirled and grabbed her shoulders, peering intently into her face.

He's going to kiss me. The realization rippled through her. *And oh, I want him to.*

His spicy aftershave smelled of promise.

Leaning in, he brushed her lips with velvet. She sank into the warm place where their bodies touched, a glow radiating through her clothes. Was this his answer? Was there an "us"?

Then, as quickly as he began, he broke away. "Yes. We do. We need to talk, seriously."

He led her to the couch, and they sat, side by side. Holding her hands in his, he searched her face with an intense gaze.

At last, he spoke, his voice raspy. "I'm sorry too. I know I've been difficult to be around all these months as I recovered from that…stupid…accident." His gaze flicked downward again and then back. "And I don't know if I'm all the way there yet. You've been more than patient with me, and I *have* been distant. I've tried not to be, but…"

A nervous little pulse thrummed beneath her skin. She stared at the slope of his cheek, the dark lock that fell so boyish over his forehead.

"I wanted to do something special, to make up for that distance. I know how hard you've worked, first to buy this ranch, and since then to build it into your dream therapy center." His gaze softened and rested on her face. "I was afraid this new group was like the Big Open guys and would try some kind of take-over here and endanger your place."

She nodded. "There has been a real estate guy hanging around lately."

"Robbins, right? Well, when you asked me to look into the APR, I began the research and dug up all kinds of secretive dealings. The station okayed doing the documentary, and I got so involved in that, I neglected you. And I didn't keep you in the loop." He cleared his throat and glanced away. "I wanted to surprise you. To please you." His gaze returned to hers. "To make you proud of me."

Her heart puddled. "Oh, Brad. I *am* proud of you. That was one heck of a documentary. And you are helping Dede and her family and all the other ranchers in that area... And by extension, the ranchers around here too."

"This is only the beginning. I'm working on a series." His face tightened. "We've *got* to stop these guys. They're endangering our state."

The powerful emotion in his words enveloped her. *Why can't he show* me *that kind of passion?*

When she didn't respond, he shook his head. "Sorry. Here I go again. I'm off on my work tangent." His voice fell soft. "This is supposed to be about *us*."

"Is...is there a chance...at an *us?* Do you forgive the foolish way I acted?" Nerves knotted inside.

"I do, Sam, I do. Can you forgive me for neglecting you?"

She dared not speak but bobbed her head in rapid succession.

His shoulders visibly relaxed. He put his hands on her upper arms and leaned forward. "Sam. I love you. I don't want to lose you. I'll do whatever it takes..." His voice choked with hoarseness.

Love! Oh, dear Lord. He said it! Joy, like sunshine, flooded her body, and the words formed and pushed their way through her lips. "I love you too," she whispered.

He kissed her then, at first softly, gently, the intensity increasing until she was afraid her mouth would be bruised. A curl of heat kindled in the pit of her stomach and twin flames of wonder and passion ignited as she melted into him.

CHAPTER TWENTY-SEVEN

Noise from the barn crew arriving brought Sam from her morning love- and sun-drenched daze. She hurriedly gathered her cereal bowl and coffee cup and dumped them in the sink. At a fast clip, she headed to the site to join the already laughing, joking, jostling group.

"G'morning, Sam," Ted called out. "I think we're on the last leg of this project."

Her gaze took in the shingled roof, the walls, the arena covering. *It's almost there.* "I think so too. Thanks, Ted. Again…I don't know how to thank you."

"Phht." He waved a hand to dismiss the thought.

Horace lifted his travel cup in a salute. "Mornin', little gal. You look chipper."

"It's a great day." She grinned at him, her insides warm and mushy after her evening with Brad. *He loves me.* A tiny squeak escaped her lips. *And I love him!*

"Oh yeah?" Her elderly neighbor peered at her from beneath his hat brim, his mouth quirking upward.

"Yeah. You were right. Brad had an explanation. I was such a ninny for not letting him tell me. It could've saved me a hay wagon load of stress and grief and anger…" She blew out a flutter of frustration at herself.

"Yup. Hindsight's 20/20, as they say." He took a sip of his coffee. "That documentary—he did a heckuva job. What an eye-opener and a huge problem for our state."

She nodded. "Well, here's hoping that with his series, eyes *will* be opened, and more people will join the Save the Cowboy group."

"They've got my support. I wrote Dede out a check last night. A bunch of us did."

"Oh, Horace, you're such a peach. Thank you for that…and thank you for always supporting me. I'll send her one too." She gave him a peck on the cheek. "Well, I better get to work. There are inside walls to be spackled and sanded and painted."

She stepped inside the structure. Men were building stalls, some putting in windows, others inside her office mixing mud to smooth out the walls. The structure—at least twice as big as her old barn—smelled of new lumber. The dirt floor was tamped hard and even, and the sun beamed through the openings, sending dust motes dancing as the crew moved to and fro. A heady breathlessness lifted her onto a fluffy cloud of anticipation.

Sensing a presence behind her, she swiveled to see Brad enter. Her temperature notched higher, and her body hummed. "Good morning."

"Yes, it is." He encircled her with strong arms and gave her a heat-seeking-missile kiss. Then he swept an arm wide. "Hot dog! Look at this. Now, *this* is a *barn*. Whooee!"

He took her arm, and they went into the tack room, where racks and shelves and hooks were being installed on weathered barnwood walls. "From Horace's old shed," she pointed out.

"Looks great." He peered through a doorway. "This your office?"

She caught her lip between her teeth as she stuck her head in. More gray barnwood paneling on one wall, with sheetrock on the others. Mentally, she arranged a desk, filing cabinets, maybe a plush leather chair or two, a southwestern woven rug… "Oh, it's going to be beautiful."

Sondra came in, carrying a bucket. "Hey, guys. This is awesome. Can't wait to see it finished."

"Me too." Sam took the bucket. "What can I do to help?"

Soon, she and Brad had trowels in their hands and under Ted's supervision, sealed and smoothed the corners and nail holes in the sheetrock. As she worked, she stole glances at Brad out the corner of her eye, full of hope and promise. She caught him gazing at her, and they exchanged a secret smile.

At lunch break, they brought their plates back to the office and sat cross-legged on the floor. "So, we're good?" Brad raised hopeful eyebrows.

"Yeah." She squeezed his arm. "One thing, though… You never did explain why you were in town when you said you wouldn't be…and why did you look like you were cozying up to Dede Hume?"

He choked on a bite of his sandwich. "Oh. That. Well, I'd been in Helena and Bozeman interviewing the 'powers that be' and got a phone call that Dede was in Billings, wanting to talk to me. So I came back early… intending to call you when I was done interviewing her." He grimaced. "Messed up on that one."

"Okay." She peered into his flushed face.

"And why we looked 'cozy' as you say…um… I'm not sure why you would think that." He gazed at the top of the wall where it joined the ceiling. "Ahh. I remember. We were studying the map. The one that showed that area the APR already has under their control."

Hmm. That would explain it. After all, I only saw them for a split second…before I ran off half-cocked. She expelled a long sigh. "All right. I can see where I could've jumped to conclusions there. Gosh, just goes to show how important *communication* is."

He studied the toe of his boot. "Yeah. I hear ya." He raised his eyes to hers. "And I'm going to try…really hard…to be better at that, I promise. I want to rebuild your trust, and I

233

know it's going to take a while to do that…if you can be patient with me a little longer?"

With her newfound headiness in the "L-word," she was nearly ready to say to heck with the past hurts and frustrations and *yes* to the future. Almost. "Yes, I think I can. But how do I know you won't leave, pull back again when things get tough? When you have that itch to go after another story?"

He cleared his throat. "I know I don't have a very good track record in that department. I guess I have found it easier to step away, pull back, put up barriers since…the accident. All I can say is that I want to try to do better. I'm working on it, still seeing the counselor. As for the next story, that's my job. I don't know what I can do about that…right now anyway."

"Okay, fair enough. I have to give you that." *No, it certainly wouldn't be right to expect him to quit his career.* "And I know you're still working through things. I understand." She chewed the inside of her cheek. "I have some things to work through too. I admit I can be a little hot-headed…sometimes."

With a grin, he pulled her close with a one-armed embrace. "Well, now that I know you do love me, and you know I love you…although I *assumed* you did know that…" he chuckled, "we can get through anything and everything—together. Right?"

A mellow peace flowed through her body as she nestled against him. "Right."

CHAPTER TWENTY-EIGHT

When in the house, Sam stopped by every window to gaze at the barn. The new structure shone big and bright, its red-painted exterior and white trim contrasting with the clear aquamarine sky. Outside, she stood at the corral fence for endless minutes, forgetting the chore at hand. She breathed in the scent of newness inside, marveled at the spaciousness, and reveled in her office.

Electra, Alberta, and Irene came every day with fabric swatches, photos, and ideas. Teresa joined in, took her to Miles City to shop for furniture—a large antique oak desk, complementary file cabinets, a pair of leather chairs. The tiny apartment above became a "pajama party" of designing, decorating, and girl-time. Electra squealed her delight when a full-sized bed became adorned with a colorful galloping-horse quilt and curtains to match. A dark brown recliner completed the living area, and the kitchenette boasted a microwave, apartment-sized refrigerator, and a hot plate.

"Ohmygosh!" Her eyes rounded. "Maybe I could come live here."

Sam giggled as her mom barked a laugh. "You. Have to live with me...that is, if you are to continue home-schooling." Alberta cocked a hip and gave a mock-frown. "Otherwise, if you move out, you're moving to town for high school."

"Nooo." The teen shrieked and dropped to one knee, her eyes raised beseechingly. "Not that! Anything but that, Mom, I

235

promise to be good." Then she cocked an eyebrow at Sam. "But…maybe when I graduate and turn eighteen…"

The women laughed again.

"Okay, okay. We'll cross that bridge when we come to it."

Sam gave the girl a tight hug. "I'd love that." She felt full and warm as if she'd stepped from deep shadow into a patch of sunlight. Her family. Her barn. Her ranch.

***

Brad spent the weekdays working on the APR documentary series, calling her every night, and coming out every weekend. Their time together was sweet and tender, navigating their way forward with this newfound relationship.

They rode together, counted calves together, marveled as the summer sun toasted the landscape varying shades of sage and gold. They talked for hours over coffee or a glass of wine, exploring the depths of each other's lives. Love grew in a place of softness as they made plans and held hands. Her heart made a funny little jump in her chest whenever she first saw him. Hope planted seeds, sprouted, and grew roots.

"It's like I'd been missing something all my life, and then I wasn't," she told Teresa. "We're still taking things slow. But we're talking. We're sharing. We're *communicating*."

Her friend nodded knowingly. "Very wise. Very wise indeed."

***

The veterans group arrived one Friday afternoon for their session and the celebratory barbecue Sam had planned to thank them and the neighbors for their part in raising her barn. Now that she had a covered arena, she alternated every other week, going to Miles City one Friday and the vets coming to the ranch the other, towing a trailer with extra horses.

Brad was there to continue interviewing and filming for the piece he was working on about the program. After he greeted her with a tight hug and lingering kiss, Garrett approached her, scuffing his boots in the dirt.

"Ms. Sam, I...uh...see that you and Brad are...sweet on each other." His face reddened. "I admire you so much, and I...uh...kinda had hopes..." His gaze flickered from her face to his boots and back again. "But I'm really happy for you. You deserve the best, and Brad's a great guy." Spinning on his heel, he sprinted to the corral.

She blinked against the sudden sting in her eyes. *What a sweet thing to say.* It had taken guts to tell her that. *How much he has grown!* She took in the sight of the group grooming, walking, and tacking the horses, Electra supervising every step. *And she has too.* Her lungs filled to the fullest.

With a bouncing stride, she made her way to where Elliot brushed Apache. He was still reluctant to ride, still had a ways to go before she considered him a success story. "How are you doing today?"

His usually-grim face wreathed a smile. "Pretty good, thanks. Nice to be back with the horses. Barn looks good though—it was fun to help."

"Thanks, Elliot, that means a lot, and I'm so grateful for that help. I hope you'll enjoy the barbecue this evening."

"Oh, I will." He stroked the gelding's mane. "Ms. Moser... I think...I'd like to try riding again today."

An electric pulse zinged through her. *Whoa! Did I hear him right?* "You want to ride? Of course. That'd be great. Do you want me to saddle him up? And, please call me Sam."

"I'd like to try myself, but you'll help me, won't you, Ms. ...uh...Sam?"

"Absolutely." She stood close by as he smoothed Apache's back before gently placing the blanket on and then the saddle, all the while talking to him in a low tone. He hesitantly reached under the horse's belly to grab the cinch.

Sam hid a smirk, seeing him glance toward the gelding's hind hooves. "It's okay. He's used to it. Go ahead and pull it tight, then test it with one foot in the stirrup."

It took a couple of tries to get the strap tight enough not to roll the saddle off, but when Elliot finally was able to mount, his beaming face nearly outshone the sun.

"Good job." She took hold of the bridle cheekpiece and led them around the arena. As they returned to where the rest of the group had gathered, Del and Garrett began a slow clap. "Oorah! You did it, man."

Elliot's grin grew even wider. And so did Sam's.

About 5:00, neighbors began to arrive, led first by Horace, then Clyde and Irene. The men brought their fiddles and guitars, and Irene had a keyboard in hand, along with a huge bowl of potato salad. Soon, the smell of charcoal and meat cooking filled the arena, and laughter overflowed.

Sam hugged herself, and a feeling of weightlessness lifted her as she bounced on her toes to the music in the background. Since the barn was finished, she had missed those sounds of the crew yelling, joking, and teasing each other.

Brad came alongside and put an arm around her shoulders. "What a group, huh?" His eyes danced as he took in the scene.

"Aah, yes. This…" she swept an arm out, unable to speak for a moment, "…this is what it's all about, isn't it? Friendships, neighbors helping neighbors, food, music."

"Yes, it is." He tapped his upper lip. "You know, I've been without this sort of thing too long. I've been isolating myself. And that's not healthy."

A sense of serenity blanketed her, like a hug from God. She lifted her eyes to the cloudless sky. *Thank you, Lord.*

Ted and Garrett approached, plates loaded, with Del wheeling alongside. "You two better go get something to eat before it's all gone." Ted chortled.

"As if. Plenty of grub left." Garrett smirked. "But we wanted you to be the first to hear our news."

Sam cocked her head. "News?"

"Yeah. Me and the guys, and Sondra too—with Ted's help—we're going to start a company to help others with remodeling, handyman stuff, small building projects."

Her mouth fell open.

"At first, helping other veterans, then maybe branching out," Del added.

"Oh my stars! Wow." *These guys, these wonderful guys.* What they'd experienced in war as an incurable wound, an unbearable hurt, was healing and had sprouted new wings. "You never cease to amaze me. I'm at a loss for words. What a great idea."

"Yeah. Taking that carpentry class at the college and then helping build your barn... It was so satisfying, and well, this is the next logical step." The paraplegic's face shone.

"And I need partners," Ted put in. "We're going to call it Helping Hands Construction."

Brad stuck out his hand to shake with the three men. "Perfect. Congratulations. I'm going to include this in my documentary."

Sam stepped forward to hug each one. "I. Am. So. Proud of you." Her eyes misted and blurred.

Brad went to his truck for his camera and soon had the whole veterans' group corralled.

Nick caught her eye and ambled over. "Look what you've done, Samantha Moser."

"Oh, no, no, no, not me." Her voice came out husky, tear-swollen. "It was the horses. And God's hand. I was just the conduit." She grasped his arm. "Thank you for giving me the chance to work with them. I've learned as much as they have. And, best of all, I know this is what I'm meant to do."

He nodded slowly, a smile on his lips. "That is the absolute truth. It's your gift, and I'm honored to work with you." He

239

looked like a proud papa as his gaze took in the group talking to Brad. "This crew is ready to graduate. Are you ready for a new class this fall?"

She gulped. She hadn't thought that far ahead. But yes, this group was ready to ride and grow and fly and build buildings. With a grin, she answered, "You bet I am."

After everyone had more than sated themselves with beef, beans, salads, and every dessert imaginable, the musicians brought out their instruments. The cacophony of tuning, conversations, and laughter quieted as the group swung into a lively rendition of "Buffalo Gals."

Teresa's beau, Alan, was the first to twirl her out onto a hard-packed "dance floor" in the arena. Other couples followed suit, and the rest clapped along to the old tune.

Ted held out a hand and invited Sam to join him in "Boot Scootin' Boogie." Garrett claimed her for a medium tempo dance, guiding her nicely despite his prosthetic foot, and Del spun her around his chair to "Can the Circle be Unbroken."

"Thanks guys! That was fun." Laughing breathlessly, she dropped onto a hay bale to rest, taking a big swig from a water bottle.

The band slowed the tempo with Charlie Rich's "The Most Beautiful Girl in the World," and she glanced up to see Brad holding out his hand. "This seems like an appropriate one," he drew her into his arms, "since you are."

Her body melted against his as they swayed, cheek to cheek, eyes closed, his hand warm against her back. When the song ended, they continued holding each other in a heady embrace as the musicians played another slow song, "Keeper of the Stars."

With the next up-tempo tune, Brad spun her away and back to him in a jitterbug. Happiness skipped through her limbs and gave her feet wings. She threw her head back and laughed, a joyous, hearty laugh such as she hadn't experienced in a long time.

After the sky had turned to indigo and a moon like a thin sickle hung in the midst of the Milky Way, Horace stepped to the microphone. "Folks, this has been a most wonderful day of celebration. Thank you all for your hard work in helping Sam build her new barn, and thank you for sharing the fun. Now, to close out the evening, we have a surprise."

A burst of light rose from the pasture beyond, exploding into a million bright colors. As one, the crowd breathed, "Ooooh! Aaaah!" as another firework followed in greens and blues, then one in reds, oranges, and golds.

Sam leaned against Brad on their hay bale, and he encircled her with his arm, hugging her close.

When the red, white, and blue finale had died down, the group gathered their spouses and friends, stopping by to give Sam hugs and shake Brad's hand. "Wonderful party. We haven't had so much fun in a coon's age. Thank you."

"No, thank *you.*" Sam wanted to pour her appreciation and love into each person. "You don't know how much I value your help and your friendship."

As the last taillights winked away down the drive, Sam and Brad remained on their hay bale, basking in the afterglow of the party atmosphere.

"What a great day." She exhaled a long and satisfied breath.

"Yeah. It was." Brad picked at stems from the bale, played them between his fingers. "Perfect."

A chitter of crickets serenaded as a breeze teased through the pasture grasses and stars flickered in the endless sky.

Brad turned his body toward her and slid down on one knee. "Samantha Moser, I love you. I've missed what we had before, treasure what is growing between us now, and I want to spend the rest of my life with you. Will you marry me?"

Her heart galloped, her blood surged electric through her veins, and her tongue tied itself into knots. "Uh…uh…" *Love. Life together. Marry.* The words ricocheted through her brain until they finally rested in the right spot. She looked into his dark chocolate eyes and knew he meant every tender word.

"Oh, Brad. Yes." Her answer whispered past trembling lips. "Yes, I will marry you."

He held up a twisted straw circlet and slid it on her finger. "I want us to pick out your ring together."

"Thank you. I would love that. And I love you."

They rose together in a rapturous embrace, an achingly sweet kiss, the air around them charged with an energy filling all the empty spots left dark for so long.

CHAPTER TWENTY-NINE

Teresa squealed like Electra when Sam called with the news. "I knew it! I could see it in his eyes! Oh, girlfriend, this is *fantastic*. We gotta get together and make wedding plans—are you free tonight?"

"Yes, as a matter of fact, I am." A euphoric giggle erupted. "I'm going to call Alberta, Electra, and Irene and invite them over too. We can have a little hen party."

"I'll bring the wine." Her friend's ecstatic voice rose. "And the *Bride* magazines."

At 7:00 Sam's friends roared up the driveway, spilling out with shrieks and laughter, bottles of wine, crackers, cookies, and tubs of homemade ice cream. Electra stood on the porch and pounded her feet up and down in a crazy, joyful drumbeat. "Sam, Sam, Sam, you're getting married, ohmygosh, you're getting married! I'm so happy, so happy, *so* happy."

She grabbed the teen in a tight hug. "Me too."

They congregated on the porch, where Teresa spilled out a grocery bag of magazines. "We gotta pick out a dress for you, go shopping, who's going to marry you, where will the ceremony be—"

"Hold on, hold on." She held up a palm. "Let's not get too carried away. I want to keep it *very* simple. I'm not into big and flashy."

Teresa mock-pouted. "Oh, okay. If you insist." Then the grin was back.

"Have you set a date yet?" Irene asked.

243

"It'll be the third Saturday in September, right here in my new arena. Brad is contacting their family pastor—"

"September! That's only two months away." Teresa's eyes saucered.

"Like I said, simple. That gives us plenty of time." Sam quirked her mouth upward. "Irene's already consented to make the cake. Will you three be my bridesmaids?"

"Yes! Absolutely! Of course!" The women's words tumbled over each other.

"I need to get invitations out soon. I'll have to send one to my folks in Alaska, if I can find an address for them." Her mouth pulled down at the corners. "I know they won't make it, but I guess I should at least let them know…"

"Well, yeah, you should. I'm sure they'll be happy for you." Teresa patted her arm. "Do you have a photo of you and Brad? I'll have my secretary design a mock-up of an invitation for you, if you'd like."

Over wine and snacks, magazine photos and ideas were presented and rejected, hashed and rehashed as plans built a foundation for this milestone.

***

One evening in August, Brad called from Billings. "The piece on the veterans' program is set to air this Friday evening."

She gulped a breath. "Okay. I'll call Billy and let him know he can expect a crowd at the Jersey that night. The vets will be here that day for their class, so I'm sure they'll want to stay and watch with us." Her tennis-playing butterflies re-emerged. How would she look in this documentary? Surely not as tongue-tied and foolish as she'd felt when Brad interviewed her.

As if reading her mind, his voice wafted soothingly over the phone line. "You're great in this. You did perfect."

She whooshed out the air she'd been holding. "I know you're just saying that. After all, you're a bit prejudiced, but thanks."

244

He chuckled. "All right then. See you Friday. Love you."

After the call disconnected, she sat for long minutes, her entire body smiling. *Love. I found my love.*

Friday evening found the Jersey Lilly packed nearly to overflowing with all the neighbors who'd helped with the barn build, plus the veterans, and a several tourists visiting the Bruckners' dude ranch.

Sam and Brad joined Horace, Alberta and Electra already seated.

"Well, here's the happy couple." Horace gave them his signature grin.

Nerves tickled her insides. She sat and picked up a menu, although she knew it by heart.

"I'm so excited, aren't you excited? We're famous again—we might as well be movie stars!" Electra gushed.

Sam gave a wry laugh. "You might be, but I wish it could've been done without me."

"Aww, you don't mean that," Alberta put in. "You were great in the last one. And look at the response it received—you were able to rescue Trixi and got enough donations to help rebuild your barn."

"That's true. It was overwhelming, and I *am* grateful, Brad." She took his hand. "I don't mean to belittle your efforts. It's just that…"

"You're a reluctant star. I know." He beamed a smile at her. "That's one of the things I love about you."

Ordering their usual steaks and burgers, they tried to eat a few bites in between friends and neighbors stopping by to congratulate them on their engagement.

At the appropriate time, Billy switched on the TV. The title "From Hurt to Healed" flashed on the screen. The opening credits rolled over a familiar scene of Sam riding down the hill on Sugar. She gasped. It was the original shot Brad had featured in the first documentary. The one she'd been so mad at him about taking without her consent. The one that had launched their relationship. She shot him a look. His face creased in a satisfied grin.

The first scene showed Del and Garrett grooming their mounts. "It all started when Garrett Webb came to visit Samantha Moser after hearing about her success in working with teens and her rescued horses…"

"Working with Sam and her horses has literally saved my life," Garrett spoke earnestly into the camera. "I was a pretty reluctant recruit, even though I sought her out, but she has the patience of a saint. And now I'm a 'regular' cowboy." He flashed a dimple and doffed his western hat.

The camera switched to Del in his wheelchair. "And Trixi, a rescue horse who kneels, has enabled me to ride. That ability makes me feel…normal, no longer confined to this iron horse."

Sam's eyes filled as each veteran gave his or her story. The film captured them at work with the horses, riding with her and Electra, and then at the barn construction site. Even the clips of her interview reassured her that she hadn't committed a faux pas, as her earnest praise of her vets group filled the room. Her young teen friend proved to be a natural in front of the camera, poised and well-spoken—no gushing run-on exclamations.

"I'm proud of you," she whispered to the girl, whose face shone with the praise.

The documentary finished with the completed barn and arena, the veterans talking about Helping Hands Construction and a plug for "Sam's Rescue Ranch."

The room erupted in applause. Someone began an off-key rendition of "For she's a jolly good fellow…" Sam's face heated, and she stared at the table, hating and loving the accolades at the same time.

One by one, the vets, followed by her neighbors, stopped by the table to shake Brad's hand and give her a hug. "That was fun," Sondra whispered, "thank you for what you've done for us."

Her heart nearly exploded with love and gratitude for "her" little group.

***

When Brad came for his visit the following weekend, he bounded up the porch steps with a canary-eating grin. He stepped into the kitchen, gave her a one-armed hug and a long, deep kiss. Then, from behind his back, he produced a bouquet of multi-hued carnations and daisies.

"Oh, wow, this is lovely. Thank you." She opened a cupboard and took out a vase. When she turned to retrieve the flowers, he flashed a piece of paper at her.

"What is this?" She squinted at the numbers printed there. "Huh? What?"

"This, my dear," he jabbed a finger at the bottom, "is the total of donations that have come in so far for 'Sam's Rescue Ranch'."

Her chest tightened and stole her breath. "Oh," she whispered through pursed lips. "For me? Ohmygosh, as Electra would say."

He bobbed his head slowly, a satisfied smirk on his lips. "We did it, my girl! You're in business. Now, you *have* to incorporate your operation."

"Especially since nobody ever found the JB guys to get my money back. Now I can get the arena closed in before winter…" she gazed out the window, "and I can give Ted that bonus I promised. And Horace told me about shipping containers we can repurpose into bunkhouses." Her cheeks hurt from the huge grin. "Oh, Brad, it's all because of you. Thank you for pushing me to do the interview, and thank you for this documentary—it's the best wedding gift you could ever give me." She grabbed him in a soft embrace, kissing him until it deepened into velvet and stars.

CHAPTER THIRTY

The RSVPs were in, her bridesmaids busy decorating the arena, with Brad setting up rented folding chairs. The weather forecast was for a perfect 78 sunny degrees.

"No fussing now," Teresa took Sam in hand after she hyperventilated about the food, who was coming and who wasn't, how to set up a sound system to play the wedding march, and how everything was going to work, down to the minute.

"You sit back and let your friends take care of the last-minute details. All you have to do tomorrow is get dressed and show up on time." Her friend smoothed Sam's hair.

"Easier said than done." She fluttered her lips. "Okay. As my maid of honor, you're in charge, and I know I can blame you if anything goes wrong."

Teresa giggled. "That's right, my dear. But nothing will."

She studied the guest list once again. Robin and the group home kids were bringing Miss Ellie, Trixi's original owner. Brad's family would all be there, of course, and her aunt Monica had called to say she would absolutely be there. She'd recently returned from a European book tour, just in time for the wedding. And childhood friend Jace would be there too!

Excitement tickled Sam's ribs. She hadn't seen her favorite aunt in a long time, the one who'd written books about her great-grandma Nettie and her rodeo career. Then a pinprick of disappointment burst the bubble. She hadn't heard a word from her parents. They lived so far out from "civilization" in Alaska that she wasn't sure the invitation would reach them, but she'd sent one anyway. *Oh well. It is what it is, as "they" say.*

She squared her shoulders and wandered to the arena where Ted and Jimmy were building a lattice archway. "Oh wow. That's going to be beautiful. Thank you."

"Our pleasure." Jimmy's face beamed. "The least I can do to help, after you've helped me so much."

Ted grinned. "What he said."

What a sweet guy. He'll make some lucky young girl a great catch. She smiled back.

Later, enjoying a glass of iced tea on the porch with Brad and Teresa, she heard an unfamiliar engine approach from the main road. She glanced at her watch. "Everyone's done for the day. Wonder who that could be?"

A dusty old blue Econoline van chugged up the drive and parked in front of the house.

She rose from the porch swing and strolled to the top of the steps, cocking her head in puzzlement.

A tall man with gray-threaded long hair and a mountain man beard emerged from the driver's side, and from the other door a woman stepped out, stretching her arms above her head. Her reddish mane flowed over the shoulders of a tie-dyed shirt in golds and browns that topped a long, rust-colored bohemian-style skirt. "Hi, Sam."

She drew in a sharp gasp. "Mom. Dad. You came!" For a moment she froze, a thousand images and emotions flickering through her. Then, flying down the steps, she grabbed them in a huge hug. "I can't believe it. You're here."

"Hey, we wouldn't miss our daughter's wedding for the world." Her dad's kind smile lit his face.

"We got your invitation, threw some things in the van, and lead-footed it down here." Mom kissed her cheek.

"You drove all the way from Alaska in *that?*"

Dad chuckled. "Yup. Runs like a top. The old ones are still the best."

"Oh, my word." Giddiness rose from her core. "C'mon up and have some iced tea. You must be parched."

As the trio stepped onto the porch, Brad rose and put out a hand to shake.

"Mom, Dad, this is my fiancé, Brad Ashton. Brad, Lisa and Kevin Moser."

"Welcome to the family, Brad. So nice to meet you." Her mom hugged him.

"And my friend and maid of honor, Teresa Knudson." More hugs and handshakes.

Sam dashed into the house for glasses and cookies and served her parents, still floating in a daze, not believing they really had shown up for her wedding. Old issues threatened the new happiness—they'd left her behind, she hadn't heard from them in months…years—would she measure up now? Brushing those conflicting memories aside, she returned to the present.

After they'd visited a while, Teresa took her leave. "See you all tomorrow."

Sam hugged her. "See you then. Thank you, friend."

As Teresa drove off, Mom leaned against the porch rail. "You have a lovely place."

"Thanks. I love it here. C'mon, you guys, let us show you my new barn that was just completed and my arena, and oh my goodness, I have so much to tell you about." She felt like Electra, gushing out anything and everything that came into her mind—her rescue horses, how she came to work with troubled teens and then with the veterans, buying the ranch, the barn fire, and how all the neighbors came together to help rebuild.

"That's great." Her dad's gaze swept the set-up, the corrals and pasture. "I vaguely remember this place when Grandpa and

Grandma had it. I couldn't have been more than four or five years old when they sold it and moved away. It's so peaceful here. I can see why you love it."

"I do. It's a part of family history, and I feel honored to continue it."

They ate steaks Brad barbecued, drank homemade chokecherry wine her parents brought, and tried to catch up for years apart in mere hours.

Brad lifted a glass. "So, what made you decide to go off-grid in Alaska? Why not Montana?"

Sam's mom emitted a snort. "Well, to begin with, we went up to escape a huge mountain of debt. Worked on fishing boats and in canneries until we were able to pay it off."

Dad picked up the thread. "By that time, the old bones were gettin' creaky, and we decided the fisherman's life was a little too hard. We had enough to buy a few acres near Healy and build our cabin."

"We raise a garden, chickens, goats, pigs, and a few cows. We have a solar generator and a water catchment system," Mom added. "Healy is under a thousand people, and we're a hundred-ten miles south of Fairbanks and two-fifty north of Anchorage."

Sam raised her brow. "Wow. And I thought I was living in the middle of nowhere."

Her dad chuckled. "Nope. I think we can claim that title. And that suits me just fine. Too many people around here to suit me anymore."

As the evening waned and headed for midnight, Brad excused himself to go upstairs to bed, and Dad headed to the barn where they would stay in the new apartment above Sam's office.

She and her mom lingered over one more glass of wine. "So, Mom..." She hated to bring up the elephant in her mind, but that hole of abandonment still hadn't been filled. "Why did you just take off and leave me behind and then hardly ever write or call or let me know if you were still alive?"

Mom smoothed strands of hair behind her ear. "Whew. That's heavy." She paused for a long beat, her chest rising and falling. "I…we…didn't intend it that way. You were always the strong, independent one and were off doing your horse thing. We needed to get our lives in order, finances back on track, and Alaska seemed like the best option. Your brother Lyle works in the oil industry, in the field and on the pipeline. We don't see him much either."

A fist squeezed Sam's lungs and her sinuses prickled. "Whenever I've loved someone, they've left. I felt abandoned, Mom, like you didn't love me anymore."

"Oh, honey." A glint of tears shone in her mother's eyes. "No, that's not true. We loved you; we still do. I guess we got so caught up in the work at first—it was hard, hard labor—and then in developing our homestead…" Her voice hitched. "I'm sorry. We did neglect you, but we didn't mean to 'abandon' you."

She reached across the small patio table and took Sam's hand. "I've often wished you could have come with us. It's beautiful there…and so peaceful. And you know your dad— he's happiest where there are the fewest people around."

The corner of Sam's mouth twitched upward. "I know. The old 'mountain man.' I think he was born in the wrong century."

"Yeah, he was. I do miss having a social life, and we did separate for a while…but we're soul mates, and where he is, that's my home." Mom drew in a draught of air. "And you kids…you know, I thought I'd have you for a lifetime, but I've realized, as a mom, it was like I was only paying rent, and the lease was up. You were never mine to keep."

"Yeah, but, a letter now and then…? That would've been nice." Sam wasn't quite ready to let it go. "It was like I was the

252

last bird in the nest. Everyone flew away for the winter and left me to deal with the depths of despair after Jace's accident."

Her mom sniffled and reached into her pocket for a tissue. "I'm so sorry, honey. We had no idea. I wish we could've done a few things different."

She had to admit, they hadn't been the worst mom and dad in the world. They'd all had some pretty good times together when she was growing up. But it almost seemed like her parents were stuck in some kind of time warp of their young hippie days.

Yearning slithered in and slammed against her ribs. *Maybe they've been struggling through the adult world like I have, trying to find their place.* She realized then that maybe she'd been holding a grudge against her younger self, hearing her own paranoid voice—not her mom's or dad's—accusing her of all the things she did wrong or could go wrong, inventing scenarios that hadn't happened and probably never would.

Her mom rose from her chair and came to sit beside her in the porch swing. "I hope you can find it in your soul to forgive us...to forgive me. I think there's something about mothers and daughters that makes us always want to hold each other close and yet at the same time push each other away. I do love you, and I've missed you." She put both arms around Sam and pulled her close.

Tears mingled on their cheeks, and they held each other for long minutes. "I forgive you, Mom, and I'm sorry I didn't write to you either." She uttered a wry chuckle. "I guess the 'Pony Express' goes both ways."

They both dissolved into laughter then, erasing the tension of the years apart.

CHAPTER THIRTY-ONE

On her wedding morning, Sam awoke to birds twittering. The sun emerged over the horizon in easter egg hues, a perfect opening for her and Brad's new beginning.

Her mom fixed a light breakfast of scrambled eggs, toast, and fruit, but nerves jittered through her stomach. "I'll eat later. There'll be tons of food."

Soon after, Teresa arrived, followed shortly by Alberta and Electra.

"Brad, out. You can't see the bride until the right moment," her maid of honor instructed. "Mr. Moser, please keep tabs on this fellow and don't let him get away."

Dad snickered. "I won't. And, please, call me Kevin. Let's go, Brad. I think there's some 'supervising' to be done down at the arena."

The men cleared out. Her mom cleaned up the kitchen and visited with Irene who'd arrived with the cake—a three-tiered vanilla, chocolate, and orange layered affair, decorated with yellow, gold, and orange roses, and topped with a silhouette of a bride and groom standing in front of a horse, embracing.

"Irene, this is beautiful." Sam admired the creation from all angles. "You outdid yourself. Thank you." She gave the motherly woman a tight hug.

"C'mon, girlfriend, let's get you into your wedding togs. People are starting to arrive."

Her old butterflies came to life and erupted in her chest. *Oh my. This is really happening.*

254

Her "honor guard" led her into the bedroom. Teresa worked on her hair, gathering it into chestnut curls that cascaded down her back and weaving baby's breath into the sides. Electra helped with her make-up. "No white pancake base," Sam teased.

"Ha. Ha. Very funny." The teen waved a mascara brush threateningly. "Ohmygosh, Sam, I'm so excited for you."

Alberta laid out their outfits on the bed. Sam donned black satin pants with flared bottoms, a long-sleeved white lace western-cut blouse that overlaid a white satin camisole. She tugged on shiny black boots, and as a concession to "traditional" wedding attire, allowed a short, simple gauzy veil to be attached to her hair.

Her attendants dressed in matching black slacks and lace blouses over colored camisoles—yellow for Electra, gold for Alberta, both with dark hair, and green for blonde Teresa.

"You are *so* beautiful," Electra breathed.

She tapped her fist against her heart. "You ladies are too." She gave each a light hug, careful not to crush hairdos and clothing.

"Let's go get you married." Teresa preceded the group outside, where Horace, Nick, Ted, and Brad held saddled horses.

Brad's eyes rounded, and he gave a whistle. "My gorgeous bride. Look at you!"

She pressed fingers to her lips, meeting his eyes.

Dressed in a smartly-tailored black western jacket and black jeans, he squeezed her hand, held the stirrup, and helped her onto Sugar's back. Her legs suddenly went weak, and for once, she was grateful to be "taken care of."

Her dear neighbor Horace, as best man, assisted Teresa, Nick helped Alberta, and a blushing Ted took Electra's hand as she giggled and stepped forward to mount Apache. One friend of Brad's from the TV station took still photos while another videoed.

She grinned as Lucky, with a large rust-colored bow tie, led the group with his three-legged hop toward the arena—Electra and Ted first, Alberta and Nick, then Teresa and Horace. As they approached the flower-woven lattice archway, the familiar, classic strains of Mendelssohn's Wedding March lifted and soared through the air.

With a collective rustle, the crowd stood and turned to watch the wedding party proceed down the aisle. She reined in her horse and sat for a minute, scanning the people. Up front, her parents and the Bruckners; Robin and the group home kids; other neighbors in bright-colored attire interspersed throughout, and toward the back, her childhood friend Jace, sitting in her wheelchair next to Del, the other vets filling the last row. *Perfect. Everyone is here.*

She met Brad's gaze with a smile. They rode together to where the attendants had dismounted and now stood by the minister. Approaching the altar, they joined hands, tapped their mounts' withers, and the horses bowed in unison. The audience applauded.

Sam and Brad slipped out of their saddles and stepped forward. She was barely aware of Clyde leading the horses away.

The pastor beamed and cleared his throat. "Dearly Beloved…"

With a fluttering heart filled to overflowing, she saw that her path, littered with dreams and pitfalls, had led her to this exact moment—all meant to be—family, friends, her ranch, and husband. Home.

God had answered her prayers.

Enjoy this book?
You can make a big difference.

Reviews of my books help bring them to the attention of other readers.

If you've enjoyed this book, I would be very grateful if you could spend just five minutes of your time leaving a review (it can be as short as you like) on the book's Amazon page.

Or let me know through my website:
http://www.heidimthomas.com

Thank you very much!
Heidi

ACKNOWLEDGMENTS
So many have been involved in making my books a reality. I thank God for the gift of the writing gene, my family for their continued support and encouragement, the teachers and editors who believed in me, my fellow Women Writing the West members, my Word Spinners critique group: Mary Bartley, Lillian Boyd, Wendy Cooper, and Jane Hirsch, and my Chino Valley critique group who have given me such valuable feedback: Sally Bates, Leta McCurry, and John J. Rust. Thank you also to Brenda Whiteside, critique partner and editor, for helping make my work better. And, of course, thank you to all my readers for supporting my writing habit.

ABOUT THE AUTHOR

Heidi M. Thomas grew up on a working ranch in eastern Montana, riding and gathering cattle for branding and shipping. Her parents taught her a love of books, and her grandmother rode bucking stock in rodeos. She followed her dream of writing, with a journalism degree from the University of Montana. Heidi is the award-winning author of the "Cowgirl Dreams" novel series and *Cowgirl Up: A History of Rodeo Women.*

Seeking the American Dream and *Finding True Home* are based on her mother who emigrated from Germany after WWII. She makes her home in North-Central Arizona.

Rescuing Samantha, Rescuing Hope, and her tenth book, *Rescue Ranch Rising* continue the fictional Moser family story.

Made in the USA
Monee, IL
05 November 2022

17116255R00156